THE PROPERTY
OF A LADY

THE PROPERTY
OF A LADY

Anthony Oliver

HEINEMANN : LONDON

William Heinemann Ltd
10 Upper Grosvenor Street, London W1X 9PA

LONDON MELBOURNE TORONTO
JOHANNESBURG AUCKLAND

First published 1983
© by Anthony Oliver 1983
434 54393 4

Photoset by WILMASET, Birkenhead, Merseyside
Printed in Great Britain by
REDWOOD BURN LIMITED
Trowbridge, Wiltshire

∾ ONE ∿

EVERYONE SAID IT was dangerous. You should never give a stranger a lift, especially if you were a woman and driving alone on a quiet country road.

Only gradually had she come to accept that she was no longer a girl. She was still attractive but the word woman no longer seemed odd. Four years ago, when she was twenty-four, she had woken in the night and realised with a shock that in sixteen years' time she would be forty. She had gone down to the kitchen to make tea and to check her mental arithmetic on her pocket calculator and it was true.

She had inherited from her mother the small house in Kensington and the .country cottage in Flaxfield together with enough money to maintain them comfortably. Taken separately her features were even but unremarkable. It was her good luck that her smile jumbled them all up under the dark curly hair. It was such a happy, trusting smile that it made her best feature her own essentially kind nature. Since her mother's death four years ago she had changed more than she knew, but there had been no one close enough to her to tell her so.

The tiny figure of the hitch-hiker was still some distance ahead. The road which led towards him was long and straight with a deceptive gradient which would have been trying for a cyclist. Even the little car would have to drop into a lower gear if she were not to appear to be slowing down at the crest giving false hope to the figure with its arm and thumb rigidly signposting the road ahead. The pack on its back made it lean forward at a surprisingly acute angle so that you could sense its weight even though the figure itself still had no face or identity.

The car radio was tuned into Woman's Hour on the BBC where an apparently sane female was describing how she and her husband had driven quite safely across Africa in a Mini Metro

1

with a trailer and four children. As Margaret's car approached the crest of the long rise, the figure came into focus and resolved itself into the shape of a young man in jeans and a white tennis shirt. The slightest pressure of her foot on the accelerator would carry her past him in seconds, delivering her from the danger of rape and robbery. She hadn't meant to look at him as she drove past but she did and stared into an open pleasant face with no hint of robbery or rape in it, nor did it appear to show any sign of resentment when she did not stop.

In the mirror she saw his arm fall and watched him hump the pack higher on his shoulders as he began walking with the afternoon sun behind him – a black silhouette with a golden pack. Not until she saw him first quicken his pace and then break into a shambling run did she realise she had stopped the car.

Ten miles away in Flaxfield Mrs Thomas was also listening to Woman's Hour, ashamed of the boredom which had reduced her to the vicarious enjoyment of other women's conquests in the kitchen and Darkest Africa. True, Africa was an improvement on raspberry jam which refused to set, but it was poor stuff for all that. No hoards of charging natives with monkey fur round their ankles, no tom-toms, only a dull account of the minor anxieties of this modern mother in the bush. The lady interviewer confessed with a low musical chuckle to a mild, but she hoped not insurmountable, distaste of snakes but she was quite happy about spiders which she thought rather jolly, friendly creatures. Mrs Thomas sighed. It was too soon for tea and far too early for Guinness. The desert of the day stretched before her.

"We tried to make it as much like home as possible," the manic mother intoned. "There was something really rather splendid about reading *Alice in Wonderland* under the stars."

"Silly bitch," said Mrs Thomas and switched off.

The village of Flaxfield in the county of Suffolk is small, quiet, compact and almost completely unspoiled by the ravages of the twentieth century. It lies in the open East Anglian countryside, a happy jumble of styles where the earliest traces of Saxon blend happily with the Tudor and Caroline, and the Georgian porches stand content next to the more solid doorways of their Victorian neighbours. Since about 1850 successive parish councils have resolutely set their bye-laws against further development and the village looks now very much as it did then. It has been invaded by Vikings, Normans, Cromwell's soldiers and Mrs Thomas.

Invader was not a word Mrs Thomas herself would have used. If she had considered her position at all she would more accurately have seen herself as a missionary. A Welsh missionary among the friendly but slightly backward tribes of England. Unlike the Scots and the Irish, whose nationalist pride bristled fruitlessly at frontiers, the Welsh had long ago abandoned such crude tactics, slipping quietly across the border to infiltrate and civilise, having long ago peacefully conquered their neighbours in a war the English hadn't even realised they had fought and lost. All over England Welsh schoolteachers, mayors, councillors, trade union leaders and civil servants unobtrusively ruled the land and Mrs Thomas was lucky to have Flaxfield to herself.

Sometimes she almost regretted selling her house in the suburbs of Cardiff and buying the cottage in Flaxfield. Ostensibly she had done it so that she could come and live near her daughter, Doreen. It was only partly true. She wasn't particularly fond of her daughter but having arrived to comfort her when Doreen's first husband had died, Mrs Thomas had appraised the village and found it good, a challenge and comfort for her in later life. Like so many of her countrymen she knew instinctively that she was wasted in Wales. Cardiff was full of formidable widows leaving her own talents largely untested and unstretched. Flaxfield, she had recognised, was ripe for a takeover, and like a general surveying the field of battle she had established her headquarters in a cottage strategically placed in the centre of the village and on ground marginally higher than that of her neighbours'. It was more of a hump than a hill but in the flat East Anglian landscape it gave her a decided advantage. From the bedroom windows and armed with binoculars, she was situated in a position of some importance. The binoculars had been a present for her fifty-fifth birthday (she was fifty-eight). To be honest, she hadn't expected anything quite so magnificent. She had indeed asked for binoculars, having ascertained from some birdwatchers in the village pub that a perfectly adequate pair could be bought for as little as fifteen pounds. Her friend, ex-Detective Inspector John Webber, had considered her worthy of something better and his present would not have been spurned by the captain of a battleship.

Mrs Thomas's hero-worship of John Webber came so close to love that she made little effort to disguise it, stopping short only of an open declaration. She was a widow, she told herself, in the prime of life apart from her legs, which, with the occasional support of elastic stockings, still gave her a bouncy mobility and resilience the envy and despair of women half her age. Her idol

3

was divorced and retired and until such time as he indicated that he regarded her with anything more than admiration and friendship she was content to bounce down the road every day to minister to his needs, to share his memories and confidences and to call herself – with pride – his housekeeper.

In many ways life in Flaxfield was a disappointment for her. She had too little to occupy her abundant energy. Webber's shopping and simple household chores she could have completed in little more than an hour although she did her best to prolong them for the pleasure of his company. But with the best will in the world she could not make more than a morning's work of it, leaving her to complete the day as best she might. True, there were delightful evenings when he would sit with her in the bar of the Bull and she would listen entranced to his stories of his service in the police force. Now that the summer evenings were beginning to lengthen he had shown a distressing tendency to spend the time pottering in his garden, an occupation she regarded as an unnecessary English vice.

She had far too much wisdom to impose herself upon him, which made the times when he actively sought her company all the more precious. But this afternoon, as too often, she was alone, surveying the wilderness of her own overgrown garden, a jungle in miniature, a refuge for every floating seed in Suffolk and a frequent sanctuary for Bunter, the black and white vicarage cat, who gratefully saluted her sanity in a village of mad gardeners and flower beds.

They regarded each other now across what had once been a lawn, Bunter sitting tidily on the sawn-off stump of a lime tree which had impaired Mrs Thomas's view to the south east. In some ways they had much in common, both content to pay lip service to the laws of the community in as much as it suited them, but both essentially a law unto themselves. After a shaky start, when both had failed to recognise the sterling qualities of the other, they had come to accept each other with an increasing respect which only their fierce independence had so far restricted to distant polite exchanges in social encounters.

Bunter's point of vantage over the garden on the tree stump reminded Mrs Thomas that if the afternoon had been so far a boring waste of time, she might well emulate him and put herself in a similar position upstairs with the binoculars. Her departing nod, not quite a bow, was acknowledged by Bunter by a subtle redistribution of his weight which, while it did not materially alter his position, was emphasised by his tail curving up to cover his

4

front paws, as in more gracious days a gentleman would have doffed his hat.

In the late sunshine of the June afternoon Flaxfield pursued its settled course. In the distant south the towers of Henworth Hall, newly restored, shivered and moved in the hot air as though stretching and aware of its new lease of life, now successfully and profitably converted into a health farm for ladies with obesity, rheumatic ailments, and money. The inmates didn't really count as part of the Flaxfield community, their strict regime effectively confined them to the Hall and its extensive grounds. Occasionally some maverick matron, pummelled beyond endurance and maddened by hunger, would evade purdah and make a cross country plunge after the discreet evening roll call to gorge and guzzle at the Bull. Only last week a large lady runaway had been found blissfully asleep in a haystack after a clandestine feast of ten sausage rolls and four double vodkas and tonics. Henworth Hall interested Mrs Thomas but she didn't consider it as coming within her suzerainty and the binoculars moved away from it and on through their accustomed routine check.

In the garden of her daughter's antique shop her son-in-law Jimmy Trottwood, known to a select circle of intimate friends as Betsey, was pegging out a Victorian patchwork quilt to dry. Both Mrs Thomas and Betsey had warned Doreen that it wouldn't wash well. They had both counselled her to have it dry-cleaned and Mrs Thomas now noted with grim satisfaction the sorry mess as each coloured patch embraced and modified its immediate neighbour. Of her obstinate daughter there was no sign and poor Betsey was left to contemplate the disaster alone, his ample form drooping in despair in odd contrast to the aggressive crew-cut of his red hair which never drooped because it was a wig. Doreen would have to be spoken to. Mrs Thomas doubted if it would do much good, but she would try. Boredom was giving way to frustration. Doreen's intransigence seemed at that moment to symbolise the entrenched stubbornness of the entire population of Flaxfield. True, she had finally forced her to agree to exhibit at the Dunwold Antique Fair and that was only three weeks away. Three weeks – she sighed and swung the binoculars to the newly cleared view of the south east.

The twice-weekly bus wasn't due for another hour and its passengers, if any, were unlikely to provide major excitements. Last week Mrs Willow had dropped an egg. There was no bus but a small car she recognised as belonging to the rather shy girl who had inherited the end cottage from her mother, the one where the

5

lane grew narrow and wandered off into a foot path. She liked Margaret Garland, the girl had possibilities.

She watched now as the car pulled up outside the cottage with the window boxes which needed watering. The driver's door opened. Margaret Garland did not open the garden gate but walked round to the other side of the car. The door opened but no one emerged. Instead Miss Garland bent down as if in conversation. After a moment or two she leaned in to help her passenger get out. Through the binoculars Mrs Thomas watched as a young man in jeans and a face as white as his tennis shirt climbed out very slowly. On his feet he would have collapsed had not the girl caught him in her arms and, kicking open the garden gate, struggled to half carry and half drag him up the path and round the side of the cottage to the front door.

❦ TWO ❧

"It's probably a bug of some sort, although his temperature's only up a bit. Could be food or good old demon drink but I doubt it, doesn't look the type for a booze-up. Wait and see, that's best. I'm not very keen on antibiotics as you know so, Doctor Nature, that's the answer. I'll look in again tomorrow. Could just be simple car sickness, of course. Did he complain of feeling sick in the car at all?"

"No, he didn't talk much, just to say that anywhere near Flaxfield would suit him. I noticed he was rather pale but he didn't collapse until he got out of the car."

"Hmm, could be a natural born fainter, although that's mostly girls and guardsmen."

Dr Collins still dyed her hair, Margaret noticed, although she might be in the process of abandoning it as the parting wandered broad and brown through the untidy yellow. She and her husband had come to the village to fill the gap created when Dr Maguire had decided to concentrate on the rich patients at Henworth Hall.

Sarah Collins humped herself into a duffel coat with what looked like old blood-stains down the front. They could have been a relic of a road accident casualty or a Sunday rabbit shoot, she herself had long forgotten which. The Collinses had opted out of the London rat-race and embraced the country life with enthusiasm and relief. She retrieved her naked thermometer from the recesses of her coat pocket returning it to an equally grubby corner in her flat metal briefcase. She snapped the catches shut, trapping the end of a green tape measure on the outside which she cheerfully didn't bother to replace. Clutching the case under her arm at the door she paused to pull on pink knitted driving gloves. She nodded up at the ceiling.

"Quite happy with him up there? I mean you don't know him, I suppose? Just a casual hitch-hiker? What I'm getting at is that I

7

should be happier as a doctor if he rested, I could lug him off to the cottage hospital if you like but it seems a pity now that he's sleeping; best thing for him sleep, up to you."

She felt more than ordinary concern for Margaret mainly because she was one of her few private patients and she always paid her bill promptly. Pity the old mother was dead, that had been very satisfactory while it lasted. Still, the girl had made it quite clear on the phone that the visit was to be considered as a private call. The patient might well be as fit as a flea in the morning. On the other hand if he did come down with something, a little money was always welcome. Margaret had not only paid promptly but, most satisfactorily, in cash.

"Oh no, of course he must stay. You say he needs rest and he really seems very nice. Rather well spoken."

Dr Collins nodded. To her, as to Margaret, it seemed a valid reason for confidence.

"Phone me tomorrow. I'll pop over if he's no better."

"It makes a change from the stick and crutch brigade," she said to her husband later over supper and Russian tank manoeuvres on television. "Rather romantic, I thought."

Dr Peter Collins made a tactical withdrawal from the Polish border and surveyed his wife fondly over the remains of a leek and rabbit pie. She was he thought, not for the first time, wildly unsuited to her profession; it was for him one of her chief attractions. With certain reservations she had taken the transfer from London extremely well. It was a pity the practice wasn't more lucrative but people on fixed retirement pensions had little to spare for the luxury of illness and private medical treatment.

"Pale and interesting was he? How old is this romantic youth?"

She grinned happily, glad to have got him out of East Germany.

"Older than she thinks. Not a teenager anyway, over twenty certainly, small build, makes him look a kid, good body. I shouldn't think he's feeling very romantic, he seemed more concerned to know where the lavatory was than anything else."

"Car sickness would clear up almost at once; the lavatory sounds more like food poisoning of some sort."

She nodded contentedly.

"Soon know in the morning."

She would have liked her husband's conversation a little longer but he had already retired to Warsaw where a group of trade union leaders were sitting glumly round a table.

8

"I'm fed up with rabbit," she said. "It gets into everything, even the lamb tasted of rabbit on Sunday."

The conference dissolved and there was a long queue of people waiting to buy food.

"Those poor devils wouldn't mind a rabbit."

"I'm fed up with Poland too," she said, collecting the plates on a tray.

"The funny thing is," she said, at the door to the kitchen. "I'm almost sure I've seen his face before."

"Very mild food poisoning," Mrs Thomas informed Doreen and Betsey two days later in the shop. "Light diet and rest and he should be up and about in no time. I bumped into Dr Collins outside the surgery on her way to Mrs Willow's elbow."

"I'm surprised she discusses patients," Doreen said crossly. "Most unethical."

She wasn't surprised at all, knowing Sarah Collins' fondness for her mother and knowing too, from long experience, her mother's ability to extract information from sources usually regarded as sacrosanct. Doreen was still sulking about the patchwork quilt.

Betsey wasn't sulking about it. That wasn't his nature. When disaster struck, whether of minor or major proportions, his instinct was always to make the best of it. He was fond of both his wife and his formidable mother-in-law, fonder indeed of both of them than they were of each other. He was essentially a peacemaker, believing that wrath which could not be diverted by a soft answer could always be dispelled by laughter. Only sometimes, when he was quite alone, would his plump body slump like a clown in his caravan away from the crowds. Then the eyes, too, were different; off-duty and sad.

This morning was no time for gentle introspection. Life was certainly earnest, but nothing he prayed that could not be coped with. Nevertheless the Dunwold Antique Fair was barely a long fortnight away and the truth was that he was beginning to have grave doubts about it. The stock didn't look too bad in the shop but, however optimistically he viewed it, he had more than a suspicion that once displayed in the Town Hall at Dunwold it was going to look quite different. It might even look tatty and in Betsey's book that was one of the worst words he could think of. The truth was that such talents as he had lay not in the erudite assessment of antiquity but in effective display and presentation. He had started life as a window dresser in Peter Jones and now, with the dread threat of the vetting committee at Dunwold looming ahead of him, he wanted nothing more than to stay in his pleasant familiar shop and do something eye catching and original in the window to celebrate the Royal Wedding.

Mrs Thomas had steered Doreen away from the delicate subject of medical ethics and now, fortified by morning coffee, mother and daughter had slipped easily into the armed neutrality of casual conversation.

"All very proper and tidy. I will say that," said Mrs Thomas delicately. "She slept on the sofa downstairs the first night but now she's back in the spare bedroom. Lights out at ten-thirty sharp and not another movement until the kitchen next morning. Black tea and toast and she takes it up on a little tray, neat as a night nurse. No, God love 'er, nothing nasty. Proper lady – not like some."

Doreen considered taking offence at what might have been a veiled reference to some of her own past indiscretions but was too interested and ignored it.

"Mam, those binoculars will get you lynched one day."

"Flaxfield," said her mother, quoting from the vicar's pamphlet on sale in the church, "is virtually a bird sanctuary in its own right, and many rare sightings have been made within the very confines of the village itself."

"Anyway what's his name and what's he doing in Flaxfield?"

They were both good questions and it was galling for Mrs Thomas to admit that so far she had discovered the answer to neither of them. Not even Dr Collins had been able to enlighten her.

"I might take a few grapes round later," she said, wincing at the last dregs of Doreen's coffee. "Don't want to seem pushy or nosey, do we?"

"Ferns," said Betsey thoughtfully, from a corner of the shop. "We could fringe the stand with ferns and they'll do to fill up the gaps if the vetting committee throw things off."

Life in the cottage with Margaret and the hitch-hiker was almost exactly as Mrs Thomas had reconstructed it through her binoculars. Even Mrs Thomas, however, had not been able to see inside Margaret's head. Everything had certainly been very proper and yet she felt far more interest in him than in a casual house guest. In the new freedom and extra space after her mother's death she had not found it easy to adjust herself to a routine where she had only herself to please. The memory of her mother was vivid and fierce within her.

10

"Margaret, why don't you stay up in Kensington for a little while? I shall be all right, Dr Collins copes perfectly well, you know that, and Mrs Woods can easily come in every day."

Some days, Margaret had gone to the lavatory at the end of the garden to sit and cry, even though it had been unused for years, and was full of spiders. It wasn't entirely for herself that she cried; the tears were for her mother, too.

By Monday he had recovered. In the days between, the black tea and toast had been replaced by Dr Collins' light invalid diet, a skill in which Margaret had been well tested. Only now it was different, and she delighted in the clean plates with nothing left over and not pushed away with an apologetic smile. She smiled herself now to think of her mother's reaction to the new patient in her own bedroom.

"It does seem just a little odd dear, that's all." That her mother was dead made the conversation not in the slightest less real. She saw her quite clearly too, sitting in the corner of the kitchen in the Windsor chair which had defied every effort to stop it wobbling and clicking a punctuation on the tiled floor as she talked.

"Why should it seem odd if he doesn't talk much? I don't suppose he's felt like talking. I hate badgering people. He can talk if he wants to and if he doesn't, I respect that."

"Well, it's your life dear, I suppose I mustn't complain, goodness knows I've never stopped you having friends of your own but you can hardly call a total stranger you found on the side of the road a friend."

"I don't know, Mother. Not yet perhaps, but I think I'd rather like him to be." Margaret was enjoying herself. "You are quite right, I do know very little about him. He's very shy but then, as you've always told me, so am I, painfully shy, you've always told everyone that. Yes, it does seem odd when I take his meals in – oh I knock first, I promise you! But there he is, in your bed and that really is odd. Perfectly respectable but definitely odd. I found some pyjamas for him in his pack, blue and white stripes and quite clean, not ironed, but clean and a hundred per cent cotton, so you should approve of that at least. And when I took them in to him you'll be delighted to know that he was decently covered by the bedclothes. There, that seems to be everything ready for dinner later, at least I think so, let me just do our final check, shall I? Veal rolled and stuffed – thyme and parsley I thought, rather than sage and onions – yes mummy, I know you dislike thyme, potatoes peeled and par-boiled for roasting, not garden peas I'm afraid, Mrs Thomas happened to be in the greengrocers and warned me they would be tough. So it's frozen peas, with cheese and fruit to follow and Dr Collins thinks a little claret could do no harm at all."

The luxury of such an uninterrupted conversation had stimulated her more than the small glass of sherry she had poured for herself, for she had forgotten it after the first sip. It stood on the draining board catching the evening sun in the glass, a still life with parsley and potato peel. She drank it slowly letting the taste drip at the back of her throat. At the bottom of the garden she could see the lavatory door hanging loose where the top hinge had pulled away from the rotting wood. She would find someone to mend it. No, she would have it boarded up.

She finished the sherry, washing the glass quickly and clearing the debris of preparation from the draining board and the sink as she heard him moving about upstairs. The old floor boards had their own pattern of sounds signalling their private progress report. She felt a sense of excitement, like a birthday or Christmas when she was a child. She felt shame, too, that she should have wanted to shock and tease the memory of her mother and to have enjoyed it quite so much. It would serve her right if she had missed any of her mother's paper-back novels when she had hastily cleared them from the room. She doubted whether any of them were as blatantly pornographic as their titles and lurid covers suggested, but the thought that he wouldn't know they were not her own choice was enough to make her curl her toes with embarrassment. They had arrived regularly in plain envelopes. Only after she had written several letters and sent an outrageously large cheque in final payment had they stopped sending them.

Dr Collins had suggested that they were perhaps only a symptom of the disease. "A morbid stimulation of desire, not uncommon." But Margaret knew it wasn't that. Her mother had simply had a dirty mind. There could have been worse faults and she had long ago accepted it as unimportant, a private, harmless fantasy of a silly, selfish woman. Now she was dead and gone and nothing whatever to do with the young man standing shyly in the doorway of the kitchen.

THREE

Ex-Detective Inspector John Webber and Mrs Thomas relaxed together in his garden after the washing up. An invitation to cook and share an evening meal with her idol always warmed both her heart and her stomach and brought out the best of her kitchen skills from the Welsh valleys of her youth.

They had dragged the deck chairs half way down the lawn to catch the last of the evening sunshine. It meant that Webber's efforts in the flower borders were behind them so that they gazed out across the well-ordered plot at the bottom of the garden where he had planted and cherished his vegetables.

"Perhaps," he said mildly, taking up their conversation in the kitchen. "Perhaps you're pushing them too hard, Lizzie. It must be a bit daunting to plunge into an Antique Fair if you've never done it before."

Mrs Thomas managed to snort and beam happily at the same time. "I'll plunge her, lazy little madam, she wants a bomb up her bum. Makes me hopping mad the way she takes advantage of poor Trottwood. No wonder the business is so bad."

"Is it bad?"

"Twelve pounds profit on a paperweight last week and the customer threatens to bring it back if her husband doesn't like it."

"They could advertise."

"Not much point if they haven't got the stuff to sell. She should be out buying in the sale-rooms. Trottwood's better in the shop than she is."

"So what will they sell in the Fair?"

"You'd be surprised what they have got if you scrape round a bit, and Trottwood's a wonder at making things look better than they are. Anyway, Dunwold Antique Fair is a bit of a joke, really. Have you ever been?"

Webber shook his head.

13

"High class junk most of it, so Trottwood says, even though he pretends to worry about the vetting committee. If they do well they can re-stock with some decent stuff later."

"Has Jimmy Trottwood got money of his own?" Webber's very bright blue eyes could be quite disturbing when he asked a direct question.

"Well yes, I think so. Mind you I've never enquired too closely and if he has, he's got enough sense to keep quiet about it, but yes, I think he must have, don't you?"

Webber nodded, making a mental note that his runner beans would want watering when the sun was off them. In the dark tent of the bean poles he could see the tell-tale patches of black and white fur where the vicarage cat had taken up a discreet tactical position in decent obscurity.

Bunter was not a cat who gave his favours easily, nor in fact did he readily attract the favour of others. For some years past he had lodged at the vicarage, being more tolerated in Christian charity than understood with affection, and the food was bad. The vicarage version of the miracle of the loaves and fishes was a sad travesty of the original, consisting for the most part of a bowl of crusts with the odd kipper skin. In Mrs Thomas he sensed a fierce originality touched with dignity and low cunning which he had observed with growing admiration. Her contempt for queues in the butchers was a masterclass in delicate foraging and the resultant scraps from her table, served simply and without comment in the long grass at the bottom of her garden, could not be faulted.

Webber had allowed himself the luxury of adjusting his chair to its lowest position, the nearest equivalent to a hammock. With Lizzie it didn't matter that it made his stomach a hillock that couldn't be hidden, or that it would be difficult for him to rise without grunting after a meal which had been calculated to give him pleasure and had succeeded. He was touched to see that she herself had placed her chair support on the highest rung and that she had not left her handbag in the kitchen, but had put it by the side of her chair on the grass as evidence that, when he should indicate the evening was over, she was ready to go.

Webber was fond of her, he liked the company of this extraordinary little woman from Wales. He was wary of her, too. At the age of fifty-six, divorced, and with a life of service in the police force behind him he had found a peace and contentment in his retirement that he was loth to disturb. Sometimes he allowed

14

himself to think back on his career of modest successes and the all too frequent disappointing failures and to wonder how different things might have been with Mrs Thomas at his side as guide and mentor. Webber was a man of generous spirit and knew quality when he found it. Lizzie Thomas, tied to a gentle pigeon-fancying coal miner for most of her life until he had died of a heart attack, had talents which ex-Detective Inspector John Webber admired without reserve. Sometimes he wished she would relax and channel her energy into the gentler art of cooking her superb meals but people were not like that, you had to accept them as a job-lot and Lizzie was entire as she was, he could not change her.

He watched her now, her short dumpy figure with legs that barely reached the grass, the permed hair parted at the side in a style she had worn since a child in the thirties and still dark for all her secret fifty-eight years. The food and the Guinness had not disposed her to relax. Webber would have liked to close his eyes. In a way, he told himself, it would be a compliment to her, a gracious expression of his pleasure and satisfaction. Her own eyes, alert and black as pear pips, changed his mind.

Throughout the meal he had sensed that there was something she was going to talk about, and since she had done him the courtesy of allowing him to enjoy it in peace, it was his simple duty now to remain awake and listen. It would be quite easy for him to indicate with a stretch and the luxury of a yawn that the evening was over. It would have been a churlish return for the egg coddled in thin cream over the layer of fresh cockles touched with saffron, to say nothing of the triumph of the lamb chops.

"I see Margaret Garland's fancy-boy is still with us."

"Fancy-boy, Lizzie, sounds very disapproving."

She nodded amiably, her hands folded gently on her lap.

"Does a bit, doesn't it? Nothing to do with sex though, whether they do or don't. Mind you, I don't think they do. She may want it, poor dab, but whether she's getting it or not's another matter. Anyway, you know me, I don't care one way or another, so long as she's happy, that's her business. She's a nice tidy girl, I like her."

"So?"

Mrs Thomas's neighbourly visit with a selected bunch of expensive black grapes had not been wasted.

"His name is Mark Carter, he's twenty-two and his mother is a patient at Henworth Hall. Nice looking boy, speaks well, bit on the shy side, blue eyes, fair curly hair not too long."

15

Webber felt it best not to comment. Whatever it was that had disturbed Lizzie Thomas – and he knew her well enough to know that something had – she would come out with it when she was ready. His only fear was that he might drop off before she got round to it. There was no point, of course, in rudely rushing her. It was only common courtesy to allow her to say what she wanted in her own time. He needn't actually close his eyes, he could rest his eyelids by lowering them just a little, just enough to diffuse the evening light pleasantly into a comforting green blur.

"I think he's dangerous," said Mrs Thomas. Webber opened his eyes.

"Why?"

"There's a vicious streak."

"A bit on the shy side?"

"When you speak to him, yes, and with her he's a nice boy. He's been in the shop, too. Trottwood likes him, of course, and so does Doreen, but that's not surprising either."

"Come on, Lizzie."

"It's a mixture, really. He's been up to visit his mother. That's the reason he's come to Flaxfield, he says."

"Seems reasonable."

"It does, doesn't it? But there's a lot of loose ends." She fished in her handbag for a handkerchief. It gave her time to sort out the words properly. It was a poor case she had to offer and only her confidence in Webber gave her courage to present it to him as seriously as she saw it herself.

"It costs a lot of money to take a cure at the Hall, right?"

"Yes, a lot."

"He hasn't got a penny. Lots of kids hitch-hike, I know, but why hasn't his mother given him anything to live on down here? Besides, he's hardly a kid at twenty-two is he? He gets everything from Margaret Garland: keep, pocket money, some new clothes too."

"Source?" said Webber.

"Margaret Garland – I asked her. Not in a way she'd notice, mind you."

"It hardly makes him vicious," said Webber gently.

In a pause which followed she rehearsed the clearest form of words to set the scene for him.

"You can walk back from the Hall two ways," she said. "You can come up that long drive to the lodge and back by the main road or you can cut out across the lawns and through Henworth Woods, the fields on this side bring you out by that footpath at the Garland

16

cottage." Webber remained silent but she saw that his eyes were open and alert.

"Last Monday, that was two days ago, I saw him walking back across the fields. He was quite a long way off but I could see him easily."

"Through the glasses?"

"Yes, plain and clear, they're very good."

Webber nodded. They had been part of a fence's stock when his men had raided a house in Cambridge. The owner, presumably a high-ranking naval officer, had never come forward to claim them. Webber had quite illegally kept them and had no regrets, they would never have been put to better use than they were now.

"It's funny, watching people alone like that," said Mrs Thomas. "Like reading about someone in a book when there's no one else to tell you about them, only the author of course, and you don't think about that, do you? You just see them, and watch them, and they've no idea."

Webber waited.

"He had his new flannel trousers and a sportscoat on, ninety-eight pounds from Marchants, not in the sale, good quality." She stared out across the vegetable patch, remembering. "He'd got his hands in his trouser pockets and then he stopped, he was staring at something I couldn't see, in a patch of rough grass near a bramble bush. He was standing near the hedge where they'd thrown the stones over from the ploughing in the other field. He bent down and picked some up, quite a lot, seven or eight, more perhaps, and quite slowly. Some he put in his jacket pockets and one in each hand. He never took his eyes off the grass. Then he started throwing and running. He was quick, like those big spiders they show on the television, all arms and legs, running like a flash and throwing like he was spitting poison. Then I could see what he'd seen in the grass, dodging and leaping out in the open across the field. I hate those programmes, spiders and lions jumping on small things and killing them. This was worse because it was happening there and then."

"He killed it?"

"No, he only hit it once. The other stones were very close. Then he was out in the open and nothing left to throw."

Webber grunted out of his chair, pulling the back up on to the top rung before swivelling it round to make conversation easier. He knew and respected Lizzie Thomas too well to dismiss what she had said as unimportant.

17

"It's the contrast, I see that," he said. "Quiet but vicious. The money's interesting too, more interesting in a way. There's no law, of course, about being poor, even if your mother's rich and presumably either mean or careful for a good reason. As for throwing stones at rabbits . . ."

"It wasn't a rabbit," said Mrs Thomas. "It was a cat."

Webber glanced at the black and white patch under his bean poles.

"That's right, Bunter. He was lucky, it caught him on the back, if he'd been stunned or lamed Mark Carter would have killed him. He wanted to kill him. I could see that."

She waited but he didn't answer. He knew she was thinking of something he had said to her one evening in the Bull when, after food and beer, she'd drawn him out, letting him talk about cases from the past. "So many of them seemed such ordinary people," he'd said. "You'd never think of them as murderers, and yet, if we'd only known . . . all the warning signs had been there all along."

"Interesting?" she asked eventually.

"Oh yes, certainly – these things are always interesting. You know something about him, and he's no idea. It doesn't necessarily make him a potential murderer." He looked at her mock quizzically over the top of his reading glasses, which he wasn't wearing. "What I'm saying is, that you haven't really enough on him if you were thinking of making a citizen's arrest."

"Worth watching, though." Her fingers curled round the straps of the handbag and she heaved herself out of the chair with surprisingly little apparent effort.

She was bored. Webber had seen that for weeks past. That was one reason he'd encouraged the Dunwold Antique Fair, throwing in his enthusiasm with hers, against the reluctance of Trottwood and Doreen. In a way this new drama of hers was a pity, but he knew her too well to discourage it. God knows where she got her energy from. At her age you'd think she'd be content to relax and enjoy such quiet pleasures as might be left to them. Oh well, it would keep her happy and she wouldn't make a fool of herself, she was far too clever and astute for that. She'd most likely find that Carter was no better or worse than anyone else, a bit of a scrounger, a ladies' man caught up in a family squabble with his mother and who happened to dislike cats. Poor little sod, you could almost feel sorry for him.

"Don't get up John *bach*, goodnight love."

"Goodnight Lizzie, see you tomorrow."

"See you tomorrow."

The light from the huge, soft orange sun pushed her shadow across the lawn to the back garden gate. In the darkness of the bean poles, Bunter had already stretched and was following her with studied indifference.

♫ FOUR ♪

WITH ONLY FOUR days to go before the Dunwold Fair, both Betsey and Doreen had worked themselves into something very near to a state of panic. Doreen really cared less about what seemed very likely to be a disastrously poor showing than all the hard work it would entail. Unlike her mother, Doreen disliked work. She took after her gentle, pigeon-fancying father, and such energy and vitality as she had inherited from Mrs Thomas she now used to heap abuse upon her.

"I wish to God she'd stayed in Cardiff," she told her husband. "You're too soft with her." She surveyed the ruins of the patchwork quilt and the motley collection of assorted pottery and porcelain, part of the accumulation from her late husband's stock that Betsey had laboriously hauled up from the cellar where for years it had lain in tea-chests and cardboard boxes covered in damp dust and green mould.

If he let her dissolve now into tears of self pity it would mean another wasted morning. There wasn't time for that. Betsey, for all his gentle, floppy appearance was capable of toughness in emergencies. An exasperated full male husband might very well have shaken her and told her not to be stupid and uncooperative. Betsey was not a full male, he had more than enough feminine genes in his nature to cope with Doreen.

"I don't think you should be working in the shop looking like that," he said firmly.

Doreen, who had indeed seriously been considering tears, forgot them.

"Looking like what?"

He surveyed her critically but kindly, the way he'd looked at her in the ladies' fitting room at Marchants when they'd been choosing her new summer coat. The note to strike with Doreen was impartiality with strength, with the kindness allowed to

20

temper the firmness, and dispel any suggestion of personal attack.

"I know business is bad but I'm supposed to be proud of you. In ten minutes it would be nice to have a cup of coffee and a biscuit, and while the kettle's boiling you could do your face and comb your hair. I hate it when you don't look your best."

"All the same, she's a selfish old cow, and you know it."

"We're all selfish old cows, dear, that's what Jesus was trying to tell us."

"She hasn't been near us for days."

"With the shop knee-deep in rubbish you can hardly blame her."

"I can."

"Yes all right, we'll blame her together – only later, do make the coffee, there's a love."

When she'd gone, he sighed with relief turning to gloom as he unwrapped yet another gaudy Imari patterned plate. He had always disliked Patent Ironstone China with its garish travesty of Japanese design and vulgar colours. The crumpled yellow newspaper around it had a photograph of a sad-faced Princess Margaret, over the story of her love for Group Captain Peter Townsend.

The boy's mother, thought Mrs Thomas, was an obvious move. Yet she could hardly go charging up to Henworth Hall and expect to extract information from a total stranger. It might have to wait until she had made at least a token effort to help with the preparations for the Antique Fair. There was a problem in that she had no idea how long Carter's mother would stay there. People, she knew, sometimes came for quite short periods, a week even, using it as a rest from the pressures of work or family, or a crash course for health and beauty. That, she decided, must be her first priority. If Mark Carter's mother was to be there for a short time then Doreen and Betsey would have to do without her help, if only for a day. Was she making a fool of herself, she wondered, as she strolled luxuriously in bare feet through the long grass of her back garden wearing only her elastic leg stockings and the winter dressing gown she had felt constrained to buy in Marchants' summer sale. What did it matter if Margaret Garland's lodger had a private face, she was old enough to make her own judgment upon him. Not every girl of her age could count on a nice pretty boy for a lodger, quiet, shy and well spoken. She paused to consider this argument. On the whole, it did not impress her.

21

The early morning dew was cool and good on her feet. She thought of John Webber's reaction when she'd told him. Analysed carefully, she considered that it had not amounted to active discouragement. Sometimes she worried that his natural lethargy might slip into a more positive trough of disinterested laziness. In fact she misjudged him. He was an old hound resting and would always prick up his ears and listen. If unimpressed, he felt entitled to tend his garden and doze. If the baying grew louder and the scent was genuine, he could still move with surprising agility. For the moment she was content to believe that her instinct was right.

It was still early, later the sky would cloud over with an advancing depression from the west, but now it was fine with the sun beginning to turn the dew on the long grass into a smoke wreath of mist. She made tea, carrying her cup back out into the garden, drinking it with keen pleasure in the anticipation of release from boredom. From the kitchen came the music from the tape she had slipped into the machine while waiting for the kettle to boil. Musically uneducated, she nonetheless had a natural taste inherited from the Welsh chapels of her youth and the wind-up gramophone of her father. A treat before bedtime.

"Dance if you want to, Lizzie *fach*."

"Mam says I mustn't dance in bloomers. She says I show off."

"Never mind your Mam, she can't hear us, she's washing up. Come on, show off with Mozart. He did it all the time."

From the dryness of the thick privet hedge, Bunter watched her improvise a gentle dance to the Mozart from the kitchen. The cup and saucer didn't look very promising but at least she was up and about. With any luck, when she'd finished showing off, she would remember his breakfast.

"I can't tell you much, Elizabeth." Dr Collins always used Mrs Thomas's full christian name. "Nothing to do with medical ethics, whatever they're supposed to be these days. Anyway she's not my patient, thank goodness."

Dr Collins was occasionally called in for a second opinion by Dr Maguire, the resident doctor at the Hall. Some patients demanded it as an optional luxury, like a room with a balcony or extra sessions with the physiotherapist of their choice.

"Couldn't ask Maguire, of course, that wouldn't do at all. He's a cagey old devil, he'd shut up like a door slam if he thought I was poaching on one of his precious battery hens. Spoke to one of the attendants though, they call them nurses, but they're only tarted up waitresses, and those two spotty boys he's got to do the pummelling and massage would be more at home with a few football injuries than female flab. The inmates are mad about them I'm told, so I suppose I'm wrong as usual."

All the staff at the Hall had originally been personable young men, without spots, it having long been Dr Maguire's sincerely held belief that the stimulus of the occasional sexual adventure could be dramatically efficacious in the treatment of both rheumatism and arthritis. The experiment had not been a success. He had quite forgotten to allow for the havoc that jealousy can wreak in the middle-aged female breast. In the event it made no difference. He sacked all his young rams and still prospered. Perhaps wild exciting rumours still echoed in the county corridors of Arthritica, but whatever the reason business at Henworth Hall continued to exceed the most optimistic of forecasts on nothing but herbs, wild fruit juices and the less stimulating forms of massage.

Sarah Collins liked Mrs Thomas. Talking to her she felt less like a doctor and more like the friendly gossiping neighbour that her nature craved and her profession made so difficult. At first she had used Mrs Thomas's legs as an excuse to drop in for a chat but she had long since abandoned that pretext and was happy to be accepted as a friend. Certainly Mrs Thomas thought of her as such and valued her.

"Yes, it's a bit disappointing I'm afraid," she sipped the coffee and accepted one of Mrs Thomas's Welsh-cakes. "She doesn't seem much different from any of the others. She's a widow, not as overweight as some but probably richer than most of them. I did find out one thing you asked about. She's on extended stay, a lot of them come for a short time, very often only for a week or ten days and she's been there for ages already, so God knows she must have money."

"You didn't see her yourself?"

"No, by the time I'd confirmed a case of mild hysteria in one of the old dears and been polite to Maguire, I was lucky to get a few words with little Annie Spicer, a Flaxfield girl, she's a nice child. I had her for acne once and mercifully it cleared up spontaneously so she tends to trust me."

"And she knows Mrs Carter?"

"She does early morning tea and stands by with warm towels after hose-baths. Last week she was afternoon relief for another girl who was off sick. That's when she met Mark Carter."

Mrs Thomas gently topped up the coffee cups. Outside, the

summer blue of the sky was retreating before a grey blanket of creeping clouds.

"When you say 'met'?"

"He was lost. The place is a warren and he was wandering around the corridors, so she took him in tow and showed him to his mother's suite."

"A suite?"

"Oh yes, very grand, there are only two of them, apparently. Most of the patients have rooms with just a small bathroom, but there are two quite large self-contained suites built over the old stables. She's in one of those and Annie showed him where it was. He was very dolly, she thought, a bit quiet and shy, but definitely dolly."

Mrs Thomas watched the first drizzle of rain drifting across the window.

"That would have been his first visit, obviously, since he had to be shown where she was. I wonder how often he's been since."

"He hasn't," said Dr Collins. "There's a visitor's book in the hall at the reception desk, I took my time signing in and flicked through. I might have missed one but I don't think so. I'm sure he only signed in once."

Mrs Thomas beamed at her with genuine affection. It was more or less what she had wanted to know. Mrs Carter was not, it seemed, likely to disappear from the Hall in the immediate future. "Extended stay" sounded comfortingly settled, at least for a little while longer. Mark Carter's abrupt break in his visits might or might not have some significance, but she could pursue that in her own time now. For the moment it would be enough to explain her interest in the matter to Dr Sarah. Not the real reason of course. What she had told Webber was private; he was her only true confidant, as always. Others, even dear, untidy, gossipy Sarah Collins should know as much as they needed and no more. Webber himself had taught her that. You kept your own counsel.

"Elizabeth, you are worried about that young man?"

The direct approach was quite certainly best countered with frankness, or at least a clear, straightforward impression of frankness.

"It's funny, no I hadn't thought of it like that." She rescued a lump of sugar which had strayed from its companions in the bowl, replacing it there with care. "No, not worried. Curious is better." She met Dr Collins' eye with a chuckle. "Nosey, my love, that's more like it, always have been, thank God."

24

Sarah Collins nodded. It was one of the reasons she liked Elizabeth. You always got a straight answer from her, you knew where you were.

"Well, I don't mind admitting that I have been a bit worried," she said. "I like the Garland girl, she had a hell of a time with her mother, but I can hardly turn round and warn her about men, not at her age. Not my role is it?"

"No, not really, you could if you were a gentle old man with silver hair and you'd brought her into the world, but that's only in American films, isn't it, not in Flaxfield. I must say she seems happy enough."

It was true. Margaret Garland was happy. She did not once stop to analyse her feelings in detail, she was more than content just to have them. She didn't know if it was love, she told the anxious memory of her mother. She slept alone in her room with the most wonderful and exciting new friend in the world sleeping each night in her mother's outraged bedroom, only seven silent floorboards away, and she was happier than she had been in the whole of her life. Sometimes, for black panic moments, she allowed herself to contemplate a day when he would go. He would tell her that he had done his best to heal the breach with his mother and could do no more, and he would thank her for her kindness and understanding and leave. Then I shall do something, she thought, something practical, but in such a way that it will not embarrass him. I shall not let him see that I cannot bear to think of a life without him. She was thankful and grateful that their relationship had not been complicated by sex. She would tell him that friendship could be so much closer than even family ties. When the time came, she would explain it all calmly and unemotionally, and in friendship. A moment chosen perhaps on a bright morning, with the early sun in the kitchen and a smell of toast and fresh tea. Talking to him about future plans, facts and figures, sensibly and wisely as she remembered the bank manager had once talked to her after her mother had died.

❧ FIVE ❧

THE DUNWOLD ANTIQUE Fair was a success. Most of the exhibitors had done well but for Doreen and Betsey it had been a triumph.

Webber had seen very little of Mrs Thomas during the last days of its preparation. He missed her food and her company and suffered it ungraciously.

Four days after the opening, with his conscience sorely troubling him, he drove along the winding road linking Flaxfield with the coast where Dunwold squatted stubbornly resisting the probing waves of the cold North Sea. In winter the wind seared the eyes and made ears ache, and even now in high summer, it was bleak and unwelcoming, like a documentary film about the hardships of fishermen. As a boy, his mother and father had taken him and his brother there for ten of the coldest days of the year, every summer. There was no coastal road when you got to Dunwold, you drove in from the comparative warmth inland and the road stopped. When visitors had had enough they turned round and drove back gratefully along the same road. Now he parked the car in the shadow of that familiar stubby phallus of the grey lighthouse. They had to build it short, was his father's joke, or the wind would have taken it. The fair was housed in the Town Hall, the only building of any size in the place. Before walking to it, he wandered down to the edge of the low cliff above the shingle beach with the wooden break-waters spoking out into the grey sea, calm for once, crinkled and crawling like elephant skin.. The bathing huts were still there, not the same ones he had suffered in as a child, wave-battered and blue with cold. Every few years the winter gales picked them up in casual handfuls and tossed them up and over the cliff for firewood. Webber shivered and turned gratefully towards the main street with its banner advertising the fair strung across it, straining at Woolworths on one side and the Town Hall on the other.

26

Inside the building, at the trestle table set up at the foot of the main staircase, he produced the printed invitation card Mrs Thomas had given him. The fair was housed in the main rooms on the first floor, the largest of which did duty for town council meetings and the productions of Dunwold amateur theatre and operatic societies. Some of the exhibitors had stands on the small stage itself, the rest grouping themselves around the walls with a cluster of them in the middle of the room. At the other end, facing the stage, a small flight of stairs led up to a Victorian architect's idea of a musicians' gallery. Here, where the organisers had set up a bar selling coffee and refreshments, Webber looked down on the people winding round the stands, sometimes pausing, a few asking questions of the exhibitors, sometimes picking things up and listening politely before replacing them and moving on, like flies escaping from poorly made webs. On the walls, huge ugly portraits of long dead town councillors and civil dignitaries some arrogant, some old and bored, stared out across the room; there was a powerful smell of furniture polish, stale biscuits and glue.

From the gallery he had no difficulty in sorting out Trottwood Antiques. They were in the middle of the left hand wall. At first it was difficult to make out anything on the stand, it was a blaze of summer flowers and ferns. When you looked carefully you could see the antiques, a few small pieces of furniture, a large kitchen dresser at the back with splashes of pottery and porcelain, some paintings on its side walls. He ought to have gone straight over when he came in but he enjoyed looking at things first. It was partly his old training through the years. Don't bother too much about the trees until you've had a damn good look at the wood.

The coffee he bought from the red cheeked woman in charge of the refreshment table was surprisingly good. He sipped it watching Doreen and Trottwood among the public on their stand. They weren't, as far as he could see, actually selling anything but there were certainly more people there than on the stands of their neighbours and rivals. Doreen looked quite attractive, he thought, in a simple navy blue dress with a white collar and cuffs, Trottwood would have chosen it for her, of course. They were an odd couple but in spite of their occasional rows they seemed happier than most middle-aged marriages he had known, his own included. There was no sign of Mrs Thomas, he couldn't see Mark Carter either.

The last days of preparation before the fair had been so concentrated that he had seen little of Mrs Thomas. He only knew that in some fashion or form Mark Carter had taken over the preparation for the fair. Just how, or for that matter why, he had no clear idea. The truth was, he told himself, he was getting lazy. Rather than question Lizzie and show an interest he had weeded his garden, hiding his sulks in an over-polite assurance that he would feed the black and white cat for her during the week she was staying at Dunwold for the fair. He had accepted his complimentary entrance ticket with such studied lack of interest that shame and a warm sun at Flaxfield had belatedly brought him to the cold sea in contrition.

"Oh Lizzie's all right John, you are a baby! She's far too busy enjoying herself." Betsey had seen him from the stand and clambered up the stairs to join him. "Coffee? Yes, well I suppose it is too early for a drink, although I'd love a gin. Oh dear! Look at them all, it's a cattle market, isn't it?"

"You're not enjoying it?"

"No, not really, it isn't me at all you know, I never really wanted to do it but Lizzie pushed us. She's a terrible pusher."

Webber nodded. "I got rather a rushed version of the facts from her. She said that young Carter had come into the shop sometime last week with Margaret Garland."

"On Tuesday. I wasn't actually in tears but really quite near them, but you can't cry with the shop full of young love and anyway they're a luxury, tears I mean. This coffee is quite good, considering."

"Margaret Garland is in love with him?"

"Yes certainly she is. We all are."

"How did it happen? His taking over, I mean."

"Lizzie, of course, how else? She gave us whisky. I'd got some gin but not enough to cheer us all up, so Lizzie found Doreen's whisky and got him talking. Have you ever spoken to him at all?"

"No. I said hullo to Margaret one morning when she was with him but he didn't contribute anything."

"That's right, he wouldn't, he used to come into the shop with her but he hardly ever spoke. She would try and bring him into the conversation, you know, like a mother does with a boy she's proud of because she knows he's bright."

"Only shy?"

"Yes shy, but then suddenly he did talk. I suppose it was the whisky, but he felt sorry for us too, I could tell that."

Webber knew better than to ask unnecessary questions when there was no need. Betsey would chat away.

"He knows more about antiques – real antiques – than I shall ever know. I like junk really, good junk if you like, but I'm lost with

28

that lot down there." The crowd had thinned, falsely tempted outside by the sun in the high windows and forgetting the chill breeze from the sea.

"Why didn't you cut your losses and get out of it? You could have cancelled."

"Yes, I did think of it but somehow I couldn't. I think to be honest that I wanted to show Lizzie that I could do it—just once anyway. She thinks that because nothing frightens her that everyone's the same. Doreen said once that she wished Lizzie would sometimes get some mould on just one of her jars of jam and I know what she means." Webber grinned so that Betsey knew he had made himself understood. "Have you ever heard of Carter and Monmouth?" he asked.

"No."

"Neither had I, that shows how little I know about this business. They're antique dealers or they were and big too, important anyway. Carter was Mark's father."

"Was? Oh yes of course, his mother's a widow."

"Yes, he didn't start with the Carter and Monmouth bit, by the way. It came out when Lizzie asked him if he liked the things we'd got ready for the fair. It was terribly interesting the way he answered, because if you just repeat what he said without seeing him say it, it sounds impossibly rude."

"How rude?"

"Well how about: 'You've got about three quite decent things, but that's all. The rest is rubbish.'" Betsey followed Webber's glance down to the stand where Doreen, elegant among the ferns, was doing her best to sell a Spode cup and saucer to a sullen-faced woman who appeared to be backing away from her.

"Lizzie wouldn't say much on the phone," Webber said, "only that she was tired and busy. She's more than a bit peeved with me, I dare say, but she did tell me that you'd had a wonderfully good opening day. Not with your original stock, I take it?"

"No, you're right, I shudder when I think of some of the stuff I had. I bought some new things, not much, as you can see most of that down there is dressing, tarted up with flowers and things, but I bought well—at least Mark did."

In the distance Doreen gazed resentfully at the back of the woman who had successfully resisted the Spode cup and saucer. The gaze transferred itself up on to the balcony where its unmistakable message was received by both her husband and Webber.

"I'd better go and show willing. She gets tetchy."

29

Webber nodded. "They do that." He smiled at Jimmy Trott-wood. "I'd like to hear the rest. When it's all over, perhaps?"

"Oh yes, but you'll come down and see the stand before you go?"

"Yes of course. I'm taking Lizzie to lunch."

"She should be around somewhere," he surveyed the hall. "Actually I haven't seen her for some time this morning, or Mark come to that. You'll get most of it from her, anyway."

The dining room at the Dunwold Arms looked out across the small town square with a fountain and a drinking trough for horses built to commemorate Queen Victoria's golden jubilee. The gaping mouths of the entwined dolphins had been dry since the war and the horse trough empty since long before that. The square was also the end of the road. Here the daily bus from Norwich swung cautiously round the fountain before going back the same way. Encouraged by the double-glazing, Webber had chosen a table in the corner of the room near the window and, on his best behaviour, had ordered a bottle of claret to help the mushroom soup and shepherd's pie.

"We were right about Jimmy Trottwood having some money of his own, then," he said.

"Doreen says it came from his mother, but she's no idea how much it was."

There was a hard rim of dried soup round his plate and traces of a stubborn blob of mustard on the edge. Why would anyone use mustard on anything in a soup plate? He wanted to say that she was wasting her time, why should they be eating muck food on the edge of the German ocean simply because she'd got a bee in her bonnet about Mark Carter? He saw with resignation that she was eating her soup with every sign of – well if not enjoyment – then indiffer-ence to the sour taste or the texture. He had started on the general composition of a conversation which would have compared her own kitchen skills to the food appearing on the tables around them but left it unsaid. She was unlikely to respond to transparent flattery. Best let her run, she would drop it when she was ready and at least the fair would be over by Saturday, in two days she would be back home in Flaxfield and there would be a prospect of decent food and more of her company.

"Trottwood is no fool," he said. "Why would he trust a boy like that to buy antiques for him?"

"Because he was in a panic, because he was too proud to cancel and because Mark is a professional."

"Mark?"

30

"From that evening in the shop," she said firmly, "I've fawned on him with the rest of them. Did Trottwood tell you about Carter and Monmouth?"

"They were quite big, he said."

"Not quite – very, and plenty to back it up, not just his word for it. Press cuttings of exhibitions, catalogues, photographs of their stand at Grosvenor House Antique Fair with Mark and his father chatting up royalty."

"Real royalty or foreign?"

"Settle for Prince Charles?"

"I'm impressed – so suddenly he's different, not shy any more."

She shook her head. "Wrong, he was chatting yes, but only about stock and antique fairs and what sells and what won't, even if it's as rare as a free-range hen. No it was Margaret, proud mummy, she showed us all the press cuttings and the photographs, not when he was there, of course."

Webber said, "Just the same, it's interesting that he carried all that stuff around with him. Mostly it's only actors who do that – you never had any doubt that it was all true?"

"You couldn't, not the way he talked. Oh yes, he'd talked about his father's business, but only to bring out some point or other, not to show off. He told Jimmy what he should buy and they went out and bought it. Not much, but all good – the best. Things you couldn't argue with, small stuff mostly, little desks, boxes, canterburys, davenports, paintings, silk pictures and a few good Staffordshire portrait figures." She paused in the middle of a mouthful of shepherd's pie, not believing that she could have eaten any of it, but forced to acknowledge that her plate was half consumed. "My God, John, this is like the war, isn't it?"

"I can remember it before the war," he assured her.

A very old waiter with a triumphant smile arrived with the claret in time for the chocolate ice cream. They drank it with biscuits and cheese instead. Both the claret and the cheddar were good, full and mellow.

She sensed a new interest from Webber; more than a polite excuse for his previous churlishness.

"Did Margaret Garland pay for any of it?"

"No, nothing, it was all Trottwood, every penny."

"You've no idea what he spent?"

"No, but I know the prices on the tickets."

"High?"

31

"We opened at eleven o'clock, there was a queue four and six deep down the staircase and out onto the road. People love antique fairs, the more rubbishy the better. By four o'clock in the afternoon on that first day they had taken over six thousand pounds in cheques and cash."

"Hang on a bit, were other people doing the same kind of business?"

"They sold, yes, but nothing like that. For one thing Trottwood and Mark had bought most of their rivals' best things, small things anyway, before the opening."

"I didn't know you could do that."

"Neither did we, it's pretty well standard practice apparently, some things change hands more than once."

"Getting more and more expensive before the public even see them?"

"Yes, that's right, Mark knew all that. Everything he told us was right, and that's just how it happened."

Webber carefully measured the last of the claret into their glasses.

"Jimmy never said he'd made a fortune."

"He hasn't, that wasn't the object. The promise was to get him through the fair without making a fool of himself. That was the promise, but only if we did what Mark said in those few days we had left."

"Which was?"

"Invest, choose good dealers, buy quality, buy small. When we got to Dunwold, do the same if there was anything good in the fair before it opened. Oh yes, and find out which of the other exhibitors was on the vetting committee and buy from them. Don't sell anything yourself before the public get in. Say you're keeping it all for collectors. Don't be greedy, take the smallest possible profit. Trust him."

"It seems," said Webber, "as though you might have to revise your opinion of our young genius."

"Our young genius," said Mrs Thomas, "has disappeared."

ɘ SIX ʚ

In London, four days after the antique fair had opened in Dunwold, Margaret Garland was talking to her bank manager. She had asked for an appointment early in the day, and at eleven o'clock with most of his routine tasks over he settled down to listen to her. Not one of his most important accounts but she rated coffee and consideration, kindness too, since he remembered her mother and hadn't liked her very much. He had known Mrs Garland as a gentle, domineering woman, with a disconcerting tendency to sudden unexpected bursts of roguish familiarity. When she had died his first reaction had been one of relief that he would no longer have to regard her as an occupational hazard. He had been glad for the girl too, it had pleased him to think of her with control over her own affairs at last.

Mr Allen liked neatness. The details of her assets and holdings were laid out neatly on his desk. The freehold properties in Kensington and Flaxfield, the shares and the saving certificates. In round figures he thought she was worth about two hundred and fifty thousand pounds. Not many years ago it would have represented a considerable fortune, now it was merely respectable. He listened to her without interrupting, his hand cupping his chin in the regulation attitude of an adviser with power and responsibility. Sometimes the gold-plated pencil flicked in the light of his desk lamp as he made a note, his face professionally blank beneath the thinning hair strained neatly across the top of his head. She talked quietly and at some length in well ordered and considered sentences ending with: "So you see, it isn't really a definite proposition, it's very much an exploratory enquiry."

"Quite," in the regulation pause which followed he numbered some of his notes and circled them neatly before replying. "The short answer is, yes, you have ample securities upon which we would certainly be prepared to lend you some money. How much

33

is another matter. You'll forgive me for saying so but I can't really enlarge upon that until you had some specific proposition to put forward. You realise that the antique trade is a highly competitive field? Yes, I'm sure you must have considered that. It wouldn't be simply a matter of suitable premises, whether here in London or in the country, there would be the question of buying stock. Now you say," he cupped his hands over the notes on his desk, "that your prospective partner is a man of some considerable experience."

"He was trained in his father's business and worked closely with him until his death last year."

"Ah yes, you mentioned Carter and Monmouth, certainly a very prestigious house. I seem to remember their advertisements in *Country Life* and so on."

"Yes, I suppose that's quite possible – I never saw them."

"Er – may I ask if you were considering a full financial partnership? In other words, would Mr Carter be contributing money to the venture as well as his expert knowledge?"

"He has no money," said Margaret simply. "His father left everything to his wife but nothing at all to his son. She sold everything to the surviving partner, Mr Monmouth."

"I see."

This time she sensed that the pause might well be followed by some advice or opinion which she had no wish to receive.

She stood and thanked him for his time and for the coffee. "It is, as I said, very much an exploratory enquiry."

"Quite, oh quite." He walked with her to the door, taking the hand she offered in farewell and retaining it long enough to deliver the regulation caution. "I'm glad you seek our advice, that's what we are here for. We used to advise your mother quite a bit, as I expect you know. She was a very sensible woman, she knew the real value of property." He met her eye without flinching from it. "You'll consult me again before you make any definite decision?"

"Yes I will, thank you." Her smile was spontaneous and happy. Happiness, he reflected as he sat at his desk when she'd gone, was all very well but it could serve you badly in business. He had seen more than one disastrously untidy mess begin with a happy trusting smile. His notes read:

(1) Potty?
(2) Going like her mother?
(3) Con man?

In Flaxfield, in the days immediately following the fair, the disappearance of Mark Carter was thought curious by some but affected most people not at all. Webber welcomed it, seeing it as the end of a disruptive episode and a gentle return to the relaxed days of Arcadia, but in this judgment he was mistaken.

For Margaret, the black panic moment had descended so quickly and so completely without warning, that her misery was beyond tears or understanding. It was cruel that he had chosen to go even before the Dunwold fair had finished. Had he left later, when they were all back in Flaxfield, she would have been able to explain it away more plausibly. A young man had stayed with her for a while and been kind enough to help her friends with his expert knowledge. With the end of a successful week he could simply have decided to move on. As it was, she had driven down from Kensington after her interview with the bank manager to pick him up at Dunwold. Unlike Betsey, Doreen, and Mrs Thomas, he had not stayed at Dunwold after the first opening day, agreeing eagerly she remembered, to commute with her in the car each day.

"Oh dear, how stupid of me," she had said, when told by Mrs Thomas. "I must have misunderstood, he must have told me about getting a lift back and I got muddled or something."

She hadn't been muddled, so why had she said anything at all? When she got back to the cottage she found he had packed and gone. It left her defenceless, without any possibility of dignity, for she rejected the idea of later inventing a reason for his flight as beneath her. She clung, half in fear and half in hope, to the possibility that his going had not been of his own choice. She told no one of her visit to the bank. The chosen moment when she would have talked to him, in early sunshine with the smell of fresh toast, had been taken from her and her carefully rehearsed phrases never spoken. When challenged by Sarah Collins she admitted to not sleeping very well and was given mild sleeping pills, which she accepted, but didn't take. She gave up searching for a note which might have slipped down behind a piece of furniture, she no longer waited for the postman. She could not bring herself to take the sheets and pillow cases from his bed. He had left nothing of his own behind when he had collected his things. She found a pencil he had used and kept it.

It wasn't only pride which made her stay on in the cottage but the real need she felt to remain where he had been. Once, when she pictured a gloating smile of false pity on her mother's face, she turned in controlled fury to the empty Windsor chair, surprised to hear how reasonable her voice sounded in the silent kitchen.

"Oh do fuck off, Mummy."

"Why doesn't she go and see his mother at Henworth Hall?" asked Webber. "Surely that's the most obvious move? She might have a perfectly simple explanation. It might not even be one Margaret would want to hear, but at least it would clear things up."

Mrs Thomas was giving him dinner in her own kitchen, flushed with enthusiasm and the glow from the fierce little coal fire, which on special occasions she still used to heat the oven of an ancient cast-iron cooking range. She beamed at him with affection before opening the oven door to baste a small golden-skinned hen chicken. He might just as clearly have said, "Well now, come along Lizzie, isn't this the life? And how simple to solve any little mystery so that we can go on enjoying it together?"

It was tempting for her, too. It was after all, as he had said, an odd little mystery but not a crime. The boy had stolen nothing, every penny and every cheque, every last silver spoon at the fair had been accounted for. People, as Webber had pointed out, disappeared every year in their thousands and they had every right to do so. It wasn't a matter for the police.

"I've kept it simple," she said, "no starters."

She put a plate in front of him, content to see him enjoy it in silence. Surrounding the chicken she had served the first broad beans of the year cooked in their pods, and new potatoes, both of which Webber had contributed from his garden, and there were rolls of crisp streaky bacon. From the table, in small jugs of blue and white china, he helped himself to pale giblet gravy and bread sauce. She liked eating in the kitchen where food and guests were under her control. It reminded her of her childhood. Even with the window and the door to the garden wide open, the warmth had made him take his jacket off and she liked that, too. At home there had always been a cat dozing on the rug but that would have to wait. You couldn't expect to tame everything all at once.

Afterwards she made tea which they both preferred to coffee. Through the open door, at the far end of the garden, he could see the motionless outline of the cat's ears and his head above the long grass. Lizzie wouldn't give up, he knew that. The fire made her face glow and her eyes on him were bright with affection. She looked, he thought, more like a young woman than someone of his own age. Sometimes he felt that the affection was spiced with an element of mockery at his reluctance to involve himself in her wilder enthusiasms. Then he felt old and he didn't like that.

36

"You can't even say that he stole anything from Margaret, pocket money and a few clothes freely given," he said over his tea cup. Considering that he'd reached the rank of Detective Inspector he could, she thought, be remarkably obtuse sometimes.

"You can hardly expect her to go trotting up to Henworth Hall to ask his Mam where he is," she said.

"Why not?"

"Oh John *bach*, do be sensible."

"I am being sensible, seems a perfectly logical step to me. If his mother can't tell her where he is, who can?"

"Like, 'excuse me but please can I have your little boy back'?"

"No, I suppose that would be a bit embarrassing for her."

"Well done, besides he didn't get on with his mother. Margaret didn't tell me why, I suppose he must have given her some reason for it."

"I'm surprised you didn't ask her."

"I did. She said it was a family matter. I didn't like to push."

"Of course not. Anything else?"

"She asked me if anything had happened to upset him at Dunwold."

"And had it?"

"I don't think so, neither Jimmy nor Doreen looked guilty enough to have made a pass at him."

"Would they have done?"

"Oh yes, I should think so, given half a chance, that's probably why Margaret came to collect him every night."

"So you think that it was an affair – with Margaret I mean?"

She shook her head thoughtfully. "No, I don't. She was mad about him of course – still is. But not an affair."

The coals settled in the grate, sending a trickle of ash on to the metal fender.

Webber lit his pipe with one of the rolled paper spills on the mantel shelf touched on to a glowing coal.

"The chicken was wonderful, Lizzie, what did you do to it?"

"Good, wasn't it? Been soaking in parsnip wine and lemon peel all night."

To Webber, at that moment, came the clear understanding of what he must do. The sooner he applied himself to the problem, the sooner he could look forward to a peaceful retirement, and the kind of meals he had come to accept as a natural right.

"Tell me again."

There was a subtle redistribution of her weight on the kitchen chair. "About that morning you came over to the fair?"

"Yes."

"It was quiet, you saw that yourself, just a few people wandering round, we'd more or less sold everything in the first few days. Mark said that would happen. He said if we were going to do well it would go early and it did. Jimmy and Doreen were talking to people on some other stands. Those who were still on speaking terms with us, anyway."

"You weren't very popular?"

"We'd bought all their best stuff."

"They didn't have to sell to you."

"Greedy, couldn't resist the cheque book and a quick profit. Mark had warned Jimmy not to question their prices. Just ask for their best trade price, he said, and accept it, and that's what we did."

She sat tidily on her kitchen chair her hands folded. "You should have seen their faces on that first day, those other exhibitors I mean. They stood round watching us sell all their things and pretending not to listen. There's a lot of hate in antiques, John."

"What kind of financial arrangement did Jimmy have with him?"

"Salary you mean?"

"Yes."

"Doreen said they gave him one hundred pounds after the first day and he was to get another two or three hundred at the end of the fair depending on how well they had done. But he never collected it."

"What made you follow him when he left the fair that morning?"

She thought back, striving to recall. "I was on the stand on my own, trying to flog some bits of Mason's Ironstone China. That was one of the few decent things Jimmy and Doreen had in their original stock. Mark made them split up a whole dinner service and sell it separately. You can ask a fortune for the stuff, goes like hot buns, and we'd only got a few chipped pieces left, even those go if you explain that they are original chips; you rub cigarette ash into them if they look too new."

"Mark?"

"Yes, he was there. It was quite early, we hadn't been open long, before you came, anyway. I'd got a terrible man from Bury St Edmunds talking away at me, so I can only remember Mark in sort of isolated flashes, while this boring old devil described every single piece of Mason's he'd ever bought since 1950. Every last detail too, including the price, and how much better and cheaper it all was than anything I was showing him. Someone came and talked to Mark, I didn't see his face but quite a big chap and young – judging by the back of his head and neck. I don't think they were talking about antiques. They didn't seem to be looking at anything on the stand, not like my rude know-all who was all over the place, standing on the furniture to reach up and price things on the top of the dresser. I remember turning to ask Mark to come and help me with the old pest. The other chap had still got his back to me so I could only see Mark's face and then, before I could say anything, Mark left and the other one followed him."

"But you Lizzie, why did you go, what made you follow him? Something in his face?"

"No – his face was nothing, just sort of blank. No, it was the way he moved. Usually he walked quite slowly everywhere. If he'd left like that I might not have followed him, but I had to. He was quick, dodging through the people. I could feel a sort of panic in him. It was like that other time, when I watched him through the glasses – like he was after something. There's something wrong, John. I know it."

৵ SEVEN ৶

THE FIRST DAY of Mrs Thomas's investigation began pleasantly.
She drank her early morning tea wandering barefoot in the jungle
grass of the lawn. In the privet hedge the cat stopped washing,
politely alert. From the tape deck in the kitchen, Papageno
instructed them in the proper way to catch birds.

By the time she had finished dressing the sun had established
itself firmly in the sky. The weather forecast proclaimed rain so
that, if it was to be relied on, she could look forward to a day of
unbroken sunshine and she had dressed accordingly. She wheeled
her bicycle out of the narrow front passage of the house and
locking the front door behind her sailed unhurriedly down the
main street of Flaxfield and out onto the Saxmundham road. Soon
she would turn off down the private drive which led to Henworth
Hall.

From the shop window of Trottwood Antiques, Betsey watched
his mother-in-law passing by with a mixture of envy and relief.
Envy and admiration for her equilibrium engendered by her
single-minded thrusting at the pedals and relief that she was
passing by.

The week at Dunwold had not been to his liking. His fears that it
would prove a humiliating disaster had been unfounded but that
had been no thanks to Mrs Thomas, whom he resented having
pushed him into the wretched business in the first place. If the
Dunwold Antique Fair represented the respected profession of
knowledgeable dealers in antiquity then he wanted no further part
of it. He tethered a rocking-horse to a brass standard lamp with an
elegant drape of tasselled white rope which had once divided the
front and back stalls of a long defunct country cinema. He liked the
rocking-horse, its ears stuck out of the holes he had cut in a straw
hat ringed with bright paper flowers. He liked the lamp too,
although no petty-minded vetting committee would have passed

either of them as antique and fit for sale to a gullible public, but the white rope he loved. For him it held magic. It had witnessed the joys and triumphs of his boyhood, seen Joan Crawford and the Light Brigade charging with square-shouldered courage against life and disaster.

"Your mother," he informed Doreen, who came in with two cups of coffee and a plate of mixed biscuits, "has just whizzed past in that pink and green frock."

Alone with her husband, Doreen was able to contemplate her mother with composure. It was only when forced into social contact with her for anything longer than an hour at the very most that she began to feel frustrated; managed and inadequate. In spite of the surface unsuitability of their marriage she was genuinely fond of her husband. Indeed, it was difficult for anyone to dislike him. She knew that and was grateful for his kindness and gentle nature. Sex had never been a part of their matrimonial contract and their relief in acknowledging that understanding had drawn them closer in companionship and affection. More than that, he could make her laugh, he not only liked her mother, but made her seem less formidable. Through him she saw a new Mrs Thomas, someone not all that unlike herself. It didn't make Doreen like her any more but it helped her to understand her. At this moment she felt drawn to him because she knew that her mother had pushed his tolerance to a fine edge of near rebellion from which only the miracle of the boy wonder had turned him aside.

"Why do you think he did it?" she asked.

"Disappeared?"

"Yes, that too, but I meant the fair, really."

He dipped a finger lightly on to the surface of the coffee, collecting the skin of the milk and placed it judiciously in the saucer. Ever since he had been a child he had done that.

"Not for our pretty faces?"

"Even if we were pretty, which we're not, we are just about twice his age. No, not that."

He sighed in mock sadness. "No."

They drank the coffee in silence and shared the biscuits, watching the morning shoppers slowing their pace to the warmth of the sunshine.

"Did he take any of that money – the cash I mean," she asked suddenly.

"I'm not very good at counting, you know that. That's why it took me all those hours to check. No, I told you, it was all there. Didn't you believe me?"

41

"You could have been protecting him."

"He was more honest than anyone in that ghastly fair. I hated them," Betsey said fiercely. "They all had that same look, it was always the money they thought about. They didn't really care for any of those things they were selling."

"Most of them weren't even proper dealers," she said, "just amateurs making money on the side, did you realise that?"

"That's why he could make rings round them, whatever else he is, he's not an amateur."

"Whatever else he is?"

Betsey brushed biscuit crumbs from the front of his shirt. "We never really knew him, did we? Not right from those first days when he used to come in here with Margaret. And she didn't know him either, not then and probably not ever – *unless* of course one day she comes to him when he's dying in a room overlooking the sea on Long Island and he begs her to forgive him." Somehow he looked exactly like Bette Davis even before he borrowed the hat from the horse. The clipped voice was exact too.

"Darling, this is too absurd. I'm simply not going to listen a moment longer. I've found the most marvellous and brilliant young doctor in New York, he looks like Montgomery Clift and I know you're going to love him."

Bette Davis blazed triumphantly at Doreen, pop-eyed and set-lipped.

"Why is he dying?" She had seen the act before but the plot was new.

"Drugs dear, of course," said Betsey abandoning Miss Davis. "Margaret picks up the golden youth – shine out little head sunning over with curls – and his tight jeans and all, she nurses him through an overdose and fights to help him kick the fatal addiction. He's been smuggling the stuff in through small ports like Dunwold, packing it into Staffordshire figures and using the antiques fairs as an outlet – simple."

"It's not a bad script but it doesn't explain his mother or the mysterious stranger yanking him away from the fair and the two of them driving off."

"I'm only the star," said Betsey with dignity, "you can't expect me to play the lead and write the story as well."

The dappled sunlight through the leaves of the trees overhanging the drive splashed on to the ruts and pot-holes, demanding Mrs Thomas's full attention. The bicycle zig-zagged its avoiding course so that from a distance rider and machine resembled the uneven flight of a vast pink and green butterfly, disguising the determination of its advance upon Henworth Hall.

On the whole she was wise, she thought, not to have accepted Sarah Collins' offer to accompany her. Very nice to have the added weight and dignity of the medical profession behind you but Sarah was best used as a source of information, to be consulted alone and at leisure. Mrs Thomas had a feeling that Sarah's presence at the Hall might well turn out to be a disadvantage.

"Oh well, suit yourself," Sarah had said. "Just thought I could smooth the entry a bit. They're a funny lot, they might well frisk you for gin or Mars bars, or they could be really bloody minded and refuse a visit at all."

The bicycle shot triumphantly out of the hazards of the drive into the open sunshine and the smooth path which circled the lawn. It deposited her at the bottom of the impressive flight of steps which led up to the Palladian terrace and the main entrance. She parked it against one of a pair of stone lions guarding the steps. On the terrace she looked out over the lawn where some distance away a group of diversely shaped ladies were being encouraged to touch their toes. The bouncing bobbing bottoms sent silent waves of agony across the callous grass. If they'd been animals, Mrs Thomas reflected, the place would have been prosecuted.

The entrance hall was handsome and big enough to make her footsteps echo on the tiled floor as she advanced towards the starched dragon at the reception desk. A refugee nurse from the National Health Service, the woman had long ago assumed the title and style of a hospital sister, wearing a uniform of that rank with an elaborate cap of stiff white cotton, like a seagull landing against the wind. Visitors were not forbidden at Henworth Hall but on the whole they were discouraged. Dr Maguire had found it difficult to make a hard and fast rule but he let it be known that he preferred the treatment of his ladies to proceed as far as possible without interruption. The dragon glanced down at the open appointments book. The morning, neatly divided into hourly sections, was blank and the admission book was equally explicit in informing her that no patient was expected.

Mrs Thomas did not wear a hat when riding her bicycle. The dragon observed her tousled hair, the uncompromising colour combination of her dress and decided that the visitor, in spite of the elastic surgical stockings, was unlikely to be a prospective customer considering a future course of treatment. When Mrs Thomas was still some yards away the woman's internal computer

43

had already programmed her features into a quite intricate blend of polite boredom and guarded hostility. Mrs Thomas absorbed the rebuff without effort, taking it easily in her last two strides, which brought her to the desk.

"There's lucky you are," she beamed confidently at the cap, "I can't wear hats, looks lovely, takes courage that, suits you too. I've come to visit Mrs Carter," she continued smoothly, before the computer could counter her opening gambit. "She's staying here, I believe."

The dragon's reply, and the rest of their conversation, was smothered by the exhausted murmur of the callisthenic ladies returning to be sweated out and hosed down before guzzling themselves on lettuce and lemon juice. When most of them had disappeared, the advantage had passed from Mrs Thomas and could be seen resting smugly on the face of the pseudo sister.

"I'm sorry, that's quite out of the question. As I said, all private addresses of our patients are highly confidential. As it happens all that information is kept in Dr Maguire's office but I'm quite sure he would tell you exactly the same."

"I might, I might." Maguire himself had appeared, perhaps lured from his office by the shrill cry of the seagull or the faint hint of sulphur in the air. "Mrs Thomas, how very nice to see you."

It wasn't, and he didn't sound as if it was, but he had known her in the days before he had left his practice in Flaxfield and instinct warned him that she was best isolated from both staff and patients as soon as possible. He guided her solicitously across the hall pausing to encourage and chat to one of the last of the stragglers.

"Such a nice woman," he said, as he closed the door of his office behind them. "They are all very pleasant, as it happens, but she is particularly nice, a Mrs Weikel. Her husband makes a great deal of money in the theatre. Not as an actor of course, he puts things on or backs them or something. I hope the good guardian sister didn't upset you, she can be a little abrupt sometimes. You wanted a patient's address, did I hear?"

"A Mrs Carter, her son's been working for us at the antique fair in Dunwold. He left suddenly – very suddenly and without his money. I thought I might get his address from his mother, but madam out there says she's left."

She was prepared to be polite to Maguire, she did not actively dislike the little man, but there was something about his dapper personality which she found unattractive. He was, she thought, like a spoiled and overfed child, clever but not to be trusted.

He walked back from the steel filing cabinet with a folder which, unexpectedly, he opened on the desk for her to see. His tiny manicured finger traced out the typed information on Joan Carter's file.

"As you can see, apart from the details of her age and her medical treatment which are in code, it is simply a record of her previous visits. The last entry shows that she left us quite recently."

The address given was Carter and Monmouth, Bond Street.

"No home address?"

"No – as you can see."

"And there is nothing to say that Mrs Carter and her son didn't like each other – not even in code?"

If she thought that might have jolted some information out of him, he was too well prepared to fall for it. Only the momentary gleam of satisfaction in his eyes, as he denied any such knowledge, told her that she was right. She was content to let the conversation drift back into small pleasantries as she walked back with him through the reception hall. When they passed the woman at the desk Mrs Thomas laughed loudly and appreciatively to let her see that she was on terms of some considerable intimacy with her boss. It gave her some satisfaction, but not much. The look of disapproving bitterness on the woman's face encouraged Mrs Thomas to go further and to surprise Dr Maguire by pecking his cheek in a farewell kiss.

At the foot of the terraced steps, where she had left her bicycle, a spotty girl was waiting for her.

"Were you asking for Mrs Carter?"

❧ EIGHT ❧

"It's best if you cycle up the drive for a bit," said the spotty girl, in her soft Suffolk voice, "just like you was leaving, but if you take that first narrow little footpath on the left that'll bring you out behind the house. Mrs Weikel's got one of those big flats round the back, an' she say please she like to speak to you confidential."

"Just a minute, Annie," said Mrs Thomas, as the girl turned to hurry away, "it is Annie Spicer, isn't it?" The girl nodded. "I thought so, Dr Collins said you'd got pretty hair so I guessed it must be you. Annie, when you spoke to Mrs Carter's son, you remember?" Annie Spicer nodded again. "Well what did you think of him?"

"I liked him, I told Dr Collins that." She didn't seem in such a hurry to get away now and walked back to Mrs Thomas and the bicycle. "Dr Maguire, he talked about him and Mrs Weikel and now you. Why? Has he done something?"

"I don't know, he just left very suddenly with money owing to him. He earned it and then left without it. He ought to have it, that's all."

The girl considered this information then suddenly laughing said, "Well that's nice to have people pushing money on you, that makes a change, I will say!"

"What did Dr Maguire ask you about him?"

"Didn't ask anything, he told me."

"Told you what?"

"Don't let him in again, said everyone had orders. Mrs Carter didn't want to see him again, he said. So something's up, that I do know. Anyway that's daft."

"What is, Annie?"

"That—'don't let him in' business—you don't have to go through the house to get to her flat or to Mrs Weikel's. You'll see when you get round the back there. There's two flats out over the

46

stables and they've both got their own entrances."

There was something about this woman with her funny sing-song accent that Annie Spicer liked. She wished she had more time to talk to her, especially about Mrs Carter's son, but she was already late for her hot towel duty. The sound of distant voices from the terrace above them prompted a final burst of confidence.

"You reckon that Miss Garland frightened him off then?"

Sarah Collins had said Annie was a local girl, so of course she would have known about the boy staying with Margaret. You could never stop village gossip, Mrs Thomas thought virtuously, but you could at least guide it accurately.

"Good gracious girl, no. She gave him a lift and then he got food poisoning, so she looked after him for a bit, that's all."

Annie Spicer nodded cheerfully. "You could see he was nicer than that other lot."

"What other lot, Annie?"

"The ones Dr Maguire used to have working here. Local boys mostly, fancied themselves, dead common lot – stuck up things."

She moved away as the voices got louder but had time to grin and fling cheekily over her shoulder, "I told my Mam. I said he's a proper little smasher, he could leave his boots under my bed any time!"

Mrs Weikel wore an expensively tailored white linen trouser suit. Her fair hair, still damp from her shower, was tied back from her forehead with a bandeau of chocolate coloured silk. Her shirt was of the same material so that with her blue eyes, tanned skin and slight figure, she reminded Mrs Thomas of a Siamese cat. The American accent with its warm nasality completed the resemblance, excepting only her disposition to instant friendship, which was definitely unfeline, more like a friendly puppy starved of companionship. It was an intriguing combination and Mrs Thomas warmed to it.

"I'm Arlene. Arlene Weikel. We met briefly in the hall with Dr Maguire – he a friend of yours by the way?"

"I knew him in the old days, when he practised in Flaxfield, I hardly ever see him now."

"Good, I don't like him much either but the place suits me so I use it, and say listen, how about Sister Succotash on the desk! Isn't she something, though? Isn't she just? Waow! I'm told she never even made it with the footballers, although to be fair it was hardly what they were paid for, poor darlings. Losing me, huh?" she enquired politely, when she caught the look on Mrs Thomas's face.

"A bit, I'll catch up. I'm a good listener."

"OK Lizzie," she paused, as if she saw Mrs Thomas for the first time. The hands clasped round one knee of the trouser suit were older than her face, she could have been almost any age between forty and sixty. When she spoke the tone was different from the bright social chatter she had used earlier. "Look, I have some questions, naturally you have every right to say get lost."

"Try me."

"I'd very much like to know why you were asking about Joan Carter. I'm sorry, but I eavesdropped shamelessly when you were getting the brush-off from Succotash. Are you a friend of Joan's?"

"I've never met her in my life."

In the beginning, Webber had once told Mrs Thomas, tell people things. You might want to leave something out but you must never lie to them. You see, you can never be sure how much they know themselves. If they hear only one lie, and they know it for a lie, you've lost them for good. When you want information you must learn to give it yourself first. Later on, Webber had said, the rules get more complicated.

Mrs Weikel proved that she too could listen, and she heard her visitor out in silence. Sometimes she got up and moved around the room, once to get a cigarette from a box on the mantel, and again to lean against a panelled recess and look out across the stable yard to where the twin flat, so lately occupied by Joan Carter, stood empty. But all the time she listened. Mrs Thomas began with Mark Carter's arrival in Margaret Garland's car and gave an accurate account of his behaviour until the moment she had seen him follow a stranger out of Dunwold Town Hall and drive off with him. She left out the vicious stoning attack she had witnessed through her binoculars.

"I've always been nosey," she explained decorously, smoothing the pink and green dress over her knees. "I can't help it, and I'm fond of the Garland girl. I just wanted to find out what was going on, because nothing seems to add up does it? It doesn't make sense. That's why I wanted to see his mother."

Mrs Weikel walked to a corner cupboard made of stripped pine. The panelling and most of the furniture was in the same wood, simple but effective against the richness of the flowered pattern of the upholstered chairs and sofas and the cream of the carpet and curtains. It looked expensive and it was. The corner cupboard, to Mrs Thomas's surprise, was generously stacked with bottles of alcohol. The trouser suit stood in front of it in silence for a moment, the thin arms akimbo on the hips of a young girl. When she spoke it was as if she had decided something: bright and businesslike, "Alrighty, what'll it be?"

"Guinness?"

"No, sorry I guess not. Lager?"

"That will do nicely, ta."

Arlene Weikel poured it and brought it with her own malt whisky and Perrier water to the table between them, lighting another cigarette before she spoke. She was very much the Madison Avenue business woman.

"OK Lizzie, one question. You mentioned your friend, a Detective Inspector I think you said, right?"

"Ex – he's retired now, has been for some years."

The hands flew up and stayed for a second, ringed fingers spread before her. "That's it! That's what I thought. I just wanted to be sure. Ex is what I wanted to hear, because I sure as hell don't want to get mixed up in any official enquiry. OK? Well now, I guess I could just tell you I was worried about Joany Carter and I am, but you really ought to know the background."

In the brief pause before she began her story, Arlene wondered if her instinct about this odd little woman in the ghastly dress was right. The moment's doubt passed; yes, she was right to confide in her, the way she sat sipping her lager beer and waiting quietly, and the way she had told her own story made her someone to be trusted and God knows there weren't many of them around. She had drunk over half of the whisky in her glass in one gulp but topped it up almost to the rim with more Perrier water.

"I met Joan Carter down here for the first time just after the place opened. You say you never met her? Well she's a big girl and she sure as hell needed to lose some. Me, I just collect fat farms, I fool around with the diet and exercises but mostly I use them as hotels where I don't have to meet my husband's show-business people. It's a good out for me, my recipe for hell is a party full of charming actors and actresses being charming. When I first came these two flats weren't here, they were converted later. I've seen some screwy ideas in the States, but Henworth Hall when it first opened was wild. Like the man Maguire had this theory, that young male attendants were good for rheumatism and morale. When I saw those kids on the welcome parade in the hall the first day I checked in, I thought I'd wandered into an audition for one of my husband's plays. Everyone as cute as a cover-boy, but not a limp wrist among the lot of them, hand-picked everyone. I found

49

out later that most of them were local boys, some from the farms and at least half from the village football team. Of course it was crazy, most of the old girls ran around like chickens with a fox in the hen house. Oh sure, some of the younger ones had a ball, but after the big fight in the swimming pool Maguire called turkey and quit."

"Called turkey?"

"Sure, when a show is a total bomb – a disaster – you get out. Who wants a screaming bunch of jealous women raising storm waves in the plunge pool? So the footballers left and peace descended upon the waters."

Mrs Thomas sipped her lager thoughtfully, she was enjoying herself with Arlene. "I suppose you didn't manage to see the fight?" she asked wistfully.

"Wouldn't you just know I'd miss it? I was on duty in London, but the word is it was like the battle of Midway. I believe some of the girls fancied the same guy but it was all hushed up and I never did hear the full story. OK. Background set, picture steady and holding. Any questions?"

"Did Mrs Carter take to any of the young men?"

"Take to! I like it, Bingo," she topped up her glass again, so that now she was drinking the spa water neat. "Sure she did, why not, if that's what she wanted. She may have been big but she could be fun and the young boys loved her for it. In those days Joan was a lot of laughs. Oh don't get me wrong, she was never a tramp like some of them but she enjoyed life and hell why not? She was paying for it and she knew how to be discreet."

"Did you think of her as a close friend?"

Arlene considered. "Sure. OK, maybe never great close buddies but sure, we were friends – I guess. We'd talk about Weikel's shows, she was interested in the theatre, and she told me a bit about antiques and all. But it was mostly polite girl-talk, houses, servants, she had a flat in London and a house somewhere in the country." She paused. "No, I guess I never knew her really well, I liked her but she was a very private person and she changed."

"When was that?"

"Maybe she thought I was prying, I don't know. It was when she told me her husband had died. I remember she more or less had to. I'd come down from London and made some polite enquiry about her family and she told me."

"Did she say how he died?"

"An accident of some kind. She didn't want to talk about it. It was then I realised how little I knew about her private life. I knew she had a son and then of course there was Billy."

"And Billy was —?"

"Right! Billy was the kid she took to. I told you she'd fooled around with some of the others before that but when Billy arrived on the scene you could see that he was her favourite and I never saw her with any of the others again. I don't know why but there was a kind of innocence about it all. He wasn't like the cover-boys. She told me they played scrabble together and I believed her leastways . . . you want some more beer?" she asked solicitously.

Mrs Thomas had been looking thoughtfully, but she hoped not pointedly, into her empty glass. "Eh? Oh! Ta, it's nice that, not too gassy. Can I ask you about her son?"

"You can Lizzie, and Arlene will tell you, but there is just one last bit of background I guess you need first."

She had refilled their glasses, perching herself like a teenager on the arm of a sofa.

"As you might guess these flats are nothing to do with the main routine at Henworth Hall. It costs an arm and a leg — one night here is a week at the Ritz — but you can order anything you like, the best food, the best anything, from foie gras to footballers. Me, I buy peace and privacy," she smiled, "and since you're too nice to ask, that's what Mr Weikel buys too, peace and privacy — only in London or New York. It works fine."

"And Mrs Carter?"

"Joany? The same, I guess, plus the most expensive game of scrabble in the world."

"She still saw Billy?"

"Sure, he was often over there, sometimes I'd meet them out in the yard, they'd go walking together, not far, she wasn't built for it. I thought it was kinda cute."

"What did you think of him?"

"I liked him, he was a bit like a labrador, gentle and sort of protective."

"Like a bodyguard?"

"Perhaps, except he wasn't there when she needed him. Remember I told you earlier that I never got to know her really well, that she was a very private person?"

"I remember."

"Well it was true, but I hadn't realised she was that way because she was scared, and that she was scared because of her son."

"That time he came to see her?"

"He came the following day too. They had refused to let him in at the front of house, so he came round the back way."

"And she saw him again?"

"No, she wouldn't let him in. He went up those outside stairs there to the door of the flat. He only knocked once and after that he just stood there, waiting and not moving. Weird?"

"She could have phoned the desk."

"Well she didn't, because no one came."

"She could have been out."

"No. I'd seen her moving around and he was waiting – like he knew she was there too. Finally, and it must have been at least ten minutes that he was standing there at that door, then he walked back down the steps. He wasn't hurried, it was all very calm and deliberate. Down in the stable yard there he picked up a loose cobble stone, big, like a tennis ball, and threw it straight through one of her windows. God knows what it sounded like in the flat, it was a hell of a crash. Then he just walked away, he still wasn't hurrying, he walked round the corner of the house and he never looked back once."

In her memory Mrs Thomas saw him walking across the fields and then stop to pick up the stones.

"Where was her friend, Billy?"

"Sure, where was he, where had he been all the day Billy boy? In fact for those two days. The days when Mark Carter came she was alone."

"Did she speak to you about it?"

"Not exactly, I spoke to her, though. It's not easy when someone's face is telling you to mind your own business while she is being frightfully British and saying, 'I'm sorry if you were disturbed, I'm afraid my son and I are not very friendly'. I don't know how she explained it but they fixed the glass the same day."

"And Billy?"

"Billy apparently had been sick for those two days."

"But he came back as usual after that?"

"Yes, it was back to square one, he'd come as usual in the mornings, about ten. I never spoke of it to her again, it was only small talk if we happened to meet. She was frightened, not just scared, but really frightened."

"Did you meet her with Billy?"

"Yes, just once, and she was still frightened to hell. They hardly ever left the flat. She stuck it as long as she could and then one day she left. She left without a word to me and she left early and alone, before Billy came. She ordered a car for seven o'clock, she paid her check and packed and left. When Billy came at ten o'clock she'd gone and the flat was clean, not even a scrap of paper left in the waste basket."

"She could have gone home – to London or to her home in the country."

"She could but I doubt it. I sure as hell wouldn't if I was that scared, besides the hire car took her to Cambridge and dropped her at the station, I checked."

Mrs Thomas swirled the last inch of lager in her glass so that the released bubbles hissed delicately in the silence.

"You didn't speak to Billy that morning?"

"No, I watched him go into the flat, I could see him moving around from room to room, then he came out and drove away. That was when I went over and then checked with the desk and the car-hire people, so now I was really worried, but there's more."

Mrs Thomas nodded. "I think I can guess. Billy came back didn't he? He came back in his little blue car only this time he wasn't alone. He came back with Mark Carter."

⚜ NINE ⚜

JUNE ENDED WITH rain and cold winds bringing in a July that seemed more like the beginning of a chill autumn. It was doubly depressing for Mrs Thomas to have to admit that, in spite of her best efforts, she had discovered nothing of any great significance. Flaxfield closed its doors and windows against the rain which drifted across the flat East Anglian landscape, soaking the fields and the streets of the village with the same dismal veil of drizzle. The one bright spot was Webber.

It was unlikely, she told herself, that the general gloom and depression would have so discouraged her that she would have abandoned what she had come to see as a personal challenge, but there could be no doubt that she no longer felt herself to be alone. For Webber was hooked, and with him to help and support her she gained courage and determination. She fed him some of her best recipes and any scrap of information she could glean.

On a night when the rain streamed silently down the windows of her kitchen they sat in the comfort of the warmth from the cooking range and she was happy to let him think in silence as she watched him eat. She gave him grilled lamb chops with a simple purée of young carrots and celeriac; and she served it with a jelly of rowanberry, crab apple and mint. Sometimes she gave him wine or beer to drink with his food, but tonight she wanted his head to be clear, he could have a drink after the meal. For his pudding she let him wait and digest while she cooked him paper-thin pancakes, dusting them on his plate with caster sugar and giving him quarters of fresh lime and a generous dash of hot rum.

"If you were back in the force and you had it as a case," she said, when they had finished the washing up and he was smoking his pipe, "what could you do?"

"Ah! Lizzie you're thinking of all my old boasting stories of the days when I thought I was God's gift to every new recruit, a bit full

54

of myself I'm afraid, very much the wise one. I expect the pipe fooled them." He grunted with pleasure as he gently disturbed the bottom of the fire with the poker, encouraging it into renewed life. "Mind you, the pipe was always useful – fill it, light it, get it going well – takes time, lets you think of something to say."

When he smiled like that, she thought, that's how he looked as a child, a little boy, charming his mother for pocket money. Perhaps he'd been like that too when he first married, until it had all gone sour and there'd been nothing left for him to ask for – except divorce.

"It isn't a case, Lizzie. Tell any policeman about it and he'd put you on to the R.S.P.C.A. They'd probably say the same – no case."

"But you don't think that?"

"When I said *any* policeman, I meant a working policeman, poor devil, with an office and a dozen jobs to work on and all at the same time, not an old crock they've pensioned off in case he drops dead on them."

The look of distress on her face made him at once regret having mentioned his heart. She was very fond of him, he knew that quite well, and it was clumsy and inconsiderate of him.

She was indeed fond of him but not blindly so. The look of distress had contained an element of disappointment that, trained observer though he was, he had quite missed. When he had been Maguire's patient in the old days Mrs Thomas had not been privy to his exact clinical condition. It had been her suggestion that when Maguire had removed his talents to Henworth Hall Webber should choose to be under the medical care of Dr Sarah Collins in preference to that of her husband. She had nothing against Peter Collins, with his mild obsession for slaughtering rabbits and his addiction to television, but as a source of indiscreet information she had found him unsatisfactory.

It was unlikely, Sarah had told her when Mrs Thomas had first tackled her on the subject, that John Webber would actually drop down dead. He was a bit overweight, blood pressure sometimes higher than she would like but nothing worth filling him with pills for. The police might well consider him best retired but there was no reason to suppose him a seriously sick man. What Mrs Thomas feared most was that he would spoil an active life and degenerate into a careful Suffolk gardener. She wasn't going to allow that.

There were times, thought Webber, as he watched her pleasant dumpy features drift from disappointment to pugnacity, when she looked very like Karsh's wartime portrait of Churchill. It was time to sing for his supper.

"What I'm trying to say," he said brightly, after refilling and lighting his pipe, "is that, with a little common sense and application, we probably stand a better chance of finding out what is going on than I would if I'd had it as a case in the force. Do you know the actual percentage of all crimes that are officially – and I'm quoting the Home Office figures for 1980 – officially solved by genuine police detective work? No? Well I'll tell you Lizzie, it is just two point five per cent – that's all. That's solved I mean by the real thing, sifting, elimination, all that; the rest of the poor sods who get nicked are shopped by informers, sometimes by paid pros but quite often by friendly neighbours."

If the weather had been anything like summer she would have suggested they walked down to the pub for a beer and a Guinness, the scene of so many of their happiest evening conversations, but she didn't like the idea of him sitting there in wet trouser legs. He could get just as wet walking home but at least he could change into something dry there. Later, when he'd gone, she would take some food out for Bunter. When the weather was fine and providing she was alone, the cat had occasionally come into the kitchen for his meals but he had always finally retired to the ruins of a battered tool-shed at the bottom of the garden wilderness where she had turned an old dustbin on its side and lined it with clean straw.

"There's bottled beer or Guinness or you can finish what's left of that rum."

He chose the rum and he talked, which was what she wanted him to do. "When Margaret told you that Mark didn't get on with his mother," he said, "she evaded your questions by saying that it was a family matter. Why didn't you pursue it? That seemed unlike you, I thought."

"I think she wanted a clean record on the gossip. She still thought he might suddenly come back and she didn't want something he'd told her in confidence to be common knowledge in the village. Sometimes you can push but not when it's like that, you'd lose a friend. She'll tell me when she's ready."

"You're probably right. Anyway, she's bound to be biased and there's no guarantee he would have told her the truth. Still, that's the obvious approach. Mark and his mother. If we can find them."

The warmth of the fire and the room were pleasant but dangerous. He would do well, he knew, to collect his points and arguments before he drifted and slept. Quite a good idea, he thought, would be to rest the heavy lids for a brief moment, having first carefully composed his face in decent concentration. He had indeed already prepared a few notes and entered them into a small pocket note-book: no harm in sorting them through mentally before sharing them with her.

"Rain's stopped," she shouted. It was odd how she did that sometimes when he was deep in thought. "Come on boy *bach*, I could do with some air and we'll stop for a beer at the Bull. No, don't bother finishing the rum, I'll put it back in the bottle, come in handy for a sauce."

In their favourite corner in the Bull, and overheard by no one except the watercolour portrait of a prize racing pigeon, Webber had both eyes and the note-book open.

"You won't get much farther down here in the village. Now, let's see," he looked at his notes. "First Henworth Hall. Well you seem to have got as much as you could from your American. What about any of the other old girls – could she have chummed up with any of those, d'you think?"

"She could but I doubt it, she practically lived there and most of the others come and go. She and Mrs Weikel used it much more like a hotel and remember she apparently didn't mix much – 'a vurry private person'."

"Except for the boy friend."

"Billy – yes I thought that was the best bet until I tried to find him."

Webber looked at his notes again.

"Billy Miller – not a local boy. Maguire insists that he was never on the staff, that he was a private friend of Mrs Carter and – let's see – oh yes, your source for that was Sarah Collins. Well in with Maguire, is she?"

"No not really, she gets pin money from him sometimes, she gets called in for the occasional second opinion. She finds him a bit cagey – so did I."

Webber grunted, she was right, Maguire was canny and secretive but he had got on well enough with him in the old days. Henworth Hall was conveniently close, he might well loosen him up a little more on the subject of Mrs Carter and Billy Miller. It was even possible that Maguire might be tempted into putting some more flesh on to the shadowy figure of Mark Carter himself. It all came back to him in the end.

"I can chase up Maguire and I might get a line on Billy boy. If he only turned up in the day he must have stayed somewhere round here." He fetched her another bottle of Guinness from the bar and re-filled his pint with Adnam's bitter. "Right, cheers, so that's Henworth Hall, and assuming that you don't get anything else out of Margaret Garland, I don't see that we've got any other leads down here. I don't suppose he confided anything to Jimmy or Doreen?"

"I didn't even bother to ask. If I couldn't get anything out of him except short lectures on antiques, I know they didn't. Doreen couldn't help chattering if she'd found out anything and Jimmy would have honoured a confidence but gone round looking like Bunter after a meal and he didn't so no, that's a dead end, too."

"Do you think it's possible that he did borrow a lot of money from Margaret and she won't admit it? It wouldn't be the first time a con victim had kept quiet through pride, in fact I'd say it was more often the rule than the exception. Why did you believe her?"

Mrs Thomas savoured her drink, rationing the sips. "I just did, she couldn't act that well. When I asked her straight out she never hesitated, poor lamb. 'I wish I had,' she said, 'it would make more sense; better than wondering if I had bad breath.' No, she never lent him big money and I believe her when she says he kept a note of everything else she gave him – a few clothes and pocket-money, even food if she'd let him."

His pint was still a good quarter full and, in spite of her rationing, the Guinness in her glass had mysteriously vanished. In such cases she had found it delicate and convenient to head for the lavatory ordering and paying for another round at the bar en route to be collected on her way back. It prolonged the evening and stopped any argument about money. She payed for the beer but never got to the loo.

"Elizabeth my dear! I thought I might just find you here. I saw your lights were out when I was on my evening round. My dear, isn't this weather ghastly and so cold! No certainly not, bless you, I wouldn't hear of it and I'm dashing away – a large G and T, Alfie please."

Sarah Collins' duffel coat was soaked and the rain had flattened her hair into a severe contrast of yellow and brown streaks, but her eyes were bright and happy in the wet face. "Goodness I wanted that, who'd think I'd be worrying about hypothermia patients in July. Poor old dears, I do feel sorry for some of them." She kicked a large wicker basket at her feet, "I've been rabbit dumping, the freezer is still half full of the brutes but sinking slowly. I'm prescribing hot stew as the great panacea this week. You never know, might be true, makes more sense than some of Maguire's daft ideas. I've still got two left, can't tempt you I suppose? Oh no,

58

of course, quite right, you told me, even your poor old puss is bored with them. I'd forgotten. Not to worry, they're still stiff, I'll sling them back in the freezer. I do wish my Peter saw them like Beatrix Potter and not destructive pests he has to put down, but he's a dedicated realist, I'm afraid."

From his seat in the corner Webber watched them talk, his pint trapped between them on the bar, and returned to his notes. It was a question of balance, he told himself. If really necessary, which he doubted, he would be prepared to exert himself and extend his enquiries beyond the convenient confines of Flaxfield. The obvious extension of the investigation was London and the only certain link there was the address Joan Carter had given, the address of the antique business of Carter and Monmouth in Bond Street. It was not all that unusual these days for rich people to be reluctant to advertise their private home address but Carter and Monmouth might be prepared to contact her in London or at her house in the country. It seemed possible that she was at neither of them but it was a lead. More interesting still, they might know where her son was.

Mrs Thomas carried the drinks across the room to Webber's table. Behind her Sarah Collins had her glass in one hand and her briefcase in the other, she pushed the rabbit basket in front of her with her foot. "Hullo, John. I've just been telling Elizabeth. I've found out why Mark Carter's face was so familiar when I first saw him."

ఆ TEN ♭

FROM THE SITTING room window of Arlene Weikel's suite in the
Ritz Hotel Mrs Thomas looked down at the traffic in Piccadilly to
her right and the pleasant view over Green Park on her left.

It had been decided that she should open up the London
enquiry and that Webber would be more useful seeing Maguire at
Henworth Hall. He had also promised to feed Bunter while she
was away. She was quite content; the fact that she knew he
preferred to stay at home didn't weaken his arguments for doing
so. She could have insisted that he came with her but her instinct
told her strongly that it would have been a mistake. To dominate a
partnership was certainly sensible, to be seen to do so was foolish.

These questions aside she would not have arranged it otherwise.
She was in London on her own terms and she had made her own
plans. Jimmy Trottwood had found himself volunteering to drive
her up from Flaxfield. He was not only to be useful as her
chauffeur. She had sorted through the ragbag of his past gossip
surprising him with the detailed accuracy of her memory. She had
seen at once that he held a key that might open back doors and
save a time-wasting assault on a forbidding citadel. He was
already briefed and on his way. Her own source of information had
reported progress, had hinted even at revelations, and was about
to appear before her. Boredom had been finally pulled from her
shoulders and only the knowledge that Arlene Weikel might
emerge from the bathroom at any moment prevented her from
dancing round the room with sheer excitement.

Some fifty yards down Piccadilly towards Hyde Park Corner
she had a clear view of a bus stop and near it the entrance to Green
Park tube station. She also had a clear view of Jimmy Trottwood
waiting patiently for a number 19 which would take him to
Knightsbridge, Sloane Square and eventually the King's Road in
Chelsea. It was obviously a bad morning for 19s, other buses

pulled up and left without him. She hoped he would look up so that she could wave encouragement to him. He wouldn't know which window she might be in, of course, but it was unlikely he would have missed the orange dress with the white facings. Yet another bus drew away without him and she watched him turn and go down the stone steps to the tube station. It was a pity, it wasn't every day that she had a chance to wave from the Ritz.

The sitting room of Arlene Weikel's suite was simply furnished, functional and comfortable, with only the occasional hint of pre-restoration Baroquefeller gleaming incongruously in some of the original moulding of the ceiling and walls. Over the sofa a Spanish dancer by Russell Flint froze precariously in the middle of a drop-kick. Head on one side Mrs Thomas considered the pose appreciatively. In her earlier days she had been much attracted to competition ballroom dancing and although her legs and her figure had been restricted by the voluminous skirts she had battled through many happy hours in the Latin-American section. She had just succeeded in pointing her toe and arching her neck with her hands castaneted above her head in a quite reasonable facsimile of the print over the sofa when Arlene Weikel slouched in from the bathroom. Wrapped in a white towelling dressing gown, she collapsed into an armchair and groaned.

"Lizzie honey, shocks in the morning I can live without." She picked up a phone and ordered coffee which arrived with impressive speed. Before it came she gathered the folds of the dressing gown around her neck with an old brown hand at her throat and marked time with an account of what she referred to as her "duty party" of the night before. Mr Weikel, in collaboration with his English producers, had launched his latest Broadway hit on the West End and had entertained lavishly. Mrs Weikel had been on duty and had not enjoyed the play or the party. Mrs Thomas sat tidily and patiently on the sofa and loved every moment of it throughout two cups of coffee. Not for some time did it dawn on her that the party had not taken place in the room she was sitting in but in a larger suite occupied by Walter Weikel. Separate bedrooms would have been impressive at the Ritz, separate suites was unimaginable luxury. It was a different glamorous world, a world that Flaxfield only glimpsed through the gossip columnists of the newspapers. It came as a shock to realise that you could be part of it and dislike it as much as Arlene.

"Sure I hate it, but I don't hate the money, I just like to enjoy it my own way. Selfish huh? Well, could be. I'm lucky with Walt, he knows how I feel and it works, has done for thirty years so we must

61

have something going for us. OK, party over, thank God – you want more coffee? Right, so I think the theatre stinks, well Lizzie have I got news for you, so does the big world of the antique trade. I've fished up all the news I could find on my erstwhile buddy Joan Carter and honey, Snow White she is not."

Jimmy Trottwood hadn't been back to London for a long time and not until he was alone in the train did he have time to collect his thoughts. He peered at the stylised map of the stations above the seats opposite, Green Park, Hyde Park Corner, Knightsbridge and then at South Kensington he would have to change and go back along the line to Sloane Square and from there he would walk down the King's Road. Sloane Square, King's Road, names too nostalgic for him to think of without slipping back through the years when he had shared a flat in Chelsea with his mother and worked in Peter Jones, the big store in Sloane Square, first in soft furnishings and later rising to the dizzy height of window dresser. Like Mrs Thomas he felt a heady sense of excitement and not solely because he might help to unravel the mystery surrounding Mark Carter. There was too, a delightful sense of freedom, a late return to times past. Even the noise of the train and the secret worlds of his fellow passengers carried him back to a time in his youth when in his loneliness every carriage might have contained a friend for life with a destination more distant than any station on the Inner Circle. In the window opposite him his reflection was disturbingly distorted by the double glazing, making his wig appear to float unnervingly an inch above his scalp. It placed his journey firmly on the Inner Circle and his destination as Sloane Square.

At South Kensington the train slipped into daylight and he sat on a bench waiting for his connection. The station looked very much as he had remembered it except that there were many more coloured faces on the platform. As a young man he had hardly ever seen a black man apart from "Sanders of the River" and the occasional American serviceman during the war, and in Flaxfield they were still a rarity. It was quite exciting, like suddenly being in Jamaica or Bombay without having to pay the fare. Perhaps they were all going to a special rally or a concert of Indian music at the Albert Hall. He would ask Dudley about it.

The train took a long time to arrive and by the time he got to Sloane Square he was already late for his appointment. It was perhaps just as well, he thought, or he could not have resisted walking round every window of Peter Jones. He wouldn't have gone in, that would have been too painful, there would be no one there to recognise him. It was gone, like the days when he could comb his hair and run up the escalators. Perhaps Dudley wouldn't recognise him either, it wouldn't have surprised him, it was many years since they had met and known each other intimately but not well. He bought a bunch of mixed summer flowers at the open-air stall in the Square, hurrying past the windows of his past triumphs and on down the King's Road which had once carried Charles II to visit Nell Gwynne.

The King's Road as he remembered it had disappeared. It had been a village street in his time, now it was a desert of hideous male boutiques with only the occasional oasis of a familiar name. The fish shop on the corner where he had bought kippers and herrings for pennies was gone and had been replaced by something called "Guys and Dolls". Here he turned right into Lincoln Street and almost at once left into Coulson Street. Halfway along on the right a gap in the diminutive houses led him into the cobbled cul-de-sac called Draycott Mews and at number 7 he rang the bell.

When they had first met as young men, Dudley Dear had been a floor manager at the B.B.C., young, fun, outrageous, with a mop of straw-coloured hair. The friendship had been fun, too, but frowned upon by Jimmy's mother. She had disapproved strongly of Dudley Dear and had left both young men in no doubt of her feelings. The friendship had faltered and died. Dudley had done well through the years, advancing to Personal Assistant and then to Director until his recent retirement as Producer. A pounding of feet on a staircase gave Jimmy a second's panic before the door opened. It had been so long; perhaps Mr Dear would be more acceptable than Dudley for his first greeting? The door opened to reveal a small monkey-faced man with a balding head studying him in silence. The face broke into a familiar happy grin.

"Betsey my dear, you gave me such a shock! I thought it was your mother. Come in, do."

His worst fears that Dudley Dear would spend hours wandering down Memory Lane so that it would take ages before he could ask him about Mark were unfounded. He listened quietly to Jimmy without interrupting. The naughtiness and charm he had loved all those years ago were still there but only, Jimmy thought, because I remember them so well. For the rest, I could be talking to a pleasant stranger with businessman's hair and a sober suit. I could have sat opposite to him on the tube and never known him.

"It was a pilot programme," he said when Jimmy had finished, "went out late one night, eleven-thirty, something like that, long past your bedtime if I remember rightly. I'm surprised you saw it."

"I didn't, someone in the village thought she remembered his face. Her husband watches a lot and it suddenly came to him. It had been worrying her."

"It worried a lot of people that face; you know of course that he's as normal as God ever made anybody?"

"Yes I know that, tell me about the programme."

"It was a try-out – a pilot as I said. You get an idea and do a sort of test programme. If it's good you hope it might turn into a series."

"And was it any good?"

Dudley Dear looked at the plump figure wedged into the armchair. Mews flats are not very big and he'd bought small sized chairs to give an impression of space. The eyes were the same, he thought, and the gentle kindness in them. The wig was ghastly, but bless him, he'd always been proud of his hair, all the same you'd think someone could have stopped him or made sure it was a better fit.

"You've told me about your antique fair so in a way you can guess the answer. Yes it was good," he fetched a vase from the small kitchen and began arranging the flowers. "I've always liked antiques, we both did I remember, but for years I couldn't afford anything really good. I promised myself that when I could I'd get the best, and so, my dear, one day I was walking down Bond Street and in the window of Carter and Monmouth I saw something so ravishingly beautiful that I just fell in love with it and knew I had to have it. No it was not, as your one-track window-dressing mind has obviously assumed, the boy Carter. I bought that little seventeenth century oak chest over there. Pretty?"

"It's beautiful," said Jimmy.

"Isn't it though? 1670 and a fortune but I've never regretted it. There – how do they look?"

"Terrible, you were always hopeless with flowers – let me – but go on."

"My God, you really are like your mother. Well, that was the start. I took to dropping into the shop whenever I could. Occasionally I bought things, nothing else as expensive as that, but it was a lovely place just to see things and listen to them talk."

"Them?"

"Mark and his father. Monmouth would sometimes appear but mostly it was just the two of them. You've met Mark, well his father taught him all that. No, that's not strictly true, a lot of it came from his father but the boy was a natural, he had that rare ability you see sometimes of just soaking up knowledge wherever he found it. You know, of course, that he didn't actually work for Carter and Monmouth?"

"No, I didn't."

"Well he was always dropping in to see his father but they didn't employ him. I got the impression that he and Aubrey Monmouth didn't hit it off together."

"So how did he earn his living?"

"In antiques of course, but on his own. He told me that even if he had been invited he wouldn't have joined the Bond Street set-up. He was shrewd, he knew exactly what he wanted, that's why he wouldn't go to a university – he wanted to know the business from the bottom up. Sometimes he helped a friend in the Portobello street market but his basic knowledge he got as a runner – the hard way. Buying cheap and running it to the best buyer, sometimes to his father but not necessarily, he went where he could get the price he wanted and he always knew where that was most likely to be. He once found a filthy dirty old oil painting of ships, he paid thirty-five pounds for it and sold it to Carter and Monmouth for five hundred pounds."

"They must have thought it was worth it."

"Of course they did, worth more than even Mark thought. It was one of his earliest lessons, he told me. It was by an English marine painter called Thomas Whitcombe. Mark had spotted a log floating in the sea and he knew that Whitcombe often signed his work on logs exactly like that. Sure enough when it was cleaned there was his signature and the date 1801. Carter and Monmouth sold it at Grosvenor House Antique Fair for twenty thousand pounds, but Aubrey Monmouth never gave him a penny more for it, a deal was a deal he said, partner's son or no. He's a tough, hard dealer, Monmouth. Mark was actually helping out on the Grosvenor House stand when they sold it too. I always thought the B.B.C. was a rat race but compared with antiques we were as gentle as Quakers."

"Why did Mark's father stay with a man like Monmouth?"

"It was a thriving business, successful. Daniel Carter had the knowledge but Monmouth was the businessman. What Carter couldn't see was that without him Monmouth wouldn't have done a quarter of the turn-over. Mark knew though; he had his father's gift and Monmouth's too. When I used to listen to Mark and his father talking it was unbelievable. They would talk about a piece of furniture or a painting and they made you feel you were listening to the cabinet-maker or the artist himself. It wasn't showing off, it was simply the most extraordinary display of expertise. That's what first gave me the idea for the programme."

"What was his father like?"

"To look at? Pleasant enough, not as devastating as his son but the same features, darker. Mark's colouring came from his mother."

"You met her, too?"

"They had a flat in Eaton Square. It was her money, of course, there was a house in the country, in Kent somewhere. Her money was inherited, her father was something very big in the city and she got the lot. I went to dinner at the flat once or twice when I was setting things up. How did you know it was my programme, by the way, if you didn't see it?"

"I didn't know, it was just luck. I phoned the B.B.C. and they told me. They wouldn't give me your address here or Mark's so I looked you up in the phone book."

"I'm sorry you missed it, but I'm not surprised at that hour. I was a good producer you know, in fact bloody good. Sometimes it's a bit lonely without it. Thank you, yes they do look better, I can never get roses to compromise. Anyway, like all the best ideas it was simple. I organised a set like a decent antique shop and turned them loose in it. They hadn't seen any of the stuff, of course. It was a mixture of pieces; furniture, paintings, ceramics—some clever fakes too—just for spice. I called it 'Guaranteed Genuine'. It would have been a winner."

"You never did the series?"

"No, Daniel Carter died suddenly of a heart attack and the series died too. I couldn't fight that. The whole point was the two of them talking together. Mark was shattered, he adored his father. I went round to the flat to see them but by that time he'd moved out to live on his own. His mother said she didn't know where he was, she didn't much care either."

"They didn't get on?"

"Mark hated her, he only stayed there because of his father. Soon after that she sold the place and I lost touch with both of them." For a moment the little monkey-face looked old and tired, it recovered almost immediately, the wide grin firmly back in

66

place. "Haven't I done well for you, though? My dear, I don't know about you, but I'm going to have a drink. Yes?"

"Thank you, yes you have done very well and yes I'd love a drink." The gin and the tonic bottles were locked in a wall safe hidden behind a painting of a young man dressed in a coloured shirt and shorts, a rugby football balanced on one knee. Not conventionally handsome, the face had the fierce intensity of a stubborn child too used to getting his own way.

"I won't bother with ice and lemon unless you'd like them?"

"No this is fine. So you've no idea where Mark is now, no address at all?"

"I didn't say that, I said I lost touch with him. He wrote to my office asking if it was possible to have a tape of the programme but by that time it had been wiped and forgotten. I was caught up with all the fuss of retiring. I left a bit earlier than I needed to but the pension is enough for us both." He caught Jimmy's eye switch to the painting. "Yes that's Michael, he used to look after my car in the local garage. He could do anything with cars, loved playing rugby and driving, nice boy, that was years ago, of course. The idea was that he should come and look after me but it's turned out to be the other way round."

"I'm sorry."

"We manage, it'll be easier when he admits he's an alcoholic but we haven't quite reached that yet. So! Hearts and flowers over, how's your drink? Oh don't worry, he won't come in, poor old love, he's in St Stephen's and they'll keep him in for a while to dry out. Cheers! Oh my dear, the luxury of a civilised drink in your own home! You shouldn't let me run on, where was I? Oh yes, Mark. No I didn't try and see him again. I'm too old to start chasing rainbows, especially straight ones. I got my secretary to write, I've got the address somewhere, he may not be there now, of course, but I'll let you have it before you go. But isn't it odd that his mother should have turned up in – where was it you said?"

"Flaxfield, it's a village in Suffolk, I married someone there."

"What made you do that?"

"I was lonely. I like sharing things – I suppose I wanted someone to nudge. Do you still like opera?"

"Yes and I still cry in Traviata."

"Why did he hate his mother?"

"Two reasons I think, the first was a plain old-fashioned business row and like a fool I got involved with that. Mark thought that if the series was made – and I'm pretty sure it would have been – then his father should sell out to Monmouth and leave him.

67

With the money they would be able to set up as partners together, Carter and Carter, as known and loved by millions as the TV antique experts. I thought it was a good idea and said so but she was against it."

"And the other reason?"

"Oh I guessed that even before Mark told me. It was odd because you'd never think of her like that. She was a big woman, quite pretty in a rather doll-like way and to be fair she could be good company but she wasn't first casting choice for a femme fatale."

"She slept around?"

"My dear, I don't think she ever bothered to lie down for it, there wouldn't have been time. I hadn't met her for five minutes before she dragged me up and down the room in a moist embrace she called a rumba. Yes, I know it sounds funny now but she was a very embarrassing lady and like my poor Michael I don't think she admitted what she was, and I don't mean an alcoholic."

"And her husband?"

"He must have learned to accept it, to understand. It's amazing what some people will put up with; perhaps he loved her. Mark didn't, he called her a fat whore who didn't even need the money."

"Somehow it's difficult to imagine Mark saying something like that."

"Sometimes he could be quite fierce, not like his father. He was different from Mark, soft and gentle. I'll find that address for you before you go, but first we must talk, and no skipping Miss, if you please. Let us start with the night your mother came and took you away at midnight. Are you sitting comfortably? Then we'll begin."

❧ ELEVEN ☙

MARGARET GARLAND SAT in the ground-floor room of her house in Kensington. Butcher Street was part of a small maze of streets bounded by Notting Hill Gate to the north and Kensington Church Street to the east. Originally workmen's cottages, they had undergone major surgery, with every inch of space pulled and prodded until the internal pressure had blown the windows out into Regency bow-fronts. In the estate agents' books they were described as desirable town houses of character. Their front doors were painted in bright Ludo colours, like discordant notes on a child's toy trumpet, lending them an air of selfconscious defiance.

The cleaning had taken longer than she had thought. She had had no one come in and do it for her when she was away in Suffolk. It was so small it hadn't seemed worth it and, however trustworthy, she disliked the thought of another woman in the place. Now it was finished. The tiny bedrooms and the doll's bathroom still smelling of her mother's scent. She had poured Dettol into the hand-basin and left it thick and milky in the lavatory. Ages ago she had given all her mother's clothes to the Oxfam shop but she could hardly get rid of all the furniture or re-equip the kitchen in the basement.

The kitchen had taken longer to clean than all the rest of the house put together. The traffic outside was never heavy but it had forced the street dust in through the window gaps to film over the fitted pine dining alcove and the yellow plastic sink unit. She had not stopped until she had cleaned every knife, fork and spoon and the drawer full of time-wasting gadgets her mother had bought and never used. Now she had unpacked and was too tired to cook herself anything to eat.

"Nonsense Margaret, of course you must eat something."

"I'm not hungry."

"It's got nothing to do with being hungry, it's simply a matter of common sense, you'll get dandruff again. You'd eat soon enough if your little hitch-hiker turned up. I suppose that's what all this spring cleaning was really in aid of? Well, I should forget that if I were you. If you had any sense you'd realise you were well rid of him. I can't think how you could have made such a fool of yourself and I wasn't the only one."

"You do talk the most awful rubbish, Mother."

"So you said in the car. You know perfectly well what I mean, why do you suppose that common little Welsh woman was asking you all those questions?"

"It's quite simple, they owed him some money and he left without taking it."

She left the room quickly and in the kitchen poured herself some gin. There was nothing to put in it, so she added some water and drank it all. Sometimes a drink would shut her mother's voice out; not always but sometimes. Sometimes too, she caught herself doing or thinking something that should surely have provoked a response, and had been surprised at her disappointment when it had not come. In her unhappiness and loneliness she clung to a memory for comfort and the luxury of irritating it with truths she had suppressed when her mother was alive and ill.

She had no more appetite for television than she had for food. It was still early but she locked the front and back doors and carried the rest of the gin to bed with the first book she picked at random from a shelf in the sitting room. With knees hunched and cradling her glass in both hands, her mother silenced, Margaret wondered why conversations with her should always be so bitter about Mark, someone she had never seen or known in life. That they were accurate she had no doubt. Other friends had been tolerated even encouraged, and yet her mother's imagined reaction to Mark Carter had been violently antagonistic, her face always twisted with jealousy. Of course! She would have been jealous! Mark was too like the wartime heroes of her mother's boasted adventures for her to have borne it in peace and acceptance. She wouldn't have minded in the least that Margaret had picked him up on the side of the road and nursed and fed him – given him little presents of clothes and affection. What she could not have understood was the reticence and propriety of the friendship. She would, in Margaret's position, have been into his room and his bed, she would have held him and never have let him disappear, because he would have had too much to stay for.

70

Margaret quite enjoyed the tears, they were more tears of laughter than unhappiness – a kind of exorcism; it wasn't only the gin that had silenced her mother, it was shame and aggravation at being so expertly analysed. She even laughed aloud when she saw the paperback book lying on the bed at her side. The green spine had led her to think of it as something respectable and comforting, like a crime novel, now she saw that it was one of her mother's. On the cover, a naked black boy with acceptable European features stood behind a blonde white girl his hands clasped over her bare stomach, fingers spreadeagled. Her eyes were half closed, the lips parted to show a hint of teeth. She had red enlarged nipples like prize rosettes at a cattle show.

<h3 style="text-align:center">Chapter 1</h3>

The Bashful Postman.

Jane was not a shy girl and her delightful sense of roguish fun soon conquered shyness in others. "How lovely," she said with a merry laugh as she unbuttoned his shirt, "the same colour all over! At least I hope so, let me help you with the jeans just to make quite sure."

On the following day Arlene Weikel sat on a gilt chair with maroon padding at a table strategically chosen midway between two enormous marble pillars flanked by potted palms.

"Tea in the Ritz Winter Garden is traditional when in London," Arlene announced in ringing tones, "it says so right here on the back of this postcard." She stood up and waved it vigorously at Mrs Thomas to attract her attention as she climbed the three marble steps up from the hallway. "My God, Lizzie, you look exhausted, come and sit. Tea!" she shouted at a passing waiter, "tea and hurry, my friend is in dire need, so move it, Buster."

The waiter smiled cheerfully, he'd known and liked Mrs Weikel for years. In quiet moments she could be gentle and kind, she always asked after his children. One night when he'd been on room service he'd told her all about his son going to prison for burglary and she'd cried with him and comforted him. In his eyes she was the new aristocracy, it was just like her to be kind to a curious little woman in elastic stockings.

"No luck huh?" Arlene said sympathetically, when the first cup had soothed and revived.

"No, my fault, too cocky, stupid of me to think I could walk into a grand place like Carter and Monmouth and start quizzing the boss about his ex-partner's wife." A faint look of annoyance frowned over her cup and down at the scones and tea-cakes on the immaculate white tablecloth. "John should have come up and done it; policemen – even ex-policemen – people listen to them. There's a cat I'm friendly with," she added in explanation of her train of thought, "I once opened a tin of cat food for him, he sniffed carefully and then slowly scratched all round it with his paw like he was covering something nasty. That's what our Mr Monmouth made me feel like this morning. Pushy too – all he cares about is selling something and the old devil soon saw that I wasn't a buyer. Lovely tea, I was parched for a cup and fair play these scones aren't bad either, lighter if they'd used sour milk, but not bad for London." Around her, the luxury of the hotel, the huge chandeliers, glass skylit ceiling and the rich carpet in pink, blue and cream, deadening all the polite tea-time voices except Arlene Weikel's. Arlene rasping on in a fury of friendship and enthusiasm, laying out the gossip of her telephoned friends like the cakes and jam and hot buttered toast on the table in front of them. It seemed to be nothing new, just variations on the same theme. Joan Carter was a big, bouncy, libidinous libertine. It was what the lay preacher in the Primitive Methodist chapel of Mrs Thomas's youth had called her sister, and by name too. "Oh Lord, in thy infinite mercy, stretch forth thy saving hand to all libidinous libertines, especially remembering our sad sister of sorrow, Blodwen Jones." Poor Blod! and nothing serious, God love her, only boys up on the mountain and no harm in it, they were lucky to get her, sweet and pretty like a dog-rose in summer. Their mother had fainted in the pew but no sorrow for Blodwen, no wonder she'd gone off to Tiger Bay in Cardiff. Wild roses were an expensive luxury in Tiger Bay and with the family genius for exploiting her talents she had made a modest and happy fortune. When the war came to the valley the billeting officer had filled Blodwen's empty room with a series of airmen from overcrowded St Athan's Airforce Station, some of them Free French without a word of English.

Arlene's voice brought Mrs Thomas back to the Ritz. "Rosie Bierburger may be a schmo but with her money nobody tells her. She puts some of it into Walt's shows so she has to be a very dear friend. One thing she has got is a memory like a tape recorder. She's too stupid to edit it, so the old lady can be useful. She has houses all over the world crammed with antiques, so I guessed she might know Carter and Monmouth and she did. It's boring but simple with Rosie, you just make sure you're lying on the bed before you call her, then press the buttons and play the tapes, she is the pits but better than a microchip. Lizzie honey, Arlene will be kind and edit. Zip – Play. OK, late fifties, Joan and Daniel Carter, they're married and seem happy, she's a slim woman, would you believe? She has the money and she buys Daniel a partnership in Aubrey Monmouth's business. He had been cute enough to buy a long lease near the corner of Bond and Bruton and bingo it's Carter and Monmouth. Cut-Cut-Cut- and you don't know how lucky you are, you want to hear about Rosie's love affair with George the Third rosewood? You do not. But Joan Carter's love affair with Aubrey Monmouth you do, and hear this, Rosie says it was no casual bedding but the full torrid rampage."

Mrs Thomas sat in earnest concentration, her black eyes unwavering.

"Mrs Bierburger – a good memory, right, I see that, but a good memory for gossip – or for facts?"

"Facts, I told you, she's oil and she counts in fields not wells. For that money you buy good rosewood and facts. She was furnishing a manor house in Berkshire, rosewood in an English manor! cute huh? She got the story from Daniel Carter himself, no less, when he went down to stay and advise."

"Why didn't Mr Carter leave Mr Monmouth?"

"Mr! – you kill me. He was too soft – a touch of the Ashley Wilkes, Rosie said, that and he loved Joan, plus there was a bonny babe – that was Mark. You saw this great lover this morning so what makes him tick?"

Mrs Thomas thought. "I suppose you could see him as good looking once. Not now, top heavy, wears a corset I think, walks careful, like a pigeon. The affair didn't last, of course?"

"Hell no, but for her it seems to have been bigger than the usual romp. She actually cleared off for six months and left both of them. Rosie met her in Cannes during that time. You want to hear about the chandeliers Rosie bought there for the Paris house? No you do not, but the meeting is worth hearing. Rosie saw her in the foyer of the Carlton and Joan Carter cut her dead."

"This Mrs . . . ?"

"Bierburger – Rosie Bierburger."

"She does sound like a very boring woman."

"She was also one of the best customers Carter and Monmouth ever had. I could tell you exactly what Rosie was wearing that day but we'll skip that. Joan Carter's dress was more interesting, though. Rosie swears she was wearing a maternity gown."

The hotel in Paddington where Mrs Thomas and Betsey were staying shared only one common factor with the Ritz: people paid to stay there. It was clean but dark and smelled of cooking fat and stale alcohol. Jimmy Trottwood sat miserably in the residents' lounge nursing a hangover and drinking tasteless weak tea. His reunion with Dudley had developed into a marathon of self-indulgent reminiscence. Pleasant at first, the day had moved on into an evening of maudlin nostalgia, with the two of them making an increasingly unsteady pilgrimage to the pubs and clubs of their youth that were still in existence. Recollections of the later part of the evening were unclear, he had an uneasy memory of attempting something called Limbo dancing and his painfully swollen ankles confirmed it as the embarrassing truth and not, as he had fervently hoped, part of his confused dreams. He'd had to ring the night bell when he finally got back at two o'clock in the morning, he couldn't remember climbing the stairs to his room. Not until eleven had he managed to drag himself out of bed to find Mrs Thomas's terse note waiting for him at the desk.

"Dirty old stop-out. Can't wait any longer. Going to Bond Street and tea at the Ritz. What news? Shall expect full report. Lizzie."

She would too. Well she could have it for what it was worth. If the boy wanted to disappear it was his own affair. The address Dudley had given him had been a dead end, as he had thought it would be. Claverton Gardens in Notting Hill Gate, a house full of bed-sitting rooms, dull and depressing, worse even than this miserable hotel. The woman in the basement who answered the bell marked Housekeeper remembered him. "Mr Carter? Yes, a nice quiet young man, rather shy so he was, but no, he'd left some time ago, didn't know where he'd gone to, it was a while now, no forwarding address. Yes, a nice young gentleman, never a trouble like some of them; minded his own business." Something he should be doing, Betsey told himself. He was fed up with London and fed up with Lizzie with her insatiable curiosity and bullying bounce. He had done his best for her, it wasn't his fault if the address Dudley had given him was useless. He wanted to slip his shoes off under the table but was afraid he wouldn't be able to get them back on again. Tomorrow he would go back to Flaxfield and Doreen. Lizzie could come or stay as she pleased, it wasn't fair to leave Doreen to run the shop alone and business was very slow she'd said on the phone. Poor Doreen, she'd sounded depressed, he'd cheer her up, make her laugh, tell her about his Limbo dancing. Well, perhaps not. London was too full of memories.

Tomorrow he would buy something nice for her – a dress or some cashmere. No wonder Mark had done so well for them at the fair. Sad about his father and his rather horrid mother. It was his own affair, no one else's, it was like prying. Busy Lizzie, she'd have to be very busy to find Mark in London, it was a big city, too big. He hated it.

When the front door bell rang Margaret was in the middle of chapter seven. In the door there was a small spy hole of optic glass so that you could see quite plainly who was standing outside. If you lived alone it was a safeguard against unwelcome visitors.

This visitor was not unwelcome. She opened the door wide for Mark Carter.

❧ TWELVE ❧

HER FIRST INSTINCT had been to throw her arms around him in the open doorway and only at the last second did she decide that in pyjamas and dressing gown she could make the spontaneous gesture less public by letting him in and closing the door on Butcher Street. Almost immediately she regretted it and the moment was lost in the cramped little hall smelling of gin and Dettol. She turned quickly so that he wouldn't get the full blast of her breath until she'd had a chance to get to the bathroom and gargle or better still give him a gin of his own. Oh God, this isn't fair! Why couldn't he have written or telephoned? No, I don't mean that, honestly I don't, it's enough to be walking into the sitting room knowing that this time it isn't a dream and that when I turn I shall see him standing there.

When she did turn she knocked over a stupid little table, one of a horrid "nest" that her mother had seen advertised in one of the Sunday colour magazines. Her hair fell over her face as she bent to pick it up reminding her that she had washed off every scrap of make-up. For a second she wondered if she was going to cry from the sheer frustration of it all, but was saved by over-balancing when she started to straighten up, sitting down heavily on the carpet and laughing instead.

"Oh dear! I'm not really drunk, at least I don't think so. I've had some gin and forgot to eat. No, I didn't forget, I cleaned up a bit and was too tired to bother. Oh Mark! You are a most awful rat, why on earth did you disappear without a word? No, sorry, that's the one thing I was determined not to ask you. Deadly calm, polite chat only, and I've come straight out with it. For heaven's sake Mark, are you going to let me sit here making a fool of myself or are you going to help me up?"

He held on to her outstretched arms and she rose with reasonable elegance to her feet, pleased and relieved at her

76

stability and clear vision. She couldn't really be drunk, she had felt perfectly sober until she had come downstairs. She was content just for a few moments to stand there and look at him, quietly demonstrating equilibrium, her face composed to express a gentle welcome without reproach.

Once before in Flaxfield she had looked at him when he wasn't aware of her doing so, trying to decide why she was in love with him. Taken separately his features were not very remarkable, the nose straight but too small, teeth white but uneven and one ear stuck out more than the other. The eyes were good, grey-blue, large and spaced wide under the untidy mop of fair hair, his figure, she decided, underneath the blue sports shirt and the cream cotton trousers, was probably perfect and that ghastly Jane in her mother's book with her delightful sense of roguish fun would have proved it in seconds.

Only when she thought of those shameless fingers and their eager dexterity did she realise that he was still holding her by both hands at arms' length, like children playing oranges and lemons. There was nothing wrong with her clarity of mind, thank goodness. With quick thinking it was obviously sensible to pretend that the position of her outstretched arms was deliberate and planned only as a charming gesture of forgiveness, and what better way to show him than by singing the nursery rhyme to him in a soft sober soprano, as she moved his arms up and down to the beat of the old tune.

Oranges and lemons say the bells of St Clements,
You owe me five farthings say the bells of St Martins,
When will you pay me say the bells of Old Bailey?
When I grow rich say the bells of Shoreditch,
Here comes a . . .
She had forgotten the rest of the words and to cover the understandable lapse of memory after so many years had decided to hum the tune and move him off into a gentle gavotte. His arms and his body remained rigid, forcing her to abandon the dance in a frustrated wobble.

"I think you ought to eat something."

"The lady is as tight as a rusty bolt so for goodness sake get something inside her to soak it up – charming!"

"Your words not mine," it was the first time he had smiled. "All right, how about, dear Peggy I'm starving, I've been wandering up and down Kensington Church Street and I forgot to eat, too."

"Much better, more like you."

"Where's the kitchen?"

"Downstairs and since you obviously don't intend to carry me – I shall lead the way."

At least she could show him that she hadn't lost her sense of humour. In the basement she was persuaded to sit at the pine table while he found tomato soup and bread and cheese. She insisted on opening a bottle of wine but the more she ate the less she wanted any of it and she was content to sit and watch him eat and drink most of it himself.

"What were you doing wandering up and down the Church Street?"

"Window shopping, what else? There's no other street in London to touch it for antiques."

It was where he and his father had planned to be together, she knew that, so it was a bold question knowing and remembering his way of telling her something and then suddenly withdrawing into himself. She risked what she had come to think of as "the look". Not fierce or intentionally snubbing. It wasn't even directed at her when it came, not a warning for poaching on private thoughts, that would have been easier to cope with, a sort of communication, even if it only told her that for the moment she had lost him to himself. Tonight he was different, or perhaps she was. She wondered at the striped blue shirt and found herself ridiculously jealous of something that was part of his life that she knew nothing about. It was clean and fresh but reassuringly unironed with the wrinkles bunched into stars where he had twisted out the water and hung it to dry. Unless, of course, he was living with a slut.

In Flaxfield she had determinedly settled into a polite civilised routine of house guest and hostess and once established the mould had been hard to break. Now he was no longer a roadside casualty and she could change the rules of the game as she pleased, and if she lost then at least she'd played.

Once as a child on a seaside holiday there had been an amusement arcade with a machine full of flashing lights and the thrilling thud of mounting numbers bumping through your fingers as you waited in an agony of last-second flipping to blast Martian invaders into outer space. She could never do it. Day after day she watched casually expert boys arrogantly saving the civilised world while her own warm pocket money doomed it to disaster. One day she ignored all their shouted advice, forgot the absurd intensity of her concentration and knew that she could do nothing wrong. She even blew her nose with studied unconcern between Raiders 1 and 2 and warded off a simultaneous attack from Venus. She had felt invincible and she was.

78

Over his shoulder she could see half of her face in the mirror over the sink. Half of her looked surprisingly sober and when she moved to include the other half it was true. Not only sober, she thought, but quite definitely beautiful. Her dark hair had fallen attractively around her face which seemed better without make-up. There was colour in her cheeks and her eyes were bright and confident. She was a magazine cover, something wholesome and domestic like *Woman's Own* or *Woman's World* with recipes for late-night snacks and useful tips on ironing. She parted her lips to show a hint of white teeth.

"That shirt is driving me mad, I can't bear to see you in it another minute. Take if off and I'll iron it for you."

She took the ironing board from the tall cupboard, Usually it dragged half a dozen things with it but for once it came out unprotesting and docile, arranging itself without fuss at exactly the right height.

"We don't have any antique shops in Butcher Street," she said.

"No, of course not, did you think I'd forget your address? Church Street's only just round the corner so I often walk past. This is the first evening you've had a light showing."

Straight into Double Score on the first flip! I can't lose.

"You never told me why you didn't get on with your mother," she edged the iron expertly round the buttons but without hurrying; concentrating. A faint but powerful scent of him rose up to her in the steam from his shirt. When, from time to time, she looked at him sitting with his bare back to the wall, his trousers hidden by the table top, she avoided his nakedness and was careful to look straight into his eyes. There was no withdrawal, no turning in upon himself, and when he talked of his mother it was without shyness or any trace of bitterness, oddly almost with enthusiasm, admiration even. Like telling Jimmy Trottwood and Doreen about Regency furniture. It had a surface elegance and charm, always popular, even the poorly made pieces with hidden flaws; it was a mistake to accept things at their surface value.

"It wasn't only chauffeurs and workmen, I mean she doesn't have a sort of rough-trade complex or anything as normal as that. As far as I could work it out she had three of the masters at my school including the assistant Head, four if you count the cricket pro, a really filthy man with a posh accent and blackheads. I was probably the only boy at school whose mother had a nickname. They called her the Female Rapist. I didn't mind, it made me quite popular, especially with the sixth formers and some of the staff, everybody kept asking me if she was coming down for half-term or the house finals. I think they must have banned her in the end because she stopped coming. I suspect it was the chaplain who obviously thought she was a bad influence, poaching on his private reserve. He didn't like me much because I wouldn't join in the wrestling romps he was so keen on. I know he said it because he wanted to hurt me and make me look small, but actually I thought he was absolutely right. 'Your mother, Carter,' he said, 'has appetite but no taste.' He hated it when I laughed with all the others."

"But you must have hated it too, surely?"

"Sometimes, but you mustn't show it or it puts you outside."

His mother, her mother – Dear God, what happened to all the nice wholesome mums in *Woman's Own*, knitting and caring and smelling of cake?

Dear *Woman's Own*,

My boyfriend's mother is a well known nymphomaniac and my own mother was deeply immersed in dirty books to the end of her life. Is this a barrier to a happy marriage?

P.S. We are both perfectly healthy and normal.

She hung the shirt over the back of a chair.

"Let it air for a bit."

She sat and shared out the last of the wine into the glasses.

"Why did your father stay with her?"

For a moment she wondered if she had pushed too hard, mistiming and losing the game, but when she looked at him she saw that his pause was not the beginning of the old withdrawal but only so that he could best consider.

"I suppose he was happy. She's a horror, of course, but she was a horror he'd grown used to. I used to see people on TV talking about their lives with crippled children and wonder how they could do it and seem so normal and happy themselves. I see now that's what we were doing in a way. Remember that his life was outside hers, he loved his work and he was good, he was bloody good."

"Did you discuss her?"

"No, we didn't – we didn't need to, the crippled child again I suppose, and remember we'd always had it with us – right back to my schooldays."

"But surely? New faces, new friends at the table for dinner – breakfast even?"

"She was a horror but not a monster, mostly she kept the really snotty ones out of the home life. And don't forget she had money, she was never tied, she travelled a lot, we liked that. I wasn't likely

80

to come out and spoil it with bright chat like, 'I wonder whose fucking mama down at the health farm', or wherever, was I? You want more?''

She nodded, pinching the crumbs of cheese and bread into a cone for trivialising the interest and the concentration she didn't want him to see. Like blowing your nose between Raiders 1 and 2.

"You're getting a biased view of her. There were loads of ordinary friends who would tell you what fun she could be and what a lovely happy family we were."

"And you stayed because of your father."

"I made him pay her for my food and keep and when I started to earn something of my own I paid it myself. She would have loved that if she'd thought of it first but because it was my idea she pretended it was hurtful. What she really hated was my independence, it was too like her own and when she couldn't get her own way she'd ignore it, pull a curtain down to hide her thoughts, so you couldn't get through to her, except sometimes if you frightened her enough and then she would run away. If you're rich – as rich as she is – you can run a long way. It was her way of keeping control."

"How did you frighten her?"

"She did it herself. She had this theory that I had what she called an ungovernable temper. That started at school, too, we used to have boxing and I hit a kid and he passed out. Actually the poor little sod had a thin skull or something, anyway he was quite ill and his parents wouldn't let him come back. She got this mad idea that I'd gone berserk so of course I played up to it." He put his head on one side and with wide-eyed mock truthfulness imitated his careful reply to his mother exactly as he must have looked then. "'Oh Mama! I don't think I could have hit him so *very* hard, of course I was a bit miffed because I'm pretty certain he took some stamps from my album but it was only *boxing*, Mama.' She didn't believe me, of course, and when I realised she thought she'd got a nut case on her hands I used to play up to it like mad. Once in the country one of her dogs got run over and had its neck broken. That happened to be when we were in the middle of one of our rows and the silly woman honestly thought I'd done it for spite. She didn't say so but I knew because she gave the other dogs away: keeping control again."

"Your father's will never turned up?"

"No, only the first one he'd made years ago. He left her everything he had. There probably wasn't a fortune in his bank account but the half share in Carter and Monmouth was in his name not hers – she slipped up there, silly Mama – lost control – except that she's got it back again."

"He wouldn't have changed his mind? About leaving it to you, I mean."

He shook his head slowly. "No, he'd had enough and after the TV thing he knew we could succeed together, even if we never made the series he knew it would work. He didn't change his mind because he told me that he had done it. Signed and sealed he said. Perhaps it wasn't true, perhaps he only said it to please me, but I believed him. I don't know. You see he was a weak man, he had the knowledge but no push. He was spoiled too, he admitted that, he liked all the luxury and he'd settled for it. He didn't fancy my life, street markets and running."

"He could still have sold out and set up on his own – without you I mean."

"No push – not enough anyway. I told him that he could have his luxury without her and I made him believe it. All you've got to remember, I told him, is that I'm her son and that I can be as ruthless as she is."

He doesn't look very ruthless, she thought, he still looks like a schoolboy: and a tired schoolboy. It was enough for tonight. The rest of the questions could wait. She wanted to tell him about her visit to the bank manager. She remembered how she had planned it in Flaxfield before he disappeared. Calmly and unemotionally and in friendship uncomplicated by sex. But he was sitting at a table not three feet away from her. She didn't want him to leave and go back to a bed-sitting room with or without a resident slut who wouldn't iron his shirts, and if he stayed she wanted desperately to be complicated by sex. It wouldn't work. It wasn't what she had planned. She had dreamed of a friendship closer even than family ties, blessed with his expert knowledge and her money, launched unemotionally on a bright morning with the early sun in the kitchen and the smell of toast and fresh tea. But if she moved now, with her face flushed and her breasts aching, the morning moment would be lost. For tonight the game was over and she had no more shots to play. Her confidence had deserted her. There was a splash of tomato soup on the sleeve of her dressing gown.

She gathered the things from the table and took them to the sink but he made no move to help her. In silence she moved the plates and glasses through the richness of the liquid soap in the bowl, feeling her warm fingers slipping and searching over the hard shapes under the water.

82

"Your shirt should be aired by now."

When she turned he was standing in front of the table facing her, the shirt was still on the back of the chair. He was smiling happily at her, not looking down as he undid the canvas belt and the zip, stepping out of the cream trousers without embarrassment.

"The shirt will make these look awfully creased Peg – would you? Not now, I mean – in the morning?"

❧ THIRTEEN ❧

WEBBER CARRIED TWO cups of tea from the counter of the kiosk on the sea front at Dunwold and took them, carefully covered by saucers, to the rusty metal table round the corner of the wooden building where Mrs Thomas was sheltering from the prevailing wind off the North Sea. She was not in her happiest mood and only with considerable tact and shameless flattery had she been persuaded that a breath of sea air would blow away the muddle of doubts and frustrations she had brought back from her trip to London.

The weeks had slipped away and already it was August, and an August for once behaving conventionally according to the establishment myth, so beloved of the English, that it was a month of blue skies where the sun shone and the clouds skidded decently out of its path. On the mixed shingle and sand of the Dunwold beach the children plunged in and out of the chill sea immune to the shock, their blood warmed and fuelled by ice cream, chocolate, and sandwiches filled generously with salad and sand. It wouldn't matter to them that it wasn't a typical August. Already they had forgotten that last year it had rained every day and for the rest of their lives they would believe, like their mothers and fathers before them, that at Dunwold, when they were young, the sun shone every day.

"It may not be the Ritz," said Webber, "but it's good strong tea." From his pocket he produced two Mars bars. He unwrapped his at once and sat munching it happily, watching the children queuing at the kiosk where the wind battered the tethered bunch of multi-coloured beach balls and the whirling plastic windmills on sticks, while the revolving display stand of picture postcards presented an ever-changing panorama of naughty pink bottoms and bosoms to the uncaring eyes of the children whose carnal appetites were as yet geared only to ice cream and lollipops.

84

He was like a child himself, she thought, back on the beach where he had played as a child. Conservative like a child too, wiser and shrewder but still faithful, as they were, to things familiar, places known and trusted.

It was endearing but dangerous and not to be encouraged. That way you could miss the world.

She misjudged him.

In her impatience to shape and hurry events to her own pace she mistook his patience and experience for laziness and lethargy; he knew it and forgave her.

She was like a sheepdog, he thought, keen, intelligent and bounding with energy which left him breathless. They were admirable animals but he had often observed them on television covering ten times as much ground as they needed to round up a stray which wanted nothing more than to rejoin the flock of its own accord without being fussed. Leave them alone. It was advice that he knew was anathema to her, but he had hopes that by patience and example she might come to accept it.

He misjudged her.

The chocolate bar and the tea had certainly put her into a more amenable frame of mind he thought. She fished in her voluminous bag for her precious binoculars and while she scanned the beach and the sparkling sea with every sign of interest and contentment he reminisced happily and interestingly about the Dunwold of his youth.

"I don't suppose it's changed much since – well certainly not since the 1860s. I've got postcards of the houses up there on the top promenade from my grandfather's time and it's almost exactly the same now. Not a single hotel amongst the lot, guest houses, boarding houses yes, but the council won't let the developers in. So, no hotels apart from The Dunwold Arms and that's the original old coaching inn so that's allowed, and the rest of the town is the same. The interesting thing is the money."

She focused along the ranks of the sheltered parents protected by the striped awnings of canvas windshields, dozing and prematurely placid in the afternoon sunshine.

"How, money?"

"It's always been rich. Look at the cars up on the front there, and in the square, more Rolls, Jags and Bentleys than Bond Street. You can tell by all the shops, too, bit dull I know, but all quality stuff. Yes it's rich all right. Not just the residents either, this lot down here on the beach aren't poor, listen to the accents of those kids over there at the kiosk. Oh yes, you get the odd day trippers but most of them won't risk the traffic jams on that single access road. No, this lot mostly come back year after year, take over a whole house for the family just like they did in Victorian years – I like that."

"But you're happier living in Flaxfield?"

"Yes of course, I was born there, and in any case I couldn't afford Dunwold. Have you any idea what houses like ours would fetch here?"

"No."

"Well, you wouldn't get a sniff at one for less than sixty thousand pounds."

"You're joking!"

"Look in the estate agents' windows, there's plenty of those too. That's always a sure sign of money, there must be three in the High Street alone."

He thought. How much a tone of voice can add to a day. For weeks she'd been restless, moody, cleaning for him in the mornings and sometimes preparing food for him at night. The quality of her cooking hadn't deteriorated but she had been unable to disguise her general air of frustrated restlessness. He'd planned the day as a treat just as, when children, Dunwold had been a treat for him and his brother. Even then he'd always half hoped that he wouldn't have to swim. He loved the beach and the roaring, roistering games, the roaring sea was different. He would paddle and run through the long curling foam praying that the others wouldn't sense his fear, and surround him in a fierce primitive ritual of manic splashing, pulling and shoving, until the cold cruel waves reached out and took him from them. It had happened every time. Mrs Thomas had listened to him as he told her the story the night before, safely inland at Flaxfield. He didn't tell her that he had news for her. That he intended to be part of the treat. He'd saved that for today.

It was always difficult to know how best to impart news to Lizzie. He didn't want her bouncing about all over the place until she'd had time to absorb it without going off like a firework, showering sparks from her overactive imagination. He tipped the last of the few crumbs of chocolate from the wrapper into his mouth while he pondered the best casual approach and she swept the binoculars slowly across the horizon. Far out to sea, a speck to the naked eye, she watched a man in a rowing boat drag quite a large fish out of the sea and hit it repeatedly on the head with a wooden club. A woman in a red dress sat under a white sunshade watching him and smiling. She must be his wife, no one else in their senses would count it pleasure to sit in a boat and smile at a man killing something. She'd be next if she didn't watch out. That would take the smile off her face and then he would tip her into the sea and the fish would nibble her face and destroy the evidence and the next year he'd come again with another wife.

"Do you think," she asked without lowering the glasses, "that Mark Carter will turn up again?"

Sometimes he got an uneasy feeling that she could read his thoughts. Lucky though, it saved laborious preliminaries.

"Yes, yes I think he will – in fact I'm sure he will."

She abandoned the woman in the boat to her fate and looked at him.

"Why?"

"He's with Margaret Garland in London."

It was almost a personal attack on her own efficiency.

"I phoned her five times," she said coldly, "and never once an answer. I thought she must be away."

"She could have been out – or busy."

"Five times?"

"In the circumstances I would think it possible," at the last moment he decided not to push one eyebrow up quizzically. Best to avoid any suggestion that she wasn't being very quick on the uptake. No point in goading her.

She plunged the binoculars back into her bag and humped the metal chair round to face him.

"Tell!"

"Margaret was a link, Monmouth was another but I thought she was more promising, so I decided to try her first."

"You phoned and she answered?"

"No, I phoned and she didn't, so I checked. There's a lad in the local C.I.D. up there. He was under me at Ipswich years ago, nice enough, bends the elbow a bit, or did in my time. Anyway he owes me one or two favours so I asked him to pop round and suss it out."

"You knew the address?"

"Voting register, Town Hall, 7 Butcher Street."

"I could have told you that."

"Yes of course, silly of me, I should have thought," better to appear incompetent than to admit a reluctance to involve her too soon.

"Suss it out, what's it mean?"

"Find out what's happening, call round, bit of a chat, friendly British coppers with routine enquiries. Unofficial of course, but who's to know that? A few random photographs from the files, old mugshots of villains. Wonder if you've seen any of these characters hanging around lately? That sort of thing. Bob's very good, he took a girl friend with him, a police lass in uniform. Simple really."

"And?"

"Bob and his girl friend – Thelma, I think she's called – thought they seemed a very nice young couple. Happy, he said. They couldn't help with the snaps, of course, but promised to let him know, although it seems they won't be in London much longer, a few bits of business to clear up before they come down to Suffolk for the rest of the summer. Bob's going to arrange for the local boys to keep an eye on Butcher Street for them. Bob had whisky and soda and Thelma took a small glass of wine with them."

"He's disappeared before; he could again."

"He could, but it seems unlikely, the drinks were for a sort of toast. They were married at Kensington Registry Office ten days ago. So if this weather holds, Flaxfield should make a very nice honeymoon for them."

This time he couldn't control his eyebrow.

She didn't notice it anyway in the rush of thoughts in her head, and he watched her face and the quickened heave of her generous bust as she gazed out at the bobbing holiday sails on the sea. Ever since his telephone conversation with Bob he had wondered how she would react. Her charm for him – or part of it – was her unpredictability. He watched and waited with professional interest.

She had planned the gesture yesterday, when he had first suggested the trip to the seaside, and so she had come prepared. It had been part of the frustration, a rebellion against the hated image of retired domesticity. She had pictured herself undertaking it with quiet deliberation and defiance as though it entailed no special effort but leaving him in no doubt of the difference in their natures. Now she would do it because she wanted to, through sheer exhilaration. The sun was shining and they were all to be neighbours again. Lovely. Too late now for, "If any man can show any just cause", Mr and Mrs Mark Carter: neighbours. She stood, and with both hands, smoothed down the front of her cotton dress, patterned in yellow polka dots. She placed the canvas bag on the table and rummaged busily.

"There's a lovely day, isn't it?" she beamed down happily and confidently at Webber, "seems a shame to come all this way and waste it. I think I'll just pop in for a swim."

In London, Margaret talked and shopped and cooked, and bought records of things they heard together on the radio. When they made love he was both gentle and passionate so that she lay under him and felt beautiful and younger than he was. In the street and in the shops, when she looked at other women, she warmed to them in sincere compassion because she felt sorry for anyone who wasn't married to him. She wished she knew more people to talk to because she loved saying "my husband". There was an unexpected bonus too. In bed she did feel younger, delighting in submitting to his fierce urgent love making and marvelling that it was so uncomplicated by the excesses described in such clinical detail in her mother's book. The bonus had come when they were not making love but talking quietly as business partners with a lifetime ahead of them. Then, to her delight, she realised that her mother's denigration of her ability to understand money had brainwashed her into accepting it as the truth. It wasn't true at all. She had simply never tried to understand because it hadn't been her money anyway, and her mother had made her feel a fool. Now it was different. Mark not only talked to her about it sensibly and with open lack of embarrassment but he listened to her and she felt wiser and more mature than he was. The balance, she thought, was exactly right. When he talked about shops and property and money she still listened but contributed her own thoughts and ideas and then he listened.

There were still some things that puzzled her; the exact details and the reasons for his flight from Flaxfield he had never explained, and her instinct told her to leave them until such time as he chose to tell her. She had enough. Even the nagging conscience voice of her mother was stilled into impotent silence. Sometimes she imagined that face set in tight lines of disbelief but she no longer had to endure the bossy, bitter voice, ringing through her loneliness. She had no time for it, for the first time she was free and her mother was dead. If she could do that for herself she could do it for him too. She had snatched her happiness and it was rich. It was their greatest asset and she would make him see that, Carter and Garland – Garland and Carter, it didn't matter which, her mother, his mother, his cheated inheritance, they were no longer of any real significance. What mattered was the future and what they did with it together. Their property was in each other. The name Garland linked to Carter proved it.

She lay propped up by his pillow and her own while already he had fallen asleep by her side. Across the room she studied her reflection in the dressing table mirror. The reading light over the bed cast deep shadows under her breasts giving an unnecessary and premature impression of droop. By lifting her arms with her hands behind her neck the shadows disappeared.

They wouldn't start their business in London. They would go back to Suffolk.

Garland and Carter sounded right, she thought.

❦ FOURTEEN ❧

ON HER NEXT attempt, Mrs Thomas succeeded in establishing telephonic communication with Margaret, and allowed herself the luxury of surprised delight at her news.

"She doesn't think it's sensible to keep two homes going," she informed Webber later, "so they've put Butcher Street on the market, just as it stands. Freehold, curtains, carpets, fixtures and fittings and all the furniture. She wouldn't get anything for the furniture if she sold it separately, she said, most of it was modern rubbishy stuff her mother had bought, quite expensive at the time but practically worthless second hand, she wishes now that they'd bought a few fine antique pieces instead. She's found a good local estate agent and they seem to think it will sell quite soon if she's not too greedy. Had one or two nibbles already, a man and his wife from Leicester and another man with a sports car and a friend. Mark had wondered if they might have sold Flaxfield instead and they've talked seriously about that, but everything's so expensive in London and she doesn't like the streets at night, only the other day they had the police round trying to identify some muggers or robbers or something. She'll be glad when it's all settled. There's a big For Sale sign right outside their bedroom window and it takes all the light away. She's ever so fed up with solicitors and agents and bank managers, especially bank managers. Mark's been absolutely wonderful and she can't think how she ever managed without him. Of course there are so many things to take into consideration, lovely to make plans and have someone to discuss them with, but all news when we meet, not too long she hopes, but she couldn't stay chatting any longer because she could hear his key in the door and she had his lunch to get, steak, salad and jacket potatoes, with baked apple and custard. I don't think I've missed anything," Mrs Thomas ended modestly. "Shame she had to break off, really. She was in a nice chatty mood."

They were walking down a pleasant country lane on the outskirts of Flaxfield, dusty from the long summer sunshine.

"And she never said a word about him leaving here like he did?"

"No nothing."

It wasn't easy to get Webber to walk simply for the pleasure of it. His garden, he told her, was more than enough exercise for him, but she liked to get him away from it when she could.

"And that was all she said – lovely to make plans and all news when we meet?"

"Yes."

"I wonder what she's asking for Butcher Street," he said.

"One hundred and forty thousand pounds, but a firm offer of a hundred and twenty might be acceptable for a quick sale. She happened to mention the name of the agent so I phoned them," she explained, "said I'd seen the board outside and thought it might suit. Tidy little sum isn't it? She's got money in the bank too. Proper little heiress, really."

"She told you about the bank?"

"No, but I've happened to notice the manager in Flaxfield when he meets her in the road. He takes his hat off."

The lanes around the Henworth estate were still unspoiled. Untouched by vicious herbicides or mechanical cutters, the hedgerows spilled down to the dry ditches, rioting with wild flowers and bees. Under the riot, deep in the stalks and leaves, small animals paused and watched them as they passed. Out of sight, in the field on the other side of the hedge, a young fox silently murdered a mouse and ate it.

The lane widened and a gap in the hedgerow held a wooden gate with a view over the meadows to Henworth Hall, a cluster of grey chimneys through the trees. Webber was grateful for the chance to rest, leaning his arms on the top of the gate. Lately he had taken to using a stick. He found it useful for disguising a limp when arthritis nagged at his knee or his hip, he was grateful that so far she had chosen to ignore it.

"Old age, John," Dr Maguire had cheerfully informed him, when he had gone up to the Hall to have dinner with him. He quite liked Maguire, he was a terrible old charlatan of course, but you couldn't help liking someone who rode roughshod over established medical practice and whose outrageous theories in his few years at Henworth Hall had belatedly earned him more money than he had acquired in a lifetime of general practice. He had come late to luxury and he enjoyed it. As a youthful medical student in Belfast he had known hardship and occasionally poverty, now he had the lifestyle of an eighteenth century squire and he lived well.

For dinner they sat in Maguire's dining room and ate venison by candle light. The furniture and paintings were culled from the best of the old owners' collection. Maguire served the wine and carved, while a slightly awestruck Annie Spicer waited at table. Annie was saving for her marriage to a boy from the local garage and only too happy to extend her duties to evening overtime. The squire was never short of willing hands. He spread his small palms and twinkled expansively, "You see I don't change, John! The best prescription in the world, good food and wine and pleasant company. I can't, unfortunately, offer any female leavening, it would never do to let the ladies see where their money goes and hardly fair to destroy their diet. No Annie, my child! *Never* cover roast potatoes they steam up and go soggy, just leave them on a low flame in the chafing dish until I've carved. You'll enjoy this John, a young stag's leg and nicely marinated. Of course, sometimes I can get quite pleasant dinner guests from the two flats out at the back there, non-dieters mostly, a rather nice American woman, Arlene Weikel, and Joan Carter could be good fun too, quite outrageous mind you, but since she so wholeheartedly practised what I preached it was difficult to remonstrate with her. How's that for a first helping?"

"Excellent, thank you. It was Mrs Carter I really came to ask you about."

"Yes, I rather thought it might be, after that visit from the good matron Thomas. How is she by the way? Such a wonderful cook, I really envy you that. How do you find the Chambertin?"

"Very special."

"Isn't it though! Sadly it's almost the last of the sixty-nine, but I've laid down some promising seventy-one."

"Lizzie's fine, she likes a challenge, you know, and this business of the Carters has rather intrigued her."

Maguire delicately cut into his large portion of venison and considered. He liked Webber, enjoyed his company and liked nothing better than to get him talking of his old battles as a policeman. He had nothing to hide but tonight Webber's eyes were startlingly shrewd and very blue and he had known him long enough to see this as an indication of more than passing interest.

"There's nothing funny going on, is there? I mean nothing that you haven't told me about, nothing – irregular?"

Webber's grin was more reassuring than any display of blue-eyed innocence.

"No nothing, I promise. I certainly don't think she's planted out in the woods somewhere, if that's what you're worried about! I just found it rather odd that she should scarper off like that, and the son too. Very odd."

"Yes – of course it was. Apart from anything else it plays hell with the booking routine, but at least she paid her bill and some of them don't always do that. To be honest, John, I just don't know what was going on. Joan Carter was one of my first patients, you know. She came down in what you might call the heyday of the boys' brigade and adored every minute of it. I liked her because I was interested in antiques. You know she was Carter and Monmouth?"

. "Yes."

"I got one or two rather good things through them. Carter was very knowledgeable. A gentle creature. I didn't care for the partner, bumptious, very much the great I am. He ran the business side. I went in with Joan once and she said she was sure he'd be happy to give me a discount on anything I liked. He did, but he certainly wasn't happy to do it. Carter was a nicer person altogether. Strangely enough it seemed a reasonably happy marriage considering her case."

"Which was?"

"Oh sex of course. I've seen it in men but that's the more usual pattern. With those two it was reversed. If anything he was a bit neuter and probably delighted she could cope on her own."

While Annie cleared their plates and brought in the pudding, Maguire chatted about less private matters, country house sales, and the iniquity of auction house premiums.

"You met Mark Carter?" asked Webber.

"No I didn't, not in London nor when he came down here. He obviously didn't approve of his mother, made rather an unpleasant scene, you probably heard?"

"Yes. Mrs Weikel says his mother was frightened of him."

"You could hardly blame her, luckily the damage was put on her bill before she left." Maguire served the last of the wine. "Curiously, her husband's sudden death seemed to affect her deeply. Perhaps that's an unkind judgment, after all something had kept the marriage going all those years – yes, perhaps not so curious; after all one grieves for friendship too."

"Did you like her? I know you said she could be good fun but – like her?"

"I also said she was outrageous," he held the last of the wine in his glass to a candle before finishing it. "I think I felt sorry for her. The sex urge was very strong in her, almost involuntary. If she'd been

94

poor she would have been a prostitute, there's quite a market for big women I believe. Middle class, and she would have been a sure candidate for those ghastly psychiatrists. However, since she's rich she seems to have resolved things without either of those sad alternatives. Money is a great soother of difficulties. The sins of the poor are merely the eccentricities of the rich, although she did once tell me that as a younger woman she'd been banned from most of the big cruise ships, with the exception interestingly enough of the Italian lines, and they actually gave her a discount. Finish your wine and we'll try something else with the egg custard."

"Tell me about the young man – Miller is it? Billy Miller?"

Perhaps the cork of the half bottle of Barsac was genuinely difficult but Maguire made the most of it before answering. He deplored anything which threatened to disturb the smooth routine of the Hall. With busy-bodies like Mrs Thomas it was easy to hide behind his non-existent medical ethics but Webber was different. Maguire had a strong sense of self preservation. It was one of the reasons he had cultivated Webber as a friend. In case of need friends could be allies, and a Detective Inspector of police, even if retired, was certainly to be numbered as a friend.

"Shall I have a go?"

"No, no it's just coming. Ah! – there – sweet wines can be very stubborn for some odd reason. Miller? You heard about him from Arlene Weikel?"

"Lizzie Thomas had a chat with her. He doesn't seem to fit in to the usual picture."

"No . . ." Maguire served the pudding at the sideboard and brought their plates to the table before he continued.

In the pause before he spoke, Webber saw Maguire's face compose itself. He's going to duck out of it, he thought. If he knows nothing about Miller he would have answered at once, but he does know something, and I think he's going to duck it.

"He was rather an ordinary young man," Maguire said at last. "Joan asked if he could come down and stay for a while. It was shortly after Carter's death and she'd calmed down a bit. They do that sometimes. There was no need for her to ask, that's the point of those flats, you do as you please if you can afford them. The boys' brigade had gone by then and I assumed that he was one of her London reserves. She was certainly fond of him."

"But he didn't stay with her in the flat, I believe?"

"No, she took one of the cottages on the estate for him. We keep a few of them for servants if they're needed, chauffeurs and so on. That's what she asked about. It wasn't my business but I did think it was a curious arrangement and frankly a little difficult. I didn't quite know whether he should be treated as a servant or a friend. He could have been both, of course, but one likes to observe the niceties."

Maguire was enjoying this evening, his opportunities for congenial company were limited and Webber was an attentive audience.

"My instinct tells me that the puritan gleam in your eye and the slight flare of the nostrils, suggest that you are about to refuse the Stilton. Yes? Well then, let us take a turn on the terrace and have our coffee later."

By standing on stretched toes on the bottom bar of the gate Mrs Thomas was able to achieve parity of height with Webber and, like him, lean with her elbows on top of it. It was fascinating information of course, but just the same, she couldn't help feeling slightly irritated by the ease with which he seemed able to accumulate facts.

"And you mean he just came out with it – down there on the terrace – without prompting or anything?"

Even without looking at her he could sense the scowl of frustrated concentration on her face. A scowl to be avoided.

"No, certainly not, not without prompting. Maguire's a coward, he likes to keep his nose clean. Truth is Lizzie, without your spadework I think he would have kept his mouth shut."

"Eh?"

He nodded thoughtfully out across the meadow. "Oh yes, not much doubt about that. You see he hadn't reckoned on you talking to Mrs Weikel and it shook him. She might have known and told you, so he decided to play safe." He smiled at her gratefully. "You did the prompting Lizzie, all I had to do was listen." There was some truth in it even though he'd only just thought of it.

Mollified and a little proud, she eased herself off the gate. "Time we started back, soon be teatime. Pity the venison was so tough, you need to be very careful with game, no good marinating it if you haven't hung it long enough. What was the custard like?"

"Rather watery," he lied, allowing her to take his arm.

On the terrace the last of the evening sun had played briefly on the Palladian pillars of the west front of the house before dipping suddenly behind the distant trees of Henworth Wood. It was past the curfew hour for patients and except for the occasional swoop of a feeding bat, Webber and Maguire had walked alone after their meal.

"So that, until Mark Carter arrived and heaved a brick at her, she seemed perfectly content with the company of this boy Miller, the chauffeur or whoever he was?" Webber asked.

"Oh yes, perfectly. We had a very pleasant dinner together only a few days before that. She was in cracking form. It was part of her charm, she could tell the most outrageous stories, even against herself, with absolutely no sense of embarrassment. It wasn't only the wine, either, although she could certainly drink a lot of it without getting in the least bit drunk. That was the night I asked her about Miller. You see, I wondered if I should have invited him too."

"And?"

"No, I was quite in order apparently. He was rather shy, she said. They were very close, but he was happy enough just to be on his own, so long as he could be near her."

"And yet she left without him and chose a hired car to drive her away."

"He wasn't a chauffeur," said Maguire, "he was her son, her son by her husband's partner, Aubrey Monmouth."

❧ FIFTEEN ❧

WITHIN THREE WEEKS it was done. All of it arranged efficiently and with a minimum of fuss by Margaret, bright with happiness and the heady discovery of her unsuspected talent for business.

Against the advice of Mr Allen, the bank manager, she had accepted an offer of one hundred and twenty thousand pounds from the man with the sports car and a friend. There had been slightly better offers but they had been hedged about by surveyors and mortgages and bridging loans. The sports car man had simply written out a cheque and shaken her hand. If possible, he said, they would like to move in as soon as convenient after the cheque had been cleared. Now that she had decided, it had suited her very well.

"I'm sure it won't bounce," Margaret told the manager, "he said he was in the fruit machine business."

And Mr Allen, who had been hoping to arrange a bridging loan for a golfing friend, had to admit that she was probably right.

Marriage, he thought sadly, had wrought a remarkable change in her, starting with the shock of that first meeting when she had made an appointment as Mrs Carter.

"Yes of course," she said briskly, "the house might well appreciate in value if the market improves, I see that. But then, I shall probably also have to pay more for my shop."

My shop, he thought, was interesting, and why hadn't she brought Carter with her?

"And by the same token," she had added smoothly, "house prices could fall. On the whole the argument does not commend itself to me. The main objection though, would be to accepting a loan from the bank."

"Forgive me Miss Garland . . ."

"Mrs Carter."

"I'm sorry, of course, Mrs Carter, but you yourself said . . ."

98

"Yes I know, but I'm afraid I was being very foolish and naive. I simply had no idea how much money you would be making out of it." There was no need for him to blush, but her direct statement had caught him unawares, and he had sought refuge in her papers on his desk.

Apart from her two houses, she had inherited a small folio of rather dull but safe shares and some National Savings issues. By the time the blood had stopped fussing his face, the gold-plated pen with the extra fine nib had added them up in neat figures to an approximate total of eighty thousand pounds.

"Round about eighty thousand pounds," she confirmed before he could speak.

"Uh – yes – I think I mentioned stock to you when we talked before. It would depend, I know, upon . . ."

"There's no point in discussing stock," she said, "until I know how much I must pay for the shop. That will, in any case, be my husband's department not mine."

In spite of himself, he smiled. She could have sounded intolerably rude but she was so obviously sincere. She was also, he had to admit, making quite remarkably good sense. His eye caught his original notes with their tidily circled numbers. The girl who sat in his office now was very different from the Margaret Garland who had prompted those observations. 1) Potty? No, she wasn't that. 2) Going like her mother? She could hardly be more different from that cloying, little-girl creature, with her head forever tilting on one side like a kitten on a chocolate box. 3) Con man? Who could tell. It was too late now, anyway.

The marriage had taken him by surprise. As bank managers go he was kind as well as conscientious. It was his duty to make such routine checks as he could on his clients' behalf and he had checked on Mark Carter at Carter and Monmouth. He had not cared for Aubrey Monmouth but had been disturbed to learn that Mark Carter had not been officially employed by them.

To have told her now, he thought, would not serve her well. In all marriages there were things best left to come out in their own time. He could have warned her about a prospective business alliance, but a marriage which was already in being was ground he hesitated to disturb.

"I shall be sorry to lose you," he told her sincerely. "I'm afraid I haven't met your bank manager in Flaxfield but I'm sure he will look after you. I need hardly say that I wish you well. I hope you will come and talk to me whenever you . . . ," he had nearly said, "need to", but aware of her new found sharpness, changed and shaded it off into, "want to".

Seeing her standing at the door ready to plunge into God knew what of a future, he felt a sudden stab of pity for her. She was more attractive than he had remembered. For years, ever since she had first come with her mother and swung her white stockinged schoolgirl's legs from the same chair she had just left, he had watched her grow out of awkward and crushed adolescence into a quiet and dominated woman. Curiously, her new image and her obvious happiness made her seem, not less, but more vulnerable than she had been before.

"Thank you, yes I will. It will seem strange to be out of London after so long."

"What made you think of Dunwold, may I ask?"

"Oh there's quite a lot of money down there Mr Allen. Mark — my husband — knows it from the antique fairs. There are one or two local shops but no really serious competition. He really is very knowledgeable you know. I mean quite remarkably so." She seemed suddenly more like the girl he remembered, quieter and hesitant.

"I hope I shall meet him."

"Yes — actually," she returned to the brisk business voice, "I'm afraid I may have misled you at our last meeting. He learned a great deal from his father, it's true, but he was never directly employed by his father's firm. He always preferred to be a freelance, you see."

He dismissed it politely. "You've had a great deal to think about. Such details are easily confused."

"I wasn't confused. I thought, if I was going to borrow money from you, I ought to make the proposition sound as attractive as possible."

Her belated frankness was commendable but he wished she hadn't tilted her head on one side.

By the end of September the brief summer had gone. Henworth Hall still held a satisfying quota of calorie counting women. Pummelled and pampered with every luxury except food, the only change in their routine was that they were allowed to wear track suits when they exercised in the chill morning air, and that they were paying more to maintain Maguire and protect him from the ravages of inflation.

In Flaxfield too, life and routine seemed little changed. Jimmy and Doreen complained about lack of business and yet he found enough money to buy the fixtures and fittings of a Victorian chemist's shop, and spent long days polishing and cherishing the deep red mahogany. It filled most of the space available in Trottwood Antiques and made an unexpectedly sympathetic stable for the rocking horse.

Webber's rheumatism improved when Mrs Thomas made him abandon his pills and sat him firmly in front of a blazing coal fire in his underpants. She was a firm believer in the efficacy of coal heat. It was a legacy from her father who had told her that only when the pithead baths had replaced the traditional tin tubs in front of the miners' kitchen fires had they developed rheumatism. Webber submitted to keep her quiet and was surprised when it seemed to work. The experiment engaged her energies and served to divert her attention from events at Dunwold. When she grew restless he brought her to heel with a limp.

He gave her a brief but impressive summary of the law of slander, a memory from his early days at the police training college. It was a time for patience, he told her, a time for discreet enquiries and just at the moment he would much prefer it if she didn't go charging off to Dunwold to play shop with the newly-weds. He agreed that it would indeed be interesting to know just how much or little Mark had confided in Margaret about his background but it could wait, and she must trust him and be patient.

Patience did not come easily to her but she trusted him. Her respect for him was deep and it was growing. She resisted the lure of Dunwold and waited. Unused to such discipline on her part he was impressed but not above teasing her.

"A perfectly normal, happy marriage," he volunteered one evening, as they waded through the uncut hay of her lawn after cold poached salmon trout and cucumber salad.

It did not escape her that if he had really believed it there would have been no need for him to say so.

"Young love," added Webber firmly, "setting out bravely in a hard and competitive line of business."

"With her money," she said.

"And his skill, his considerable skill, don't forget. How can someone of his age know so much, do you suppose? Oh I know all about the street markets and his father and so on – all the same, what is he? About twenty-two?"

"Nearly twenty-three, December the second. I asked him that same question once, during the fair. He told me that it didn't seem strange to him after nearly twenty years' experience."

101

Webber paused in his systematic prodding of the long grass ahead of them with his walking stick.

"Even with my limited maths I make three an early age to start."

"He spent most of his time with his father. It was the earliest game he could remember, the only game. Museums, shop windows, books, magazines."

"Game?"

"Always the same. Who made that? Painted this? What date? What wood is that? What's the period? When he was older they would sit and do the catalogues together."

"How did that go?"

"His father had kept complete sets of sale-room catalogues going back for years. He would tell Mark the date of the sale and then read out the description of a lot number – show him a photograph if there was one. Then there would be two questions. How much did it fetch? And then, How much is it worth today?"

"You'd need a good memory."

"Yes."

Webber's stick had been searching for the ancient line of bricks where the path had once edged the lawn. He parted the grass to reveal a space where it had been squashed flat like a secret nest.

"Bunter," explained Mrs Thomas, "he sleeps in the grass when it's warm. There's quite a few of them, he gets a bit closer to the house as the nights get colder. One night he'll come into the warm."

"That cat bites the hand that feeds it. Did you know that?"

She nodded equably. "If you take anything away from him or he thinks you're going to. Is that what you did?"

"Out of common courtesy. I was simply moving his saucer to a better position."

"Oh well, of course – a misunderstanding."

"Has it occurred to you – it's just a thought – that at some point he might have misunderstood our child prodigy? Cats who bite sometimes get stones thrown at them."

"And mothers?"

"Mothers," said Webber, "can give you a very nasty nip sometimes. You're right, it's getting chilly. Shall we have a nightcap at the Bull?"

Autumn probably comes earlier to Dunwold than anywhere else in England and if this is statistically untrue it is still firmly believed by the local residents. Margaret never noticed the cold wind from the sea edging through the streets. For all she cared it could have been spring.

The shop had been built in the main High Street of the town in 1825 and that date was picked out in flint pebbles on the wall above the centre doorway. It had been successively: a linen drapers, an ironmongers, and finally a chemist's shop run by an ancient husband and wife, for whom even the occasional sale of aspirin or cough mixture was proving too much. There was no living accommodation, the rooms on the floor above the shop had long ago been used as storage space. They had put it on the market at sixty thousand pounds for the freehold. It had been almost the first property that Margaret and Mark had looked at. Within two days they had decided and she had made out the cheque. The other possibility had been a shop, long empty but temptingly cheap, just ten yards off the High Street. They both turned it down for the same reason, laughing and delighting in their unanimity like clever children.

"Of course you think it's a bargain," said Doreen, looking around helplessly at the wealth of mahogany fittings with the ivory knobs and the gilt titles of the Victorian pharmacopoeia. "You thought the rocking horse was a bargain and you haven't sold that, either."

Jimmy Trottwood was the only one who had been officially invited to inspect the new shop at Dunwold and that had been partly for business reasons when he had bought the old chemist fittings. Every day Margaret and Mark drove there in her car, the same car which had originally brought them together.

"They want to get it all straight first," Jimmy said, "and when they get back here at night they're probably too tired to want to go out much. I think it's very romantic. You mustn't mind."

"Well invited or not, I'll bet Mam's been over for a good snoop round."

"Only through her binoculars from the steps of the fountain in the square, she did admit that, but no closer. She can be quite tactful, sometimes. She watched the builder's van delivering loads of wood. No harm in that. She says that she and John Webber want to respect the children's privacy."

"It sounds like John, doesn't sound like her. Why didn't they buy that empty shop in King Street? It's half the price they're paying. She must have more money than sense."

"You can't see it from the main road, that's why. They said that a shop in the High Street gets all the passing traffic, very important, especially for antiques."

"No wonder he took the money we owed him from the fair."

"Oh come on love, he did earn it."

"We're on the main street here and it doesn't seem to do us much good."

"You're tired, I'll help with the table."

"I do think they might have come to dinner, I'd have bought lamb chops instead of that damned expensive joint if I'd known. First them and now John Webber's cried off too – Mother on her own! I can't bear it. It's really not fair. Did she say why he couldn't come?"

"Webber? He's been called up to London, quite suddenly, on business."

❦ SIXTEEN ❧

WEBBER TRAVELLED UP to London by coach. Before he retired there had nearly always been a police driver to take him about his business. Now he disliked driving himself, especially in London. The railway in Suffolk had long ago succumbed to the planner's axe and what was left of it was expensive and unreliable. The coach surprised him, it was comfortable, cheap, and left Flaxfield at the exact minute promised in the time table. He watched the flat fenland of East Anglia travel slowly past the frame of his window, until his attention was caught by the rustle of the white paper bag being offered to him by his travelling companion.

"No good poking around," said Mrs Thomas, "they're all the same. Old Fashioned Mint Humbugs, they last longer on a journey."

He might have known she would come with him in the end. Not that he minded, he was glad to have the company, and at least if she was with him she couldn't be racing around putting up hares all over the place.

"Doreen cross about the dinner?" he asked.

She nodded happily, the nostalgic flavour of the mint humbug adding to the enjoyment of the journey, his company, and her daughter's fury.

"Tamping mad she was, knew she would be, bossy little bitch, good for her. Mind you, fair play, it was my idea."

"The dinner party?"

"Umm, I thought it was about time." She saw Webber waiting for more information but not asking. "Well, why not? You said not to go bothering them at Dunwold and I didn't, not so's they'd notice anyway. Well, the shop's finished now; almost finished. The last of the wood and new fitments went in last week. They've cleared out all the upstairs rooms for storage but nothing in them yet. The shop looks very handsome. Plain green felt on the walls, fitted shelves and generous cupboard space, new floor, parquet blocks, only veneer but beautifully laid so you couldn't tell it from the real thing. Want another?"

"You went snooping."

"Certainly. There's a nice, tidy little man in Gun Street, just round the corner from them. Sells junk mostly, second hand books and old bottles, got a daughter married to a milkman in Slough. I bought an old wine bottle from him for twenty pence. I guessed he might have gone in to see them, you know what people are like."

"Anything else?"

"Not much about the shop, except, as I said, they've bought no stock for it yet. There's a cellar but it's damp like all of them in the High Street. He said they'd be better ignoring it and he thinks they probably will."

"What does he think of them?"

"He took to them. He's a nice old thing, says he's seen them late at night kissing in the lighted shop, covered in paint and still holding the brushes. Nice?"

"I told you, young love . . ."

"I know – setting out bravely – you said. Then what are we doing going up to London?"

"Because we don't quite believe it and so we might as well hear what my tame sergeant friend has to say."

She wondered why he couldn't have heard that on the telephone. Perhaps he had wanted to get away from her for a while. She knew she sometimes irritated him. She fell silent.

The evenings were drawing in and the light lay low over the fields, softer now in Essex, with moulded slopes and the trees standing straighter without the wind from the sea. Colchester, Chelmsford, the telegraph wires rose and dipped. Webber tried his crossword again and gave it up. There was always one clue he couldn't do. Four across: two words; three and five letters, "Limits of human understanding".

She sat wishing the journey would end. The seat which had been so comfortable at first seemed to be pushing her bust up into her neck so that the thin white bows on the turquoise blue dress thrust out under her chin like crab claws.

He pocketed his pencil and tossed the newspaper on to her lap.

"Hopeless, too grand for me, something stupid out of Greek philosophy I expect. I'm not sure how long we shall stay but the hotel's not full, I checked."

"A chat with your sergeant shouldn't take long."

106

Webber helped himself to another sweet from the bag on her lap. "I'm glad you're coming, Lizzie."

All doubts gone, the crab claws thrust forward nipping at his words as she turned her head to him.

"It would have been a bit much for me on my own, perhaps," he continued. "This evening we'll talk to Bob Raglan, my old chum, then tomorrow I'm going to see Aubrey Monmouth. Yes I know, I should have done it in the first place."

"Why didn't you?"

"Laziness," he said simply, "I thought it might not be necessary. Then when Bob phoned I felt I should come up and do the two together. I had another enquiry too but I have an idea that you'll do that better than I would. Landladies terrify me."

"Claverton Gardens?"

He nodded.

"I may be wrong but I have a feeling that Jimmy Trottwood could well have missed something there. Do you mind?"

She assured him that she didn't, curling her toes with pleasure.

They were edging their way through the eastern suburbs of London, soon they would arrive at the Victoria bus station. Webber looked out at the East End with interest, he hadn't seen it for years. In his early days as a young police constable on the beat the shops had been almost exclusively Jewish, now only a few familiar names caught his eye, all the rest were Indian or Pakistani, the names and advertisements in script as exotic and alien as the brown faces crowding the pavements. He was a tolerant man; he was indignant and angry when he read of the injustices of racial discrimination. It occurred to him that tolerance was an easy virtue if you lived in Suffolk. He was glad he was no longer a young policeman on this manor. First Mosley's blackshirt mob and the Jews, now the National Front and this lot. He sighed. Best to stick to small puzzles.

Mrs Thomas watched the changing expressions flitting across his face and smiled. Sometimes he made things more difficult than they were. He caught her smiling at him and grinned sheepishly.

"It's all right for you, you old Welsh mole, your lot had enough sense not to invade in force."

"Twickenham Rugby Finals?"

"Only a raiding party, these poor devils have made a ghetto for themselves."

"That's the policeman talking." She pointed out at the respectable orderly crowds in the streets. "You see trouble when it's quiet and peaceful."

107

"Oh I love that coming from you! Perhaps you're right, we see things and judge more by instinct than by trying to understand them."

"Limits of human understanding?" She passed his crossword puzzle back to him. "Not difficult; not Greek philosophy, either. Common sense. 'Toe Nails' – fits in nicely. My God, I wish there was a lav on this bus."

Margaret telephoned Sarah Collins from the cottage in Flaxfield. She had come back early from Dunwold taking the bus and leaving the car for Mark, who had to wait for a man to come and fit some new locks.

"My dear, don't be silly, you're practically my only private patient and much cherished. I'll come round and see you after the last of the stick-and-crutch brigade have gone, say about five o'clock?"

The man wasn't coming with the new locks until half past four. "Well if it's not a fuss," Margaret said, "that will be fine."

Almost as soon as she replaced the receiver she regretted making the call. It wasn't disaster, she could invent a vague depression for herself through overwork, let Sarah Collins cluck a little sympathy and prescribe something innocuous if she wanted to. Perhaps it was just that and nothing more. She really was tired and they had both been working ridiculously hard. She should have insisted that they get someone in to do all the painting and decorating after the builder's men had finished. And that's what it would be with him, too. He was exhausted even before they had bought any stock. It was nothing but her own tiredness that had made her imagine a change in him. Nothing to run to a doctor about.

She moved around the house tidying away paint-stained clothes and washing up the remains of their hurried breakfast. She would just have time to prepare something for their evening meal before Dr Collins came. She tried to remember what it had been like when he had been a guest in her mother's bed. The shy invalid in his pyjamas, guaranteed one hundred per cent cotton, and the sheer blazing excitement of peeling potatoes while she listened to the floor boards when he went to the bathroom or the lavatory.

"This delicious fish pie may be cooked from frozen in a pre-heated oven 375F, Gas Mark 5."

Sometimes when her mother had been alive they had driven over to the harbour at Dunwold and bought fish, fresh landed by the local men who came chugging in from the sea in small boats smelling of mackerel and flopping plaice. Like Webber she was afraid of the sea.

It was odd that she no longer heard her mother's voice and, curiously, she missed it. She missed that blind, impotent anger so easily goaded to vulgar excess but now it was silent, the voice was her own.

"You can't say you weren't warned. Any sixth form schoolgirl would have had more sense. No wonder the bank manager tried to slow you down. The boy drops his trousers and takes off his underpants and the next minute you're backing him with every farthing you've got in the world. Different? Of course he's different, you could hardly expect him to stay sweet and shy for ever, could you? Well you wanted him and you've got him, but not quite as you thought. No wait, wait, wait, you'd better settle for what you've got. You're not going to find it quite as simple as you thought, so, if you're clever, you'll accept it. Accept Carter and Garland over the shop and Carter in bed, you're lucky, it's a bargain. Love is a bargain, you can never pay too much for it. Of course he's upset about losing his share in his father's business, who wouldn't be? You mustn't keep thinking of it as an obsession, a persecution complex, it isn't that. If you lose an inheritance, you say and think terrible things. Why do you suppose romantic novels are so popular? Sarah Collins isn't due for twenty minutes. You're being silly. It will be all right, it will be *all right*. Listen," she told herself, "it's a test, if you can peel the potatoes and chop the parsley and lay the table before she comes then it really will be all right, he'll forget about his mother and Monmouth and his half-brother and his father's will and we'll rest and not be tired and buy stock and have sex in the bath and people here for dinner and he can have the new Citroen estate car for country sales and he can . . ."

"Coo-ee! Can I come in? Not too early I hope? Only two sticks and a hernia turned up so I thought I'd come and save your life before teatime."

Sergeant Raglan and his girl friend, Policewoman Thelma Pipe, sat in a quiet corner of the pub with Webber and Mrs Thomas. On the table stood two pints of draught beer, a vodka and bitter lemon, a glass of Guinness and a photostat copy of a newspaper cutting. Webber picked it up and read it again.

"There was nothing in the national papers?"

Thelma Pipe shook her head. "Nothing that I could find, anyway."

Webber grunted.

"No, why should there be, people die of heart attacks every hour of the day. If Daniel Carter had died in hospital, there probably wouldn't have been an inquest at all," he looked at his ex-sergeant. "And you say nothing in C.R.O.?"

"No, clean as a pin, no record of any sort. You didn't expect anything though, did you?"

"Not really, though I've known routine checks turn up some odd things in the Criminal Record Office."

While Webber was at the counter buying another round of drinks, Mrs Thomas read the newspaper cutting again.

CORONER'S SYMPATHY FOR SON'S ORDEAL

A son who tried to save time by driving his father to hospital himself, instead of calling a doctor or the ambulance service after his father had suffered a heart attack, was certainly misguided but more deserving of sympathy than censure, said the coroner at the resumed inquest on Daniel Carter, an antique dealer of Eaton Square, Belgravia.

Mrs Thomas wished that she and Webber were alone. In books and films, drinks arrived at tables without fuss or bother, people walked up and ordered drinks from happy joking barmaids. There were at least four people waiting to be served before Webber, and the barman was slow and surly. To her relief, Raglan and the girl stood up to leave, calling Webber back from the bar.

"Best leave it John, we ought to get back, you know what it's like."

She said goodbye to Thelma, even urging her to stay for a while, and watched her join Webber and Raglan chatting at the door. Both Raglan and the girl, she thought, looked like police officers in plain clothes. Webber looked like a farmer.

Seeing a gap at the bar she was into it like a terrier and brought the drinks back to the table where Webber sat alone.

"There's glad I am I asked her if she couldn't stay a bit longer," she murmured, placing his brimming pint carefully in front of him, "and there's glad I am she didn't."

"Don't be so ungracious."

"I know, I wanted to talk. What do you think?"

"You read the verdict, Natural Causes. There was a long history of heart disease and the post mortem confirmed it."

"Why was the inquest postponed originally?"

"Standard practice – more or less – the post mortem for one thing, and of course in those rather unusual circumstances the police would have made routine enquiries. Bob said the local boys did that."

"Like?"

"Oh, what sort of relationship he had with his father. Whether he stood to gain from his father's death. Routine."

"Did he?"

"His father's will left everything to his wife."

They drank slowly and a machine in the corner started playing a bright jangling tune with incomprehensible lyrics.

"Terrible time for a car to break down," said Mrs Thomas, "no wonder the coroner felt sorry for him."

❧ SEVENTEEN ❧

MARGARET FELT ASHAMED of herself for allowing her tiredness to exaggerate a whole series of trivial worries into a major panic and grateful that she had told Sarah Collins nothing.

Now that the shop was finished she had persuaded Mark that it would be good for them both to relax for a few days before he started buying stock. Last night he had sat with her quietly after their fish pie. Helping her with the few plates, he had listened without interrupting while she had gone through the bills and expenses. There was no sign of what had worried and disturbed her sometimes when they had been decorating the shop. Like the times when he had so bubbled with enthusiasm that she had found it almost impossible to concentrate his attention on any single subject for more than a few seconds.

Now that the last bill, the one tendered for the new locks, had been added up with the others, he had taken the pile of papers and re-checked the figures, agreeing with her on the final total. They had a working capital of just one hundred thousand pounds.

And when they had gone to bed he had curled up close to her holding her gently in his arms. Her arm went to sleep before she did but she lay still and quiet in case she woke him and spoiled his rest. Before he slept she had heard him murmur, scarcely audibly, "Poor Peg, you must be so tired."

It didn't matter, she thought, which one of them said it.

Now, in the morning, she had left him sleeping. She had almost forgotten the luxury of a day in Flaxfield. How on earth had she managed to fill her days before Mark, she wondered.

It was early, with a clear sky and no wind but with little warmth in the autumn sun. She wished she had put a coat on but hesitated to go back in case she woke him too soon. A few early morning shoppers drifted slowly along the pavements, most of them with empty baskets going towards the shops. Jimmy Trottwood met her coming the other way with heavy baskets dragging down both arms.

"Don't even think of it dear! Queues everywhere, all the silly old things go to the butchers early to avoid a queue so this is the only time of the day there is one. I've left Doreen with five yards of pavement to go before she even gets inside the shop, with Henworth Hall and the vicar's wife lengths ahead of her. She'll be hours yet. My God, I shall have arms like a gorilla if I gossip much longer. I've been sent back with the heavy stuff, beer and potatoes. Thank goodness she's off her diet this week. How lovely to see you. Come and have coffee. Don't argue I beg of you, I'm in agony."

He made her sit in the shop in a comfortable Victorian armchair, button-backed in green velvet.

"The kitchen's like an ice box, you'll get the sun through the window in here and the stove will soon warm it up. What about this weather! You don't know what to wear, do you? Mind you, I'll bet we're warmer than Dunwold. Shan't be a tick."

He beamed fondly at her and disappeared into the kitchen.

Sometimes she felt that all the surface brightness and chatter was only a cloak of protection.

It was the first time she had seen all the old fittings from the Dunwold shop in their new setting. He had polished them until the wood gleamed. Some of the little square drawers, labelled in gold with shorthand Latin tags, he had pulled out to make supports for pots of green trailing house plants. Leaning against one of the few gaps on the wall was an old enamelled advertisement he had bought when the railway station closed down.

Anaemic Girls Need Virol.

When he came back he carried a butler's tray, the legs of which he expertly dropped, to place it in front of her. On it he had set a steaming pot of coffee, large French coffee cups, biscuits, toast and honey.

"Now dear, you can call it what you like. If you've had breakfast – which you haven't – it can be early elevenses."

"Why shouldn't I have had breakfast?"

"Don't bully dear, it's too early. Some people look as though they've had breakfast and you didn't. I'll be mother. How's Mark?"

Afterwards she wondered why it had been so easy to talk to him about Mark when, with Sarah Collins, she had merely complained of her own tiredness and settled for taking it easy and a tonic. She ate the toast and the honey too, while he sipped his coffee and listened without interrupting her.

113

"I don't see how you can expect to know him yet," he said at last. "It would be terribly dull, my dear, if we could all know each other so easily. It's part of every marriage. He doesn't seem to have been very happy with his family from what you've just said. It takes time to get over that. It takes time to know that you're happy. He's lucky to have you to teach him."

"I expect some people in the village think he married me for the money."

"I haven't heard them, but yes, I expect they do. But then imagine what they must say about Doreen and me! Or about Lizzie Thomas and dear John, if it comes to that."

"I hate gossip."

"You're quite wrong you know, gossip is one of the great luxuries. Oh, I don't mean *bad* gossip, like spreading deliberate lies about people. Speculation now, that's *quite* different. If you don't wonder about people you might as well be a stone or a door post." He sipped his coffee happily. "After all, if people hadn't gossiped about Jesus we'd never have had the Bible."

"Yes, people were bound to wonder about Mark, weren't they?"

"Most of the village, except those very near to death, poor things."

"And you?"

His round face creased into an immediate smile.

"Wildly biased of course! One of the privileges of growing older, you can say what you think without giving offence. Now let me see. I think he came into the shop here for the first time with you at twenty past four on a Tuesday afternoon and by half past both Doreen and I were madly in love with him. And that," he said, tidying the cups and plates on the tray, "was even before he saved our lives at the Dunwold Fair, so you can hardly expect a word against him from us, dear."

"Oh Jimmy, why does everything have to be so complicated?"

"You don't even mean that, you know. What you really mean is, 'Oh dear, he's not absolutely one hundred per cent as I thought he was', and so you're enjoying the luxury of a mini-panic and you've come to your poor Aunt Betsey for reassurance with toast and honey. My dear, you wouldn't be human if you didn't have the odd doubt. You are very lucky Margaret, if you knew how ill-matched some couples are you'd be very, very grateful."

"You see I worry in case he's not happy about Dunwold."

Why was it that women never listened to what you told them.

"Has he said anything?"

114

"No – well not exactly. It's difficult to know what he thinks. One minute he's planning for the shop and then sometimes, almost in the same breath, he's talking about one of the big antique fairs in London."

"Don't let him rest too long."

"What?"

"You said you were going to make him rest. Take my advice and don't. You're like one of those girls in a Victorian novel. Sure as fate they'd land up choosing the liveliest horse in the stable – mettlesome they were always called. That's Mark, you'll have to let him have his head."

"Like you and Doreen did."

"That's right. I nearly fainted sometimes at the prices he used to pay. Oh come along dear! You've got yourself a beautiful racehorse. It doesn't matter where you run him, he's a winner. Now listen, in two minutes Doreen will be here, I can just see her rounding the corner so there's not much time. First of all, and you don't have to answer but I hope you will, are you all right for money? For stock I mean? You haven't overspent on the shop?"

"No, we're all right, at least I hope so – but we couldn't think of . . ."

"Not a word, she's only got twenty yards to go and she's got her butcher's-queue face on. Now when she comes in you are to go straight up and give her a kiss on the cheek. She likes a kiss – a peck will do. Say she was sweet to ask you to dinner but you've been worried about Mark overworking or something like that. You might just as well butter her up and she's a good ally given a push. Oh yes, and for heaven's sake admire her new handbag, I bought it for her in London and I don't think she likes it very much."

"Won't she want to know what we've been talking about?"

"Yes, but just ask her how her mother is and she'll forget it. Right, here we go. I should get the kiss in first while she's got her arms full."

It was an odd time of the year for a thunderstorm, yet it had disturbed both Webber and Mrs Thomas in their rooms at the Glockemara Hotel. Nevertheless she was pleased to see that he had come down to breakfast without his walking stick and no sign of a limp. They had already planned their day, agreeing that they would make no effort to meet before the evening. Webber had secured an appointment with Aubrey Monmouth after lunch. In the morning he had promised himself time to choose some new pipes and restock himself with the special tobacco which he reserved for peaceful evenings and weekends. Mrs Thomas preferred, she told him, not to decide how she was to tackle her own assignment until later. The day lay before them new-minted with washed pavements.

In Henworth Hall, Dr Maguire took morning coffee with Sarah Collins, summoned by him as a precaution.

"It's something you wouldn't have to consider, my dear Sarah, but I promise you, it could be a very real problem in my case. I really can't be too careful."

"Well she's not potty, if that's what you're worried about – a bit fragile but so are most old girls of eighty-five. I take it she doesn't go clumping over the lawns with the others?"

"No, no, of course not. She's lonely, that's all. I've got about six in her age bracket. They come for bridge and company but only for a few months in the summer."

"And she wants to come and live here permanently?"

"Out of the blue. About three weeks ago she asked Sister if the Carter flat at the back was free and that same evening she asked if she could move in for good."

"Well if she can afford it – I imagine it's not cheap – why not?"

"She can certainly afford it, her husband invented something to do with aeroplanes and had the sense to patent it. I got the impression from her bank manager that her income is – well – impressive."

"Her bank manager! How very enterprising of you."

Maguire's little squirrel eyes fought with the rest of his face spoiling the expression of gentle reproof.

"Mrs Barnstable naturally offered references. She is a very businesslike old lady. She understood perfectly my point of view about her having an independent medical examination."

"I'll bet you didn't say I would be assessing her senility as well as her blood pressure."

"Certainly not – really Sarah you make it all sound – well, underhanded and I must say I don't much care for that. If an elderly widow tells me she intends to sell her house with everything in it and come and live at Henworth, then I do feel I have a right to protect myself."

"Oh take no notice," Sarah Collins said, cheerfully humping herself into her duffel coat. "Point taken – gossiping relatives, undue influence and pressure on poor bewildered old great auntie,

116

yes of course you're right. Well, in my book she's as sane as a trout, although she must be barmy to pay your rent. Pax! A joke, I swear it! I rather liked her, I only hope I wear as well at her age. Why sell up, anyway? She may not like the arrangement. Too late then."

"I gather it's one of the chief reasons for coming. The house is a bit isolated, a converted farmhouse full of her bits and pieces, she doesn't want the responsibility. Even with her money reliable servants are hard to find. Luckily it's only about ten miles away, near Saxmundham."

While he spoke he reached into a desk drawer for a cheque book and began to fill it in.

"I haven't seen it yet, but of course I shall go over with her and help her to get things sorted out."

His finger nails were not really dirty but they had a sort of threat of grubbiness in their greedy grouping at the point of his pen. Honest dirt had never worried her but she was happier with cow dung than ink stains and the cloying smell of stale whisky and after-shave. Ridiculously she felt as she had as a schoolgirl waiting in front of a mistress's desk to receive her copybook marked and scored with encouragement or blame. Yes of course he would go over with the old woman and help her to get things sorted out with his greedy, money-grubbing little claws. In a way she felt demeaned by allowing herself to be a party to any of his oily little plans. Why should he live on the fat of silly rich women while she and Peter struggled to cope with the flotsam and jetsam of his old Welfare State patients in Flaxfield?

When he handed her the cheque for twenty-five pounds she would take it and tear it up. Not fiercely and dramatically but calmly and with dignity so that he would see and understand that she was acting from principle.

Glancing up he saw something of the struggle in her face but misinterpreted it. It was Maguire who tore up the cheque and reached inside his jacket for his wallet.

"That's what comes of chatting. I was forgetting how much more acceptable cash can be. Come to think of it, nothing gets any cheaper. I think we might make it thirty pounds from now on."

The moment of protest passed, and with relief she cheerfully thrust the notes into the pocket of her duffel coat. He was quite right, nothing got any cheaper; least of all scruples.

Scruple was not a word which often occurred in Mrs Thomas's thinking. In the Palace Dairy on the corner of Claverton Gardens, she had drunk her solitary cup of morning coffee and laid her plans.

She rang the bell in the basement of number 52. Her open, honest face smiled happily at the suspicious scowl of the woman who opened the door.

"Don't you worry my dear! I'm not selling anything. God knows I get enough of those myself. I'm Mrs Morgan from Victoria, used to have Mr Carter for a lodger. He left an old shirt, said I could use it for dusters, and the silly boy left a fifty pound note in the top pocket. Chilly old day, isn't it?"

"You'd better come in," the woman said.

❦EIGHTEEN ❧

IT HAD BEEN Mark's idea that they should drive over to Dunwold. She had not told him of her talk with Jimmy Trottwood and he had seemed surprised that she had not tried to keep him to his promise of some quiet relaxed days before they returned to the shop.

They stood on the opposite side of the road and looked at it. Carter and Garland faced them in neat white letters on the black background; simple and uncomplicated. He took his keys from the pocket of his jacket and held them up, the large new shop keys catching the sunlight. For an instant she had a wild idea that he was about to do something dramatic like flinging them down into the drain and running away. She didn't know what made her think anything so silly and unlikely. Instead he grinned happily at her, letting the keys drop for a second before sweeping his hand down, clutching them out of the air and returning them to his pocket.

"Will you be warm enough?" he said unexpectedly.

"For what?"

"Let's walk, you're right, the shop can wait."

She wasn't cold, there was still some warmth left in the sun and they walked inland protected from the wind off the sea. Away from the High Street there were only a few twisting roads lined with big houses set in walled gardens, glimpsed briefly through the wrought iron gates. The houses settled into an orderly line at the edge of the common. There they stopped short, overlooking the summer cricket ground and now, in autumn, the goal posts without nets of the town football team. Beyond lay the open country with the land falling away in gentle folds to where, on the horizon, the water of the estuary from the sea lay salt and silver under the dwarfing arc of the sky.

Once past the level ground of the sports fields, the common gave itself up to deep coarse grass, flattened by the wind. It blew through their hair snatching suddenly at it and slapping it against their faces. Down the slopes ahead of them, the ground evened out again into a meadow with softer, greener grass. In winter it was

119

often flooded with the brackish water from the estuary, but now it was drained and bright emerald green, dotted with black and white cows like a child's painting pinned up in a classroom.

For a moment they paused, standing on the top of the slope holding hands, and caught in the excitement of the wind tugging at their clothes.

It's like a film, she thought. She could see them both, as through the eye of a camera. All the film location crew intent on their every move, like they showed you sometimes on television, with the director shouting across the moving grass.

"Fine! Wonderful! I like it! Keep holding his hand, Margaret. Now turn and look at him, remember there's no dialogue, it's all just you two with the wind and the music. It's your thoughts, darling, just your thoughts. You've never been happier in your whole life than you are at this moment. Remember you've lost all your doubts about him, remember the scene in the Trottwood shop, 'You wouldn't be human if you didn't have the odd doubt'. That's it! you're human! I love it! OK – but now slowly he turns. Take his other hand darling. Divine! OK my darlings, but very slowly he comes in with his head to kiss you – slowly – slowly – and, NOW! You break and run down the hill. RUN! RUN! Both of you." Faintly in her head she heard him shouting at them as they raced down into the meadow, "Wonderful. I like it. Print it. Wonderful!".

It was wonderful. Like a film, but more real than any film she'd ever seen. More exciting because it was only the beginning and she didn't know how it would end. Only that this was a good scene, panting and running down into the warm sheltered air of the meadow, smelling of grass and cows and laughing helplessly. And Mark laughing too as she turned and dodged until, unable to gulp courage enough to run through the cows, she collapsed into the sweet scented ground and felt his face pressed cold-nosed into her neck with his hair soft in the palms of her hands. High in the clear sky above them she watched a sparrowhawk hover with short fluttering wings, defying gravity and the wind.

"Well just for a moment then," Mrs Thomas said, comfortably settling herself into a lopsided armchair at the side of the unlit gas fire.

"Would you take milk with the coffee?" the woman asked her. She was thin with a tired face and a tartan skirt, a pale blue pullover with a polo neck hung stained and loose over her flat chest.

"If it's no trouble."

"I'll borrow a cup from the Pole in number 3," the woman said. "He takes in two pints every day," she added as she left the room. It was difficult to tell whether she was offering this as proof of the affluence of the Pole in number 3, or as an assurance that they would not be depriving him.

Even in the morning light the basement room was gloomy. The window, heavily barred against Victorian burglars, looked out onto a damp area with a coal shed under the stone steps descending from the street. The room had once been part of the original kitchen and along the wall above the gas fire a row of round cast-iron caps, like saucepan lids, blocked off the flues where the kitchen range had once been.

Mrs Thomas looked around her in disbelief that anyone could live in such a room and not try to clean it up. The remains of breakfast crockery still littered the table where newspaper sheets served as a tablecloth.

The woman boiled the kettle on a gas ring in the hearth next to the fire. She seemed almost too listless to be cunning or avaricious, yet Mrs Thomas knew that only the mention of money had gained her entry.

"Is it your own place you have in Victoria?" she asked, pushing down on her bent knee to help her stand from the hearth. Only a woman of substance, she thought, could afford such honesty over a fifty pound note.

"No, no, I just look after it, sheets and so on. The owner," Mrs Thomas explained, accepting the cup of grey liquid without a shudder, "has a flat on the top and lets the rest off as bed-sits."

The tired woman sat at the cluttered table and looked at her visitor without embarrassment. So it was a bribe, she thought. It was to be fifty pounds for information. Perhaps the boy had left owing months of back rent, or he'd broken open the telephone coin box. Perhaps the old fancy man in the red wig, the one who hadn't offered her any money, perhaps he was the landlord in the top flat in Victoria. She would have to think carefully if she was going to get her hands on the fifty pounds.

"Dear God, isn't memory a terrible thing," she said, screwing up her eyes at the mottled ceiling in concentration. "Wouldn't it be the grand thing to have a memory like a book. Wonderful entirely," she added wistfully. And then when these overtures produced no reaction from her visitor, "Ah dear! I get so many coming and going, but I've a mind that he gave me his new address on an inch of paper. Sure it'll be in a drawer and as safe as

121

a secret with a priest. I could send the money on to the lad, so I could."

It was unpleasant to have to watch anyone lying so badly. Through common courtesy, and because she hoped she might not have to drink the coffee with its wrinkled grey skin, Mrs Thomas came to the point more quickly than she would normally have considered prudent.

"Of course, that would be the answer," she put the untouched coffee on the table and lifted her handbag on to her lap. The clasp clicked open holding the woman like a snake.

"It would, it would," she said, "or he might well stop by himself for comfort and pity, poor soul." In the silence she raised her eyes from the handbag to Mrs Thomas's face.

"Don't worry, I'll leave the money," she said to the woman gently. "Why pity and comfort?"

Released from the charade of remembering something she had never been told, the woman abandoned the Celtic twilight and without it seemed to lose some of the wheedling tiredness.

"Are you the police?"

"No."

"Or from the girl's family, perhaps?"

"No, nothing like that, it's nothing official, I promise."

The woman seemed suddenly aware of the mess on the table and carried the things over to the already crowded sink under the window.

"You can't have the curry, I told them, and you'll have to pay extra for the room if it's to be permanent. He often had the girls back, of course. They all do and you can't stop it, but a permanent, and with a risk of the curry clinging to every sheet in the house, I had to speak out."

"She was Indian?"

"Brown anyway, a child. She'd run away from home. Southall, she told me. She'd knock on this door for company if he was late back. I felt sorry for her, there'd been talk of an arranged marriage at home so she left and helped people selling silks and that in the Portobello Road. That's where the Carter boy met her. One day she'd seen some friends of her family roaming round the market. She thought they were looking for her and after that she stayed away from the market, she'd only go out to the corner. She earned a bit washing up for the Palace Dairy caff, enough to pay for her share of the room. To be honest, I don't think it was that. He wasn't as short as that, not dealing down in the market, and everything a cash deal, so it was. No, he was glad of her out of the house for a while. I had it in my head that she was like a shadow he hadn't bargained for and didn't the child tell me one night in this very room he was the only husband she'd ever want?"

With the sink full she stacked the last of the breakfast debris on a plastic draining board.

"She was possessed entirely with Carter. They say a new hatched duck will follow the first moving thing it sees for life and didn't she just put one in mind of that, poor soul."

"She followed him when he left?"

"I don't know the way of it. Maybe he took his things when she was at the caff and she did try to follow him. She could have seen him pass by the dairy. All I knew was the rent in an envelope under this door, and the room empty of them both. Not a button or a stitch of stocking to show where they'd been, though you could have put all her things in a shoe box, so you could. Separate or together I never saw them go."

She fell silent, her eyes dropping for a moment to the open handbag on Mrs Thomas's lap before, with an effort, she shifted her gaze to the neutral ground of the barred window.

Mrs Thomas held her peace. The woman knew something more, she was certain, and instinct told her that if she made no further move to prompt her with direct questioning the lure of the money would be too much for her. She sat, like the woman, silent and unmoving.

"He was never a trouble like some of them," she said at last, "he minded his own business."

Mrs Thomas recognised the words as the same whining parrot cry she had given to Jimmy Trottwood. She had no intention of paying fifty pounds for them, they fell a long way short of explaining "pity and comfort".

Without moving anything but her fingers she squeezed the clasp of her handbag shut.

To the woman at the table it sounded uncomfortably loud; like someone slamming shut the door of a safe. Without speaking, she crossed to the sink and opened the drawer where she kept her cutlery. It clattered as she retrieved a piece of newspaper she had used to line it with. Silently she handed it to Mrs Thomas and sat again at the table.

It was half a page torn from a local newspaper. In the top left hand corner was a poor quality photograph of a dark-haired girl. Her skin could have been any colour but the features were unmistakably Asian. She looked awkward, as if ill at ease before the camera. At the side a small headline read:

123

DO YOU KNOW THIS GIRL?

The body of a young woman of Asian appearance was recovered from underneath a train at Notting Hill Gate underground station on Thursday 15th. In spite of intensive police enquiries the unfortunate girl remains unidentified. Her clothes bore no laundry marks and the labels on some of them indicated only that they had been bought at a branch of Marks and Spencer. No handbag or luggage was found and the deceased had nothing in the pockets of her clothes. At the inquest, as reported in an earlier issue, no blame was attached to the driver of the train. The station platform was crowded during the evening rush hour and no one appears to have noticed the girl immediately before the tragedy. Medical evidence was given that death was due to multiple injuries but that in the absence of any eye witness reports there was no way of telling whether the death was due to suicide or accident. Further evidence was given by the police pathologist that the girl was not pregnant. The coroner instructed the jury to return an open verdict. The photograph is a police reconstruction.

"Can I keep this?"

The woman nodded warily and accepted the fifty pound note, folding it and placing it carefully in a zipped pocket of the tartan skirt.

"You're sure it's her?" Mrs Thomas asked.

"I am, God rest her soul that's gone from that poor dead face, but it's her right enough. Nor has she gone back to the dairy, though much they'd notice with the place full of black, brown and yellow."

At the door she suddenly became businesslike, announcing in a matter-of-fact voice: "I won't have trouble. If it's the family or the police, you do know I'll deny every word in this room?"

"Yes I know that."

"You're a sensible creature so you are, I can see that, with an interest I'm not asking a word about, and not a sip of coffee past your lips. Ah sure I don't blame you for that. I borrowed it from a friend in number 12, a woman with no palate at all."

Mrs Thomas smiled kindly. She almost caught herself saying something catty about the woman being able now to repay the friend in number 12 with good expensive coffee. But she looked at the worn, crafty face and felt only pity for her. She thought, too, of an Indian mother in Southall.

She put her hand on the woman's arm. "Go and see your priest," she said.

❦ NINETEEN ❧

IN THE PRIVATE office of Carter and Monmouth in Bond Street Webber faced Aubrey Monmouth across an impressive desk.

He had at first considered representing himself as being a fully fledged Detective Inspector of Police, still serving his time and not retired. Now, meeting the man for the first time, he changed his mind. With some people it would have worked with no fear of discovery, but this man could make trouble. He'd seen the type many times before during his career. Self important, confident, watchful, their essentially unpleasant natures groomed over with quiet cultured accents and after-shave lotion.

He listened courteously while Webber talked.

Webber kept it simple. He was an old friend of Margaret Garland, Margaret Carter as she now was. A village community was close and since her mother's death he had taken a fatherly interest in her. Her friends were happy for her and Mark Carter seemed popular with everyone. With everyone, that is, except apparently his own mother, and that was vaguely disturbing.

"It's no true business of mine at all," he said, "and I shall perfectly understand if you tell me to mind my own business, nevertheless, as I say, I'm fond of her, and since I happened to be coming to London for a few days . . ."

He had deliberately given no indication that he knew anything else, neither the circumstances of Daniel Carter's heart attack nor of Monmouth's affair with his wife and the son who was a half-brother to Mark. Of the stone throwing, he said nothing.

At one point Monmouth rose from his chair at the desk and stood gazing down on to the crawling traffic of Bond Street, his hands clasped lightly behind his tailored back. Webber had the impression that he'd often done it before and he was right. Sometimes, Monmouth knew, you could come back from that window after a long silence and offer a thousand pounds less than the asking price.

Now he was thinking about Webber. Aubrey Monmouth was not a fool, a blank refusal to discuss his partner's son might be stupid. He didn't trust policemen. What was he? Acting privately for Mark Carter? He thought about the telephone calls from the boy, half hysterical, half pleading about that myth of his father's will. There hadn't been a new will. Whatever nonsense Danny had filled the boy's head with, it wasn't true. They only had to check with Higgins the solicitor, he would tell them the same. No it wasn't that. What then?

In the distance he watched a furniture van unloading at Sotheby's. It still amazed him that you could buy a piece of fine furniture at Sotheby's and sell it in your own showroom for whatever you thought a client would pay. It was even more satisfactory to buy in the country if you could, fewer awkward questions about profits, but it came to the same thing in the end. You polished it up and sold it. It was his private joke (which he never shared) that he sold the most expensive beeswax in London. Since his partner's death there had been no price tickets at Carter and Monmouth. He sold fakes too, another thing Carter would never have condoned. Fakes, reproductions, but only the very best, and never from the front sale-room. Well that wasn't illegal either. The descriptions on some of his receipts were, of course, but then he prided himself that he was a good judge of a fool, especially a foreign fool. It couldn't be income tax or his VAT returns, he was too clever to try and cheat the government when the public was so obligingly gullible.

Unless – unless his judgment had let him down and this man was nosing around on behalf of some irate customer. It was unlikely, but the man's eyes were disturbing.

"I must congratulate you, Inspector," he said at the desk, as Webber finished. "An admirably simple exposition of your inquiry and, if I may say so, a refreshing frankness in stressing its purely unofficial nature."

Just the same, Webber thought, you wouldn't be chatting away to a milkman.

Monmouth decided to further establish his base of respectability. He picked up the card Webber had presented to one of the elegant women in the showroom downstairs.

"Detective Inspector John Webber," he murmured. He replaced it carefully on the desk. "Now retired," he added, smiling as though they were sharing a private joke. "I confess I had to think for a moment. I am acquainted with quite a few of your Metropolitan colleagues – purely socially, of course." The smile broadened and stopped just short of a chuckle. "But the name Webber escaped me."

Not bad, Webber thought, quite well done really.

Monmouth cleared his throat and his voice matched the new serious expression under the careful grey hair.

"My late partner's wife is a remarkable woman. You never actually met her? No?" The soft hands rested lightly on his writing pad. "I see her less now that he is sadly gone from us, but we have been friendly for many years. She knows her own mind, Inspector, and when he died she did what she felt was best. I quite liked young Mark, a most personable boy, but there was never any question of his working here. His approach to the business was quite different to ours. He will do well in the country, I imagine."

He smiled gently and the hands opened like a pink butterfly with manicured wings.

"He would never have settled, he likes the rough and tumble of trade. Oh a remarkable knowledge! A little timid on prices perhaps, but he has a lot of his father's expertise. However, not a Bond Street man *au fond* – what shall I say – too restless? His mother knows that quite well. His father did, too."

He looked calmly into Webber's impassive face wondering if Mark had told him the same story about his father changing his will. He couldn't decide and the pale blue eyes were no help at all. Try candour.

"Mark seems to think his father intended to make him his sole beneficiary. It isn't true, embarrassing, but not true. When Danny Carter died he left his share of the business to Joan Carter and she sold it to me. It's as simple as that."

"Do you happen to know her present whereabouts?"

As he had intended, the directness of the question took Monmouth by surprise and it showed in his eyes.

"No – no I don't. She no longer has any connection with the business, as I've explained."

"I thought that perhaps – as an old friend."

"I'm sorry."

Webber was certain that he was lying but he would get no further with it. He switched back abruptly.

"So your partner never suggested – proposed – his son for the business here?"

"No, never." The voice was flat and definite with an edge of concealed anger. "He knew that I would not have been agreeable to it. My liking for the boy did not extend to welcoming him as a business partner. I have always made my feelings quite plain on that score."

Years of training warned Webber that the man was tensing up. He was losing him; tension led to blank walls with no doors. He tried an old trick. He stood politely, collecting his parcel with the Dunhill label from the floor beside him.

"I'm afraid I've taken up a great deal of your time but I am most grateful."

"Not at all, not at all."

Webber sensed his relief and made time by putting the parcel on the chair while he took his gloves out of his overcoat pocket. He spoke gently.

"Don't you find it odd that with his background he seems to have no money of his own at all?"

"Really Inspector, you can hardly expect me to comment on that. Even if it's true, and I assure you I have no knowledge of his financial status, the question is one you should discuss with him, surely?"

Webber nodded pleasantly, glancing up from his gloves. "Of course, or with his mother? Yes, I would have liked a chat with her. It's sad isn't it? You'd expect his father's death would have brought them closer together. Are you a family man, Mr Monmouth?"

"No I never married – the business . . ."

"Quite so," Webber smiled understandingly and made himself shake hands warmly.

Monmouth walked with him to the door. Webber had left him feeling nervous and unsure of himself, as though he had in some way answered questions he had been at pains to avoid.

"They never did get on you know, Mark and his mother. There was bad feeling between them always, long before his father died. Confidentially, I used to chide her about it. Oh yes, I took the boy's side there, and I often told her so. She had a quite unnatural fear of him, almost paranoid, one might say. I always thought it very sad. He can be rude, unreasonable – unpredictable even, but for her to suggest that he was capable of violence seemed grossly unfair. No, not violent. I'd stake my life on it."

She stood, brushing the bits of grass from her skirt and looking down where he still lay, hair tousled, his hands clasped behind his head, smiling up at her. She had an uneasy feeling that he might be laughing at her for fussing about her clothes. Perhaps he'd had sex

128

with other girls in fields and they hadn't bothered even to think about green grass stains or being tidy afterwards but just stretched out next to him, chewing buttercups like he was now and laughing. She wished that she hadn't got up, but felt that to lie down again would somehow make her look ridiculous. To her dismay she felt the blood rising up into her face, pulled up by a kind of frustrated anger at herself and a stab of jealousy for a part of his life she didn't know about. The sudden misery was made complete by the cold damp patch on her bottom which she hoped was just clean damp and not cow dung.

"Peg stop it!" He was on his feet, his face and eyes still smiling and stopping her reply with his fingertips on her mouth. "It's too good to spoil, so forget it, whatever it was. Come on." He took her hand and started to walk.

She was so relieved that she kissed him, smiling and brushing back her dark hair from her face.

They walked quickly as though he was impatient to reach the bright water of the estuary which dipped and rose in the distance with the uneven meadow beneath their feet. Sometimes when the pace was too slow for him he broke away and ran ahead to the next rise in the ground, shouting encouragement and urging her to catch up, hand outstretched to pull her up the last few feet of the slope; excited like a child afraid that they would miss the holiday train.

He never referred to her mood after sex, confident that he had exorcised it as if it had never been. He talked almost all the time, happily and with exuberance. He jumped from subject to subject as though there was no time to waste in the slow give and take of ordinary conversation. Yet she sensed that, in a kind of paradox, he had relaxed, and that the tension she had sometimes felt in him had gone, released into the energy of his thoughts and their own wild dash across the meadows.

"What's the best line of poetry in the world, Peg?"

"For me?"

"You, me, anybody – no that's silly, for us, now – at this moment."

"Tell me."

"Over the hills and far away."

"Yes, it's beautiful."

It's restless too, she thought. Like always wanting to be somewhere else, anywhere but where you were. She hugged his arm covering it with her other hand, half protection, half possession.

129

"It's a bit escapist, though."

He considered it seriously, looking down at his feet pacing into the grass.

"No it isn't, no I've done that already – we've done it. What's that?" He pointed to a tall, ugly concrete tower away to the left of them.

"It's a water tower, you see them all over the fen country, it's because it's so flat or something."

What did he mean, "We've done it", done what? Escaped? He'd said something like it when they'd been painting the shop too. He had a way of saying things to her as though there was never any need to explain them, as though they were the logical conclusion to problems they had discussed and debated many times over a lifetime of marriage.

"I like towers, do you think it has little rooms inside all the way up, like a lighthouse?"

"I don't know, I've never really thought about it. Machinery perhaps, for pumping the water up."

"It's higher than anything for miles, you could see the ships right out at sea, and the town and people all over the common, perhaps even as far as the shop."

"Are you pleased about the shop now?"

He looked surprised and slightly puzzled as if she hadn't been listening to him.

"That's what I mean. We've done it. The London thing was silly, a dream really, I see that now. The clever thing is to get away from them all. You can't fight a plot like that, not when they're all in it together. You get out, get away from them, that's the clever thing, and we've done it. We're there now. 'Over the hills and far away.' They won't get us now. Look at all the boats on the estuary, aren't they splendid? I like them all anchored and tidy like that, like a great litter of puppies."

The pub sat back from the water's edge separated from it only by the forecourt of shingle and shells long abandoned by the sea now safe behind the walls of the harbour. Sometimes when the winter gales combined with a flood tide it broke out of its prison, surging up the estuary to claim its lost sea bed. It drowned cows in the meadows and left its salty mark contemptuously under the bedroom windows of the pub and the scatter of fishermen's cottages on either side of it.

In the summer the shingle would be crowded with the cars of holiday families who had crunched their way along the pebble road from the harbour. The tables then would be covered with the

130

drinks of the mothers and fathers and the packets of crisps of their children. Now it was deserted, left to the cries of the seagulls and the metallic clang of the halyards slapping against the masts of the boats at the water's edge.

He fetched beer from the bar and they sat at a table sheltered from the wind. When he was silent, as he was now, she knew it wasn't because he felt awkward, only that with her he could relax. He seemed to think that she was so completely attuned to his thoughts that there was never any need for him to explain or elaborate. She would have to accept it, even learn to profit from a status he had given her, it seemed almost casually, but with certainty and trust.·

She wasn't, she told herself, skilled in marriage. It was an art and she would master it. It was a question of finding the right – what? Role? Balance? In the giddy release from her mother she had assumed at first a control and a command that she now doubted. She thought of the bank manager and how simple and exciting it had been to dominate her own affairs. She didn't want to dominate Mark, only to love and understand him. It was terribly difficult, made worse because on the surface he seemed so open and uncomplicated. She looked at him now, his eyes screwed up against the sun reflected from the water and felt ashamed that she had made herself miserable for nothing. If there was to be a balance she would accept him as he was, clever and beautiful and – miraculously – hers.

"Come and look at the boats," he pulled her to her feet. They walked across the shingle to the muddy bank where the masts swayed and bobbed on the water.

"You can't really believe that they were all plotting against you?"

"Yes of course I do, silly – I've known that for years. Peg, look! Every single mast has its own seagull sitting on top of it. Isn't that fun?"

"But why? Why were they so against you?"

"They hated me, simple."

Seeing her expression, he laughed and faced her like a tolerant teacher happy to explain to a favourite pupil. He counted on the spread fingers of his hand.

"I told Mama she was a mean fat whore, so that's one. Two, Aubrey wanted full control of the business again and was terrified I'd inherit from father."

"Your father was on your side, at least."

"I used to think so – yes probably – he was just weak. They persuaded him against the new will. I see that now." He sent a pebble skimming hard across the water.

131

"Plots Peg, plots."

"It seems such a horrible, unnatural thing to do to a son."

"Yes."

"Why is Billy's surname Miller and not Monmouth?"

"She went to live in a mill in France when she was in pig. She and Aubrey had his name registered by deed poll to stop gossip. Romantic?"

"But you don't hate him like the others, Billy I mean?"

"Oh little Billy. Mama's little Billy boy – no you can't hate Billy – he's just wet, they had to make him an accountant in the end. That's all he's good for; adding up figures like his father. 'Oh Billy, do go down to the health farm and sort Mama out, she's being a most frightful bore with all the pretty boy attendants.' No, God help us, I don't hate that poor little sod. Besides he was useful, he always told me more than he realised, like a mole in a spy story, except of course he thought he was working for them. He's pathetic. That's why he came screaming over to Dunwold for me when she did a flit from the flat at Henworth. 'Oh Mark! Mama's gone again! I'm ever so worried about her. Did she say anything to you?'"

"And did she?"

He laughed delightedly.

"No of course not. I'd got the mean old cow into a panic, so she did her usual disappearing act and waddled off with her cheque book. I think little Billy thought I'd buried her somewhere."

"Where would she go, do you think?"

"France, Spain, Palm Beach, God knows. Shows you how much she trusts darling little Billy, she wouldn't even tell him. Oh come on, let's finish our beer."

He brought sandwiches out to the table.

"Only cheese I'm afraid, it's all they had." He bit into one hungrily, chewing and talking with his mouth full.

"Yes of course I'm glad about the shop. We can start buying. Just think Peg – the two of us together! Safe!"

The cheese was good, strong and nutty. A small piece of it fell inside his shirt and he pulled his chin into his neck to look down and retrieve it.

"It's good to be able to talk. You couldn't tell most people about things like that – they'd think you were insane or something."

She moved along the bench closer to him for warmth and comfort. "It's over now, it's like you said, the two of us."

He nodded happily. "It feels so good, Peg, not having to plan any more."

৶ TWENTY ৻

WEBBER WAS SERIOUSLY worried.

His interview with Aubrey Monmouth had been inconclusive, but now back in Flaxfield and soberly assessing the rest of the picture, his instinct and training forced him to consider the appalling possibility that Mark Carter was mad.

With that conclusion Mrs Thomas was in complete agreement. What she could not understand was Webber's reluctance to act.

"For God's sake Lizzie! He hasn't done anything."

"He hadn't counted on that poor Indian girl becoming so possessive. She was spoiling things, just by loving him too much, so he pushed her in front of a train."

"Prove it."

She ignored him and continued quietly but with insistence. "He wanted Carter and Monmouth. He's brilliant and he knows it. The first step was his father's partnership. He thought he'd got it, so he made sure his father would die of his heart attack. He died of natural causes but the boy murdered him just the same. He ought to be in Broadmoor."

It was a measure of her distress that she had not cooked an evening meal for them, pleading lack of time after she had read the books she had ordered from the public library in Ipswich. They sat in their corner of the Bull, eating mushy peas and chicken pie. Webber forked at it without enthusiasm. Half convinced himself, he disliked his role as devil's advocate.

"It could just be true that he let his father die for a half share of the business but you can't expect me to believe that anyone in their right senses would calmly push a possessive girl friend under a train simply because he couldn't get rid of her."

"He's not in his right senses and he did get rid of her."

"You know what I'm trying to say. It's not logical, it doesn't make sense."

133

"It does if he's potty."

"Monmouth doesn't think so."

"Then why is he determined not to have Mark anywhere near him in the business?"

"Greed; my guess is that he always regretted letting the Carters in, in the first place. He put up with Daniel Carter because of the affair with his wife. And that's another thing, what about their son? Billy. Suppose Monmouth brought him into the business – as he has every right to do. What's our little monster going to do then? Kill them too?"

Mrs Thomas pushed the plate away, the food almost untouched.

"I know what you're doing and why you're saying it. It's the police in you. You say there's no case, but you know I'm right."

He let the chatter of the pub wash over them, quiet and civilised with occasional bursts of laughter from the bar. Ordinary complicated people, using an authorised drug to escape from being alone for a while, worrying about pensions, and cancer, and family rows, and the price of petrol. Sometimes kind and loving, sometimes frustrated and mean; but they didn't kill people.

"The books are full of big words," Mrs Thomas said. "But all of them say the same in the end. You don't have to act daft to be mad. Sometimes it starts when they're quite young, little things, nothing much taken one by one. But it's a pattern and it gets worse. You can look normal and be bright as a button. 'Impressively intelligent, even brilliant' one book said. It's called Paranoia."

She was right and he did believe it.

"What we've got, because of you Lizzie, is terrible, and – yes, I know it's true. If we had all the other bits, heard what other people knew about him all through the years, school masters, friends, his half-brother, his mother."

"You couldn't trace his brother?"

"There's nothing at Henworth. They only keep records of patients and I'm damned if I'm ploughing through the phone book for Miller."

"You didn't ask his father?"

"No and he wouldn't have told me, he'd closed up on me by then. He knows where the mother is, too. She's the one – if we could find her. What do you want? Another Guinness?"

She watched him queuing patiently at the bar. He was right, of course. How could you say to a nice girl like Margaret, "Listen love, I'm ever so pleased you're so happy, with a lovely new

134

business and a sweet-faced, brilliant boy for a husband. Only thing is, he's a bit mad and might kill you". No of course you couldn't. You couldn't say it to anyone. If you were wrong it was vicious gossip; evil and irreparable.

When he brought the drinks back she noticed that he was limping again. Before she could ask him about it he said,

"And by the time you'd done all that, built up a case to convince two doctors to commit him, what is he doing in the meantime?"

"It is true John, isn't it?"

"Yes, I think so."

"So what can we do?"

"Not much, God help us – watch him, and wait."

"Christ Almighty."

"I hope so."

The autumn which had seemed about to slide straight into a bitter North Sea winter suddenly relented. Over the rest of the country it was cold and wet but from the Wash down to the Thames Estuary an unpredicted and obstinate ridge of high pressure defied the weather men and poured golden days of sunshine on the fen country.

In Flaxfield the old ladies and gentlemen carried their deck chairs back out into their gardens and stopped thinking about Christmas. Bunter abandoned his plans for sleeping in Mrs Thomas's kitchen and retreated to his summer quarters at the bottom of the garden. Even Dunwold was warm, children still swam in the sea and the beach kiosk re-opened to sell tea and ice-cream. Webber tended his garden and listened to such reports as Mrs Thomas brought to him. She had nothing to tell him, or nothing which could have added to their doubts and fears, so that at times he wondered, and allowed himself to hope in the sunshine.

At Henworth Hall, Dr Maguire rejoiced in a flurry of late bookings and ordered four dozen of vintage port. Arlene Weikel escaped from the theatrical rat-race and came down to take up residence again in the unexpected bonus of the Indian summer. Peter Collins to Sarah's relief abandoned rabbit shooting and was taking golf lessons. Betsey came perilously close to selling the rocking horse to an interior decorator from Los Angeles but managed to talk the man out of it. Mrs Barnstable put her house and contents into the hands of a local estate agent and auctioneer and moved into the Hall. Maguire invited her to dinner with Arlene and gave them champagne, caviar, and roast pheasant.

135

Mrs Thomas alone did not relax. She went back into light summer dresses but the weather did not beguile or divert her vigil.

For Margaret it was a time of wonder and magic. From the day when they had walked over the common to the pub on the estuary she never worried about Mark again. He started buying stock for the shop. She bought the new Citroen estate car and they watched the man from the garage drive the old car away. There was no time for sentimental regrets about it and in any case it reminded her more of her old life with her mother than it did of Mark. She told him how she used to hold long imaginary conversations with her mother until the day he had come back to her in London and changed everything, he listened and was sweet and tender, kissing her in the kitchen with her hands covered in flour.

He wouldn't let her stay in the shop, saying she would learn more if she came out with him in the car. The shop could wait until they were ready. They drove all over Suffolk and Norfolk only rarely venturing inland to Cambridge or Essex. She forgot the times when she had been depressed, when she had worked herself up into a state of panic, wondering if the antique fair at Dunwold had just been a lucky fluke for him. In her worst panic of all, imagining that his stories about paintings and furniture and the television programme with his father were all lies and that he had known her for a fool and married her for her money.

Now, watching him when they walked into someone's shop, she felt ashamed of herself. She loved watching the faces of some of the old antique dealers when it dawned on them that they weren't talking to an innocent young husband but to a professional buyer. He never showed off, never displayed knowledge for its own sake, never interrupted their sales talk or contradicted them at the end, only asking politely when they had finished if he could examine the piece for himself. He took drawers out of furniture and used a torch to look at the back or lay flat on the floor to shine it up underneath. Oil paintings he liked to carry into the stronger light of the doorway or even outside if they raised no objection. Sometimes he bought, more often he thanked them and left empty handed.

He loved the car and drove it with pride.

"You never ask them any questions, except the price."

"That's all I need."

"Do they tell lies?"

"Some of them. Some of them just don't know; amateurs trying to eke out a pension, ex civil servants, army officers. They're not crooks, just ignorant. It's important not to argue, stay polite, you might find they've got something you want one day. When they come to us – and some day they will – that's different."

"How?"

He pulled the car off the road into a grass clearing looking out across a newly ploughed field to a line of trees, their leaves almost unchanged from midsummer in the warm sunshine.

"Never sell to another dealer if you can help it. Other dealers are bad news, it's something you'll have to learn, it's not always easy to spot them but after a bit you get to recognise the clues. The amateurs will just want to pick your brains, to find out what you're asking for something. Quite often it's something they've seen you buy at auction and didn't have the knowledge or courage to bid for themselves. Or they might have something they think is very similar in their own shop and they're terrified of underselling it. They're not important but very boring and time wasting. You'll soon learn to spot them by the questions; quite often they'll try and trick you into quoting prices on the phone and the rule is simple – don't."

"Suppose they are genuine enquiries – customers?"

"Ask them to write – dealers never do but customers will if they're serious enough, anyway it's better to lose a customer than be robbed by a dealer."

She was aware that what he was saying was important to him and that he was very serious. She could see that, even though his tone of voice was light and almost casual, clinical, like the teacher at the art class which she had once joined to get away from her mother in the evenings. Afraid that he would think her inattentive – a poor pupil – she assumed a puzzled expression of enquiry.

"It's your money and my knowledge, so it's stealing," he said.

"And the professionals?"

"They are the worst. They steal customers, collectors usually. They don't care so much about prices, except to beat you down, of course. They'll try and buy your best pieces so they're stealing your prestige as well, and the customer loses because he pays more. They're bastards, scum, parasites."

Because he said it quietly, and without any outward show of anger, the illogicality of what he was saying didn't occur to her. She accepted it as she accepted Mark himself. Later she would

137

remember that conversation in the car. Now all she could think of was her love and her pride for him.

October came, and although the trees had reluctantly acquired some autumn colour the weather remained fine. Only in the mornings and when the sun was setting was there any hint of the winter to come. Then there was an edge to the air, keen and sharp in the lungs. In the evenings there came a mist from the sea. Thick on the coast at Dunwold, its long fingers drifted inland as far as Flaxfield, touching and probing it gently during the night until the morning sun rolled it back over the land and the waves. Every day it came to rest a little nearer to the beach and waited for the night.

In that first week of October Mark told her they had enough stock and the shop was ready.

"OK, perhaps not quite enough, but the tourists have gone and we'll have to wait for the locals to discover us during the winter. We've got enough for that, it's not sensational but it's right, every piece of it is right."

"Suppose no one buys anything?" said Margaret.

She looked round the shop where the quiet pieces of English furniture sat against the green felt walls. In the centre of the polished parquet floor they had put a dining table. Mark had told her what to type on the card. "Late Georgian three-pillar support. Circa 1820. No restoration." It took up nearly the whole of the shop. There were some Staffordshire figures on the shelves and just three oil paintings, a horse in a landscape, an old man reading a book, and a portrait of a girl on a marble seat holding a rose. In the window was one piece of furniture, a table which was opened out to form a pair of library steps.

That night they sat with the receipts and the bank statements. They had spent forty-five thousand pounds and they had fifty-five thousand pounds left.

In the morning the local paper carried an advertisement for a sale by public auction of a converted farmhouse near Saxmundham, together with all the contents as it stood, by order of the owner Mrs Jessie Barnstable of Henworth Hall.

❦ TWENTY-ONE ❧

WHEN MRS THOMAS burst into Webber's sitting room without knocking he was sitting naked in front of a blazing coal fire.

"Lizzie, for God's sake!"

"Don't be so daft, put your pants on if you want to be so fussy. I'll go and make some tea."

She tossed the book she was carrying into an armchair and left him clutching a cushion.

Silly old fool, she thought, as she waited for the kettle to boil, a man of his age too, you'd think he'd be proud of it. Webber often put crumbs on the kitchen window sill when he made tea and an alert blackbird flew down from a tree expectantly.

"He may be a bit rheumaticky," Mrs Thomas informed it confidentially, "but he's beautifully made."

It wasn't the main reason for her feeling of occasion and excitement.

When she carried the tray in after a delicate tap on the door he was dressed and examining the book.

"You are a menace."

"You ought to watch yourself, you've got starving birds in the garden. Where's the pain?"

"In the hip again, the fire helps. It's not too bad. What's all this about?" He held up the book.

She smoothed the lime green skirt under her bottom with practised hands and poured the tea.

"Do you remember that little girl up at the Hall, Annie Spicer?"

"Yes, I told you, she waited at table when I had dinner with Maguire, she's the one who put you on to Arlene Weikel."

"That's right she did. She's bright too, she knows that we've been trying to trace Joan Carter so she turned up about an hour ago with that book and a conscience, seems she 'borrowed' it from Joan Carter's flat and then couldn't return it because she left in such a rush."

Webber finished tucking in a piece of his shirt and took his tea from her. He nodded at the book.

"An odd choice of reading for Annie – *A Better Class of Person?*"

"She's engaged, marrying above herself I gathered, a boy from the local garage, runs a posh motor-bike, went to grammar school. Her mother told her she'd better start learning how to behave nicely – a few social graces. Annie thought it was a book on etiquette."

"Ah!"

"She found this letter folded up inside it. She thought it might tell me something."

The paper was pale blue, expensive looking with an embossed address. The handwriting was precise and angular and signed Marie Camous. The letter was in French.

"Alpes-Maritimes is about my limit," said Webber handing it back to her. "I believe the vicar's wife is quite fluent, she might help."

"It's from a servant of some sort, sounds like a housekeeper. She has received Madame's instructions and will arrange matters to her satisfaction. The house will be ready to receive Madame and she will tell no one of her presence. She begs Madame to accept the expression of her most distinguished salutations. More tea?"

Webber looked at her with open admiration. "I didn't know you could read French."

"I don't, not very well. I'm better at the speaking. We had some Free French Airforce boys billeted on us during the war. Nice lads, a bit rough some of them. There was a boy called Armand, came from Marseilles, he was a bit of a monkey! I picked up quite a lot from him."

"I can imagine. Where's this place Pegomas?"

"I looked it up in the atlas. It's quite small, a village I should think. It's up in the hills above Cannes. It sounds as though she's rented a house there, or near there anyway, and I'll bet that's where she is now, cootched quiet. I'm going down there to find out."

When Mark and Margaret had finished viewing the contents of Mrs Barnstable's converted farmhouse they left the car parked in the paddock set aside for that purpose by the auctioneers and went for a walk in the grounds. The house was isolated and it had been Margaret's idea to take some sandwiches. They found a summer house at the end of the garden, dusty with a smell of leaves and damp. It had cast iron furniture with brown rust showing through the ancient paint. A label tied on to the leg of the table had Lot 408 marked on it.

Margaret had enjoyed her morning. It was an odd feeling prying legitimately in someone's home with most of the rooms left as they had been when the owner had lived there. On a shelf at the side of Mrs Barnstable's lavatory she had found a copy of Jane Austen's *Emma* under a pile of copies of the *Radio Times*. Some of the programmes were marked in green ink, symphony concerts and gardening talks. She tried to imagine what it would have been like to live alone in the big house with only the radio for company and Jane Austen in the lavatory.

Mark was eating a bacon sandwich, absorbed in the catalogue of the sale, a cheap sheaf of stencilled papers stapled together. There were no illustrations, just the lot numbers followed by a brief description. Some country sale-rooms had been taken over by the big London auction houses. Their catalogues were much grander with glossy photographs and they sent them to a selected list of buyers all over the world, both to dealers and important collectors. This catalogue was on sale from a table in the hall of the house and cost fifteen pence.

"Peg, how much money have we got left?"

"I was just thinking. Enough to buy you some more clothes, anyway. I don't think the boy genius of Carter and Garland should go viewing in jeans."

"Seriously."

"You know, more or less, we worked it out, about fifty-five thousand pounds."

"How much more?"

The question was so quick and eager that it took her by surprise and it showed instantly on her face so that he made his explanation more casual and less important.

"You said 'more or less', I just wondered if you'd done all your sums right – you know, counted all your mother's shares, and there was something in a Building Society wasn't there?"

"I counted everything, you know I did, we went through it together – Mark what is it? Have you seen something in there?"

"It's all quite good, I wish we'd known about it earlier but it doesn't matter. She's got some nice things but nothing better than we've bought already. Except that."

He pointed to a page and a lot number:

Lot 160. An attractive small mahogany desk. Style of
        Chippendale, early 19th century.

"Do you remember it? It was in the corner of the breakfast room. We'll go back in a minute and you can see it again but don't show too much interest in it."

After the food they went back into the house. Only a few people were wandering around, most of them she suspected were local farmers and their wives, curious to see how a wealthy widow lived. Once she thought she recognised one of the old men they had visited in his shop but most of the slowly milling viewers were unknown to her. Mark didn't come and stand with her but wandered off on his own.

The desk didn't look much she thought, some of the pieces they had bought seemed to her to be much more attractive. The wood was rather red, three small drawers on either side with brass handles were separated by a recessed cupboard leaving a space hardly big enough for one knee, certainly not two. Not comfortable for writing, she decided. One long drawer ran across the top decorated with three carvings like scallop shells or open fans. They were quite large, the middle one was scooped out and the other two reversed in bold relief over the side-drawers below. Pleasant enough but perhaps a bit dull.

On the way home in the car he told her.

"It's not English. It was made in America about 1770. I'm not sure who made it, either a man called John Goddard or one of the Townsend family. There was a group of them working in Newport, Rhode Island. They had a special way of making things, it's called block front. They made some of the best furniture in America and it's rare – very rare."

"You're sure it's right?" Already she was beginning to use the jargon of the dealers.

"Yes, quite sure. There's no staining anywhere and it couldn't have been made in England."

"What will it fetch?"

"It depends. In that sale with that catalogue and that description perhaps five to eight hundred pounds – unless someone else realises what it is."

"How much is it really worth?"

"Christie's sold one in New York about two years ago. It fetched seventy thousand pounds."

"What could you sell it for?" She was quite proud of her control.

"Today? I don't know. Perhaps double that. There's a lot of money in America."

They had come through the narrow country lanes which led from the farmhouse to the main road. Ahead of them the A12 ran long and straight, rising slowly to a crest in the distance. She wondered if he would remember standing there with the pack on his back and his arm extended as she drove towards him with no intention of stopping. It seemed a very long time ago. They reached the crest in silence and beyond it the landscape lay flat before them running on to the smudge of Flaxfield in the distance and further still, but far out of sight, lay Dunwold and the mist lying and waiting on the sea.

It didn't matter that he hadn't remembered, nothing mattered except that he was sitting beside her in the car. It was selfish of her even to think of it when she could see that his mind had no room for anything but a piece of furniture that someone had fashioned in Rhode Island when America was still a colony.

"We might be lucky," she said.

"We might. I don't like relying on luck, not for this, it's too important."

"We could get backing from the bank, raise some money on the shop and the stock – the house too, if you want."

He shook his head.

"You'd have to tell them what you wanted it for and even if you didn't it would make them wonder. In a place like this people talk, it's not worth the risk."

"We could buy it on commission for someone. There's an American woman at Henworth Hall, a Mrs Weikel. Lizzie Thomas says her husband is a millionaire."

"Still too risky and why should we settle for a pittance when there's a chance of all that profit?"

For the first time since they had bought the Citroen he drove quickly, not easing the speed on corners, his face, she noticed, was pale and set and they.didn't speak again until, to her relief, they drew up in the lane outside the cottage. Not until they had eaten an early tea with toast and poached eggs did he mention it again, calmer now, and more relaxed.

"I don't think we'll lose it, Peg. Even if one of the local dealers thinks it's better than the catalogue description he's not likely to go as high as I will."

"You're counting on none of the London dealers finding out."

"It's a terrible gamble but I've got to take it. Can't you understand that?"

"You mustn't be angry with me. I know you have more understanding of these things than I do but I can see how important this is for you. That's all I was trying to say."

"It is important, yes – important for us. It could establish us in months. Without it, it might take years."

"I wish I had more money."

She had washed her hair before the meal and it fell down across her cheek, soft and dark in the afternoon sunlight. He came and stood behind her his hands encircling her waist.

"I didn't marry you for your money."

It wasn't, thank God, a protest, only a quiet statement.

"You know, Jimmy Trottwood has money and you told me he likes you."

"Too near home, besides he's a dealer – a sort of dealer."

His cheek was cool against her own, his hands pulled her closer to him. She felt the shape of his thighs and his body stirring against her.

"Anyway what is this, you shameless woman? Are you trying to procure me or something?"

She turned so that they could hold each other. "You shouldn't tease me, I was trying to help."

"You can help better than that."

Later, lying on the bed with a bath towel covering him like a toga he said: "No, not Flaxfield, that's for certain, nobody here. There is someone in London though. The man who did the TV programme, he'd accept my judgment, sight unseen too. He must have some money, his family owned three butchers shops in Yorkshire, he told me that once and I've always remembered it. I wouldn't suggest a share of the profits though. I shouldn't say anything about profits, just a tempting interest on a short loan. I'll tell him enough to whet his appetite."

"Would he do that, lend you money, I mean, without any questions?"

"Oh yes, Dudley would, he's gay and greedy; retired on a pension and loves antiques. I may not get a fortune out of him but he's safe and it'll help – just in case. Why do you always do that?"

"Do what?" she said, her head emerging from a roll-neck pullover.

"Put your clothes on from the top down."

"Do I?"

"Yes always."

"I don't know; habit," she walked to the bed and sat. "Do you love me?" she asked him softly.

"Yes."

"Yes – I know you do," she jumped up. "Come on, are we walking? The sun's not gone yet."

"Let's take the car and drive out to Dunwold to the water tower."

144

He loved the tower. He had found a broken lock on one of the doors. Sometimes they climbed up the stone stairway inside, winding past locked doors with peeling paint and no sign to say what lay on the other side of them, until at last they could walk out on to an open balcony into the cold air above the common with the land and the town and then the sea stretched out before them. Once he had said to her: "Now we really are safe".

In the car she said, "We've left it a bit late, the mist will be coming soon".

"Yes, I know, don't worry."

"So will you go and see your television man?"

"Yes, it's important. I'll drive up tomorrow. You know, I've been thinking, perhaps the top of the tower stays above the mist. Wouldn't that be wonderful?"

✌ TWENTY-TWO ✌

In the morning they woke early. He found Dudley Dear's telephone number in his diary.

"Did you get him?"

"He'll see me this morning about twelve o'clock. I should be all right."

She found him a clean shirt which he wore open-necked, refusing a tie. With his sports jacket and grey flannel trousers he looked, she thought, ridiculously young. He seemed relaxed but disinclined to talk. He didn't eat very much breakfast and by a quarter to eight he had kissed her and left.

For a moment after the car had disappeared she stood in the silence of the little hallway quite unprepared for the sudden wave of panic which hit her almost like a physical blow. Everything around her, the crooked lintel over the door to the sitting room, the pattern of ferns on the stair-carpet where she had sat mutely for long hours waiting for him to come back to her, all of it reminded her of the terrible time when she had at last been forced to believe that she would never see him again.

When it passed she made as much work for herself as she could in the house, welcoming the howl of the vacuum cleaner and the sound of the tumbling water in the washing machine. She worked without stopping, restoring the neglect of the weeks she had spent helping him to decorate the shop. Not until she had scrubbed the kitchen floor and filled the clothes line in the garden with sheets and as many of his shirts as she could find did she stop and make herself some coffee.

It was almost half past eleven. Perhaps the traffic had been good and he was there already. Last night on the tower he had made it all sound so simple, as though preparing to spend all the money they had in the world and borrowing more on top of that was an ordinary everyday occurrence.

146

"And it won't worry you," she asked, "bidding as high as that?"

"I may not have to, no it doesn't worry me. Not when I know it's good like that. It doesn't often happen. Look Peg! Look at the mist! I was right – see? It's lying low on the sea and there's no wind but it's moving! How can it move like that?"

The lights in the houses of the promenade were the first to fade and disappear, then other streets nearer to them in the town, until in the silence only the houses on the edge of the common were left. And when the thick white blanket had covered every one of them it rolled on towards them like something alive with a secret power of its own. Then they were an island above it in the moonlight, with only the distant tower of the church to tie them to the land below.

"You were right," she said, moving close to him and holding on to his arm, "and it is wonderful – beautiful. Mark – suppose – suppose someone else recognises the desk and knows how rare it is – it could happen couldn't it?"

His face shone in the moonlight, reflected bright from the solid whiteness of the mist. "Yes it could happen, but we don't think about that. That's all in another country down there; somewhere all covered up, and we're above it. You'd think all the boats in the harbour would rise up and float on it like the sea but they won't, they'll stay down there where they can't see us or watch us or know what we know, because we're safe and the only ones who can see properly. When the sale is over and the mist has gone we'll buy a boat and go sailing, Peg."

In the days gone past, before she had known and understood him as she did now, such talk would have seemed wild and strange, even frightening, because it was like listening to someone speaking in riddles. Now it was no longer frightening for her, she accepted that he thought and explained himself in an exceptional way because, quite simply, he was exceptional.

She had become used to his quicksilver change of thought, his way of jumping suddenly from one topic to another so that he could be discussing rare furniture one minute and in the next second planning to buy a boat and sail on the sea. It explained something else, too. Sometimes when she talked to other people who knew him she had a strong feeling that they had somehow found him strange – even that they didn't like him, but couldn't, for common politeness sake, tell her so. John Webber and Lizzie Thomas had given her that feeling, and there had been others. At first it had upset her, now in a curious way she found it not only understandable but comforting. She wanted to tell them that Mark was wonderful, a rare person not to be judged by anyone

147

they had ever known before. She didn't do that because it wasn't something she could explain easily. They would have to discover it for themselves as she herself had done.

Her coffee was cold in the cup, untouched on the table of the clean kitchen. Suddenly the house and the silence oppressed her and she longed for the fresh air and the sunlight.

Golf, decided Sarah Collins, was a definite advance on rabbit shooting. It was irritating that she found herself quite incapable of hitting a ball but gratifying when she found that she wasn't expected to do so. Peter Collins seemed perfectly content without any incentive of competition, and in the late summer evenings she was happy to trundle the trolley of clubs round the course for him and discovered a new skill in pressing back divots of dislodged turf. It was an infinitely better way of identifying with their new life in the country than slaughtering rabbits and it solved the problem of disposing of the corpses. Lately she had taken to raiding the deep-freeze cabinet in the garage when he was out on his rounds and surreptitiously burying the icy carcasses at the end of the garden. She was silently grateful that he had chosen to move to golf and not gardening. A furry layer of perma-frost could have suggested an element of deceit in her nature which would have upset her because she loved him. She admired Peter too, he was a better doctor than she could ever be. Once she had met an old acquaintance of his who had known him as a brilliant fellow student in their old hospital days. The woman, now a successful consultant psychiatrist, had professed mild astonishment that Peter had chosen general practice. Smart and well-groomed, she had managed to give Sarah the impression that his marriage to a frump had been the most probable reason for his wasted genius. Sarah had not liked her.

She knew it was true that even as a London G.P. he could have made more money and she had accepted his decision to abandon even that modestly successful practice which they had established together without complaint. She was happy, and if she sometimes secretly felt that he had wasted his life she never allowed him to know it.

The golf course ambled through the meadows to the north of Flaxfield, the view from the veranda of the clubhouse overlooked the last green and the public footpath from the village. The late summer heat had eased the pressure on the surgery and Sarah and Peter often had time to wander round a few holes and take a modest lunch of sandwiches and beer at midday. Today they had the veranda to themselves. In the distance they watched Margaret Carter walking slowly along the pathway. She seemed pre-occupied and never looked towards them.

"Does she ever come to see you?" He nodded at the figure in the distance.

"Margaret? No, not much, not professionally anyway, not since her mother died. Oh, and briefly, of course, when young Mark had that touch of food poisoning." Sarah looked down at the wooden planks of the veranda floor, astonished at the amount of mud and turf she had deposited there from her shoes. "I must say it's all worked out very well."

"He came to see me the other day."

"Mark Carter? As a patient you mean?"

"Not specifically. You know that old set of surgeon's instruments we found in a cupboard when we took over the London practice?" She remembered them; the exquisitely fashioned tools of a grim age when speed with saws and knives were the chief skill of a successful surgeon. They had ivory handles and fitted into an inlaid box of mahogany and satinwood.

"I happened to mention them to him in the pub one evening. He seemed to think they might have some value so he came round to see them. They weren't doing us any good stuck out in the garage, after all."

The mention of the garage with its lighter load of frozen rabbit gave her a quick pang of guilt, but he didn't refer to it and she kept her face blank.

"Did he buy them?"

"He said they were quite good of their kind. I had no idea what to ask for them. Yes, I think he'll buy them, he took them with him, anyway. He said he could find out what they might fetch at auction and send me a cheque. We might get quite a pleasant surprise."

She pushed some of the dried mud down through the cracks of the veranda floor. "You said, 'not specifically' – as a patient, I mean."

"Perhaps the instruments were an excuse, he seemed a little concerned about Margaret."

"In what way?"

"He thinks she might have been trying to do too much, overworking, that's why I asked if she'd been to see you. He said she'd been behaving rather oddly sometimes."

"It wouldn't be too surprising, I suppose. She has worked hard helping to get that shop ready but she seemed to be enjoying it. The marriage seems happy enough, of course she's older than he is. She had a bad time with her mother but she should be over that by now."

"He told me that she heard her mother's voice sometimes, not in her head, but quite clearly as if she was still alive and speaking to her when she was alone in a room."

Sarah watched the distant figure as it disappeared around the notorious gorse bushes guarding the seventeenth green. She was out of her depth with mental illness. In the mild cases of senility she occasionally encountered she relied on a bright cheerful approach and mild tranquillisers. On the whole, she had more faith in the former. Margaret Carter was not senile. Sarah thought back over the few times she had chatted to her since her marriage. What Peter had just said had so surprised her that she reacted with a mild sense of outrage.

"Well she certainly hasn't complained to me about any voices, she did say she was a bit tired. *Is* she complaining?"

"No, I don't think so, it was very much a conversational throwaway. That's par for the course, it's very often a close relative who seeks reassurance, not always the patients themselves."

"She's as sane as I am," Sarah said vehemently.

"From the little I've seen of her I would agree," Peter said mildly, smiling at his wife's outburst.

"What did you say to him, does he want you to see her?"

"No, I told you, it was all very casual. I got the impression that he wanted confirmation of his own diagnosis, which I was quite happy to give him."

He looked at Sarah's face, still slightly flushed and angry, with affection.

"My dear, I wouldn't dream of interfering, not only because she is your patient but for what I believe to be far more cogent reasons. I don't know whether they are simplistic, cynical or perhaps just old fashioned laziness. It doesn't matter, they make sense to me. You know what I've always felt about psychiatry; at best a pseudo-science, but more often a dangerous menace made worse by the people who practise it, most of them certifiable if God delivered them into the hands of their colleagues."

She knew his views. Sometimes she wondered if they were a subconscious defence, but she knew that for whatever reason he held them sincerely.

150

"The only real advance," he continued amiably, "came from the law not from medicine, and that was when they stopped locking people up because they were different – a bit potty perhaps but it was a terrible price to exact for the odd social embarrassment."

"A dangerous psychopath is rather more than that."

"Yes of course he is, but there aren't many of those, thank God. Oh yes, lock those up by all means, poor devils, always providing you can spot them in time and that's not easy, I'm afraid. But then look what happens, some wretched mad dog has his bite and they shove him, quite rightly for once, into prison or Broadmoor and do they keep him there? No they do not, the silly buggers let him out to kill again! I give up."

It was, she thought, exactly what he had done.

"Oh no," he was saying cheerfully, "not for me. If your poor Margaret Carter is psychotic, which I am inclined to doubt as much as you are, she will either get worse or get better and in either case will do so without any help from us. Overwork will suit very well. He tells me that they're thinking of taking up sailing – his idea to give her a new interest, he says she's quite keen. The sanest treatment possible and I told him so."

"She's a nice girl. I'm fond of her."

"Yes I know."

"Do you like him?"

"He's very bright."

She had lived with him long enough to read shades and nuances of meaning into his words that others would have missed. With Peter, brightness could suggest shadow, too.

That evening the sea mist which reached Flaxfield held the first hint of the autumn frosts to come. By the time Mrs Thomas left Webber's house and walked home through the failing light there was a noticeable nip in the air.

It had been a good evening, warm with friendship and concern on his part and full of affection and love on hers which she had contented herself in expressing by cooking him a meal calculated to make certain he missed her while she was away.

There could be no question of his being able to go with her. The severe attack of arthritis would improve, Sarah Collins had predicted, but it would take time and, temporarily crippled as he was, he could only be a burden to her in France. His sum total of usefulness, he told her wryly, would be restricted to looking after the cat for her. He hated her going on her own but there was no help for it and he had faith in her judgment. The fact that she had never been abroad before did not seem to deter her in the slightest. Her French might be rusty, she conceded, but it would do. On one thing they were agreed. If there was a chance of meeting Mark Carter's mother they could not afford to lose it.

Bunter, the cat, sat waiting for her at the back door, his fur gleaming with the mist, his eyes solemn and expectant. Usually after she had fed him he would politely ask to be let out again into the garden. Tonight, aware of her plans, he chose to sit on the hearthrug staring into the glimmer from the ashes of the fire. Tomorrow she would take the bus to Victoria and then, because she wouldn't fly, she had booked on a train which would be the beginning of her journey to France.

❧ TWENTY-THREE ❧

AUBREY MONMOUTH WAS not a nice man but he wasn't a fool. After Dudley Dear's visit he sat at his desk and thought very carefully about their conversation while it was still fresh in his mind.

People thought they could be very clever with antique dealers when they deviously sought information but Monmouth, like all dealers, had encountered the ploy so many thousands of times that he could not possibly be mistaken. What never ceased to amaze him was the unoriginality of their approach. It was almost as if they had bought a book with a section on "How to pick an expert's brains without being obvious." Perhaps they had.

From his over-elaborate opening gambit of, "I was just passing and couldn't resist your delicious window", Dudley had chatted away in a carbon-copy conversation during which, had he ever faltered for his next move, Aubrey Monmouth could have prompted him with ease. From the traditional display of interest in things which did not interest him in the slightest, Dudley had moved unerringly to the true reason for his visit, and that was to discover the rarity and current price at auction of American furniture. He knew nothing about it, but the odd piece he had seen had always rather appealed to him, he said. Actually an aunt of his had one or two quite nice examples, she'd lived in America as a young woman. She was quite old now, he supposed that one day they would come to him. Of course his space in a mews flat was severely restricted so he'd probably sell most of her things. Dudley in his innocence had thought that little bait a rather clever touch, especially as he professed a dislike of sale-rooms. However all that sounded horribly like scavenging. Poor Auntie! No he certainly wasn't going to count on her demise, that would be really too mercenary. But suppose – just suppose – he were to treat himself to a small piece, nothing too big. Auntie, he remembered, had a rather nice little American knee-hole desk. What sort of price would he have to pay for something like that today? Not from a sale-room of course, you could never be sure of what you were buying there unless you were an expert, but say from a reputable dealer, like Aubrey Monmouth?

When he'd gone, Monmouth was reasonably sure of two things. The first was that Dudley Dear knew of a very rare knee-hole desk, probably made in New England, that would shortly be offered at auction. There was nothing coming up in the immediate London sales and a series of telephone calls to the main auction houses gave no hint of anything in the foreseeable future. That only left the rest of England, but he felt he could narrow the field considerably, because the other thing he was reasonably sure of was that Dudley Dear's information had come from Mark Carter.

Monmouth remembered the undisguised simpering attraction on Dudley's face in the old days when confronted with Mark in the shop. If he hadn't been fully aware of Mark's present whereabouts Dudley could not have resisted enquiring. No, he not only knew where he was, but he had shown no surprise when Monmouth had casually mentioned Mark's marriage, so he must have had contact with him quite recently. Mark Carter was looking for money.

Monmouth cast his mind back to his conversation with John Webber, what was the name of that village? – Flaxfield, yes that was it, Flaxfield in Suffolk. That would do for a start, a place to avoid if he didn't want to alert Mark, but somewhere in that area there would be either a country auction house or a private sale of house contents. In that sale he would find what he was looking for, an American knee-hole desk, and almost certainly wrongly catalogued or it would have found its way to Christie's or Sotheby's. In his diary was a list of his country contacts. He consulted it and reached for the telephone.

On the whole Dudley was well pleased with the results of his mission. He had discovered what he wanted to know and, rather cleverly, he had managed to do it without arousing any suspicion. After Mark's visit he had given the matter his earnest consideration. There was no question in his mind about trusting the boy's judgment but there could be no harm in acquainting himself with a little more background on the current state of the market for American furniture.

In fact, background was all he had got from Monmouth's standard prevarications. Such things, he had admitted, were indeed of great rarity but actual prices? Ah well, that would depend upon so many imponderables. He would be only too happy to visit Dudley's aunt and value her knee-hole desk when he would be able to tell Dudley exactly how much he might expect to pay for something in a similar condition, but he quite understood that her frail state of health made that impossible.

Nevertheless, Dudley was satisfied that they were talking about something quite exceptional, they were talking about a great deal of money. The amount Mark had mentioned was indeed just that. Not so long ago, when Dudley was still at the BBC, and his parents were still alive, ten thousand pounds would have been out of the question. With their death within six months of each other he had suddenly found himself a wealthy man, wealthier indeed than he had ever expected to be. His father had been a close, taciturn Yorkshireman not given to discussing his financial affairs and Dudley had been surprised how much more money there was in meat than culture.

Mark's telephone call, out of the blue, had surprised him too, but it had come at the right time. Even though it was over a month now since that terrible day when he had gone to the hospital to visit Mick and they had told him that he was dead. He had been improving and there had been plans for him to come out quite soon. Somehow, they never found out how, Mick had managed to get hold of a bottle of vodka. By the time they discovered it he had drunk it dry and choked to death on his own vomit. It was ironic that just when Dudley was in a position to help him most, his money was useless. They would have gone to Switzerland, he told Mark, there was a clinic there which had performed miracles with cases like Mick's; hideously expensive, but what did money matter when you loved someone?

He was touched by Mark's sympathy and understanding, he told Dudley about the nightmare of the journey when he had tried to rush his father to.hospital and his feelings when the car had broken down and no one would stop in the pouring rain when his father was dying in the front seat beside him. Dudley had forgotten how sensitive the boy could be, there was a link of sorrow between them. The death of his own parents had left him largely unmoved but Mick and Mark's father were the two people they had loved. Lonely and unprepared for pity, Dudley had broken down and cried. Only later, when he remembered it, was he surprised that Mark had taken him in his arms and comforted him. The day had held a kind of magic for Dudley. It was Mark who had seen that they should leave the flat and its memories. A walk he'd said, was better for them if they were to talk of happier things. They had walked for miles into Hyde Park and Kensington Gardens and there, sitting on one of the garden seats outside the Orangery,

Mark talked and Dudley was the one who listened and gave comfort.

He already knew about Mark's relationship with his mother. What he had not realised, immersed in his own affairs as he had been, was the deep and tragic sense of loss the boy had suffered when his father had died. Mark, in spite of his brilliance, was an innocent, that much was obvious to Dudley, and in spite of his fierce defence of his wife and his touching loyalty to her, the real tragedy was the fact that he had sought comfort in a totally unsuitable marriage. If they hadn't been in a public place he would have wept again, but this time for poor Mark and not for himself.

Now sitting alone in the mews flat he knew he had been right to find out what Mark might be up against. If the boy was right there might be no need for him to call on Dudley's money but he was glad that Mark now knew of his changed fortunes. The possibility of a handsome return on his investment was pleasant to contemplate but friendship was a higher profit than money.

In Flaxfield, Jimmy Trottwood sat contentedly looking through the catalogue of the Barnstable sale and drinking morning coffee with chocolate coated wholemeal biscuits. The wholemeal was a concession to a healthy diet and the chocolate was an indulgence. He liked to use the shop as an extension of his living quarters. Customers, he felt, should feel that they were being welcomed into a home to discuss the furniture and admire the things he loved himself. There was some truth in Doreen's contention that the more they admired them the less inclined he was to sell them. It was a dilemma he had never succeeded in resolving to his complete satisfaction. What he sought most of all was peace and quiet.

"She's up to something," said Doreen.

There was no need to ask who she meant. That morning they had conveyed her mother to the bus stop and had bidden her farewell. Destination unknown.

"She's a grown woman, she doesn't have to account for her every move."

"I'm her daughter, why should she be so secretive?"

It was true, he thought, Doreen was indeed her daughter. A younger version of that extraordinary product of the Welsh valleys. Lacking her mother's saving grace of humour she was undeniably from the same mould. Gossipy, inquisitive and just as

156

reluctant to be kept in the dark. Nosey was as good a description as any.

"She might have gone up to London to visit her sister," he said.

"She wouldn't go near Auntie Blodwen unless she was dying."

"Perhaps she is – or ill, anyway."

"She's as strong as a horse, besides I phoned her to make sure. No, Mam's going further than that. I think she's going abroad."

"Why on earth should you think that?"

"I checked in the chemist. Two extra pairs of elastic stockings, laxative, mosquito cream, and seasick pills. She's got herself a passport, too, I happened to see it in her handbag when she was in the lavatory. Apart from that, look at her clothes. That was one of her serious going-away outfits if ever I saw one."

She was right. Mrs Thomas that morning had presented an awesome sight in a biscuit coloured skirt under a dark brown nylon jacket edged with white fur fabric. She had looked like a determined chocolate eclair.

"Not a happy choice, I admit. It's easy to make fun of her but your mother is a remarkable woman."

Doreen grunted.

"Whatever she's up to, she's got a good reason for it and if she doesn't want to tell us, it's not our business."

This time Doreen didn't even bother to grunt.

In Dunwold, Webber met Arlene Weikel in the newly opened antique shop of Carter and Garland. Having done his duty of attending to Bunter's breakfast according to Lizzie Thomas's detailed instructions, he had travelled over to Dunwold by bus, finding it less painful than driving. He had met Arlene with Lizzie several times and liked her; groomed, intelligent, she was, he thought, no man's fool. He could see why she had taken to Lizzie. Mark Carter was showing her a child's sampler and Webber watched them while he made a show of talking to Margaret.

Webber didn't pretend to any great knowledge of salesmanship although he reflected that it was perhaps not so far removed from his own field. Through the years many people had tried to sell him things – mostly their version of events in which he had reason to be especially interested. This chap was good, Webber could see that, had he been listening to his story across an interrogation table he would have marked it down as truth and Mark Carter as quite certainly sane. Dates, style, history, quality of stitchwork, all of it was impressive but delivered without any obvious attempt to show off. The information he gave to Arlene Weikel was succinct and helpful. If she was interested then these were the answers to questions she would want to know. They were facts and not flights of fancy. The sampler was good of its kind, not of any great rarity but she might, he told her, search for a long time before she found anything else in that condition and at that price.

"It's one helluva price; an arm and a leg," Arlene announced cheerfully.

Rich people, Webber knew, were very careful with their money and Arlene Weikel was most certainly rich. Even without his knowledge of her through Lizzie Thomas you couldn't miss that unmistakable smell of wealth.

Mark Carter was obviously not to be swayed by her alarmed protestations of what Mr Weikel would say to her if she paid that price for a child's sampler, however attractive. Without actually saying so he was managing quite well to suggest that the decision, now that she was in possession of all the facts, was entirely her own. He even gave the impression that he would be quite relieved if she decided against it. In the end after a token battle she gave in and bought it. It seemed to Webber that she had quite enjoyed the bargaining even though it hadn't done her any good. More interesting still he got a definite feeling that it was not her first encounter with Mark Carter. There was a teasing intimacy about their financial banter that suggested she had been to the shop before.

Webber was glad she was there and occupying Mark Carter's full attention. It gave him a chance to look round the shop and talk to Margaret. He admired an old map of Suffolk. She had obviously done her homework but she could see that the name of Christopher Saxton as a map maker meant nothing to Webber and that in any case the price was beyond him. It didn't matter, she liked this slow, gentle man with his quiet kindly manner and his intelligent blue eyes. He was probably younger than he looked she thought, but that was probably because of the limp and the stick he used to help him walk. She warmed to his interest in the shop and her new life as an antique dealer. She was quite unaware that he encouraged her sympathy deliberately and while Mark was completing his business with Arlene she delighted in showing him round the new premises and pointing out all the work they had done in cleaning and decorating it together.

Webber was a good listener and years of experience had taught him the value of small talk. He admired the quality of the paintwork and their good sense in doing it themselves. Builders, he agreed, were an expensive luxury and he was suitably appalled at the estimates they had received for retiling the roof and damp-proofing the cellar.

"These new floorboards," she pointed out when they were upstairs in a storeroom, "Mark laid himself. He told the builders to leave the wood and he'd do it himself."

It looked to Webber a very competent job of work, and he said so admiringly.

"He did the roof too," she told him proudly. "Once he got up there he found that only about half a dozen tiles needed to be replaced. That saved us four hundred pounds alone. We gave up on the cellar though," she laughed ruefully. "But we were warned about that before we bought. They're all the same along here so we've cut our losses and just shut it up, that's what everyone does with them, apparently, even Mark couldn't cope with that."

Webber told her about his damp patch under the stairs and how, after the builders had gone, it was coming back as bad as ever. He had asked another man to come and look at it. He was not, he confessed, a very practical man.

"I'm very lucky," she said.

She was happy too, he thought, as they went down the stairs to the shop.

Arlene Weikel was just leaving, Mark carrying her parcel out to the car for her. Webber accepted her offer of a lift gratefully. He was surprised that she had been content to hire a modest Ford. Somehow the elegant clothes and the expensive jewellery would have seemed more at home in a Rolls or a large Mercedes. She drove well, fast but safely.

"What do you think?" she asked him.

"The shop? Impressive, they've worked hard."

"Not the shop, the boy, don't tell me you went there to buy a map. You were on duty, sure as hell you were."

Webber didn't know how much she guessed but he knew that Lizzie had not fully confided in her because he had asked her not to. That way you didn't muddy the water more that it was already. She knew no more than she had at the beginning of it all. He avoided her question, but opened the subject up a little.

"Not your first visit, I take it?"

She looked at him with respect and grinned.

"I don't persuade easy but he knew I wanted it. It was a good excuse to go back. You wouldn't take him for a hell raiser would you?"

"Not a hell raiser, no."

"I guess we were wrong, marriage must have sweetened him. Either that or he's calmer without his mother. And, of course, money fascinates him."

It seemed such a non-sequitur that Webber knew she wanted to intrigue him, break down his defences. She wouldn't do that but he could let her think so.

"Has he suggested borrowing any? I gather the shop has proved more expensive than they expected."

She changed down into a lower gear to negotiate a difficult bend in the road.

"He thought about asking but changed his mind. No, he didn't ask," then she added, "I've been rich a long time, John. I know the signs. In the old days I used to think that if they didn't ask it was a compliment. At my age I'm not so sure."

They drove in silence until she pulled up at his garden gate.

"And where in hell is Lizzie? Why doesn't she answer her phone?"

At that moment Mrs Thomas was walking unsteadily down the gangplank of a cross channel ferryboat and about to take her first shaky steps on French soil.

✥ TWENTY-FOUR ✥

MRS THOMAS SAT in a quiet corner of the Calais brasserie recovering slowly. The Channel crossing had been rougher than she could have believed possible and she had tottered from the customs shed with her suitcase to the nearest chair she could find on dry land. The motion of the ship had released its grip on her reluctantly so that at first she had half expected the heavy ashtray to slide off the red gingham tablecloth and go careering along the heaving floor of the room. The wind driving the rain against the steaming window was gradually losing its force, allowing the streams of water to run down vertically and the brasserie to sail into calmer seas. Mrs Thomas released the edge of the table and looked about her with interest. She was in France and she was alive.

A notice on the door had said "English Spoken", so she took them at their word and ordered tea. The tired girl who took her order seemed to have no difficulty in understanding her and edged her way back through the tables to a zinc-topped bar displaying a colourful array of bottles and a formidable woman behind a till.

The tea when it arrived was weak and the girl brought hot milk with it. Mrs Thomas drank it because it was wet. Most of the customers were paying their bills and leaving. They looked like dock workers and they left the air thick with the smell of Gauloise and coffee and stale sweat. Now that the general background babble of voices had gone she could tune in to some of the conversation at the tables that were still occupied. To her dismay, apart from the odd word, she could not follow any of it.

It was a moment when she was tempted to abandon her journey through a foreign country where she couldn't speak the language and go back to Flaxfield and tea with cold milk. The mood was depressing but it passed, she thought of the way the ferry had plunged and bucked in the boiling green water and thanked God

161

for dry land. There was also the interesting discovery that she was hungry. Unwilling to trust her ability to order in French she pointed out soup and an omelette on the grubby menu scrawled in purple ink.

While she waited, the last of the incomprehensible workmen went out into the rain leaving her alone in the café. The girl brought her the soup and some good crusty bread and started to clear the clutter from the tables. The soup was undistinguished and could have been hotter but she drank it gratefully, becoming aware as she did so that the woman with the dyed jet-black hair behind her fortress till was eyeing her with curiosity. The omelette was overcooked, brown on the outside and dry throughout, she wished she had ordered a glass of wine and was about to see what was on offer on the menu when she heard the woman tell the tired girl to get a move on with clearing the tables and then come and suggest a reason why the total on the bill for table four included coffee for only two people and not for the three customers who had been sitting there. With a leap of bright joy in her breast Mrs Thomas realised that she had understood every word. The workmen had obviously been talking in a broad local dialect but the woman spoke the language that she understood. She decided against the wine and pointed to coffee with a bright trusting smile.

"My God!" the woman said to the girl, "what does she think she looks like?"

Mrs Thomas studied the cascade of rain running down the window. The girl clattered the coffee on to a tray and studied the Englishwoman with pity.

"She's had a bad crossing, poor thing. One could hardly expect her to look like a fashion plate after such a storm."

"A fashion plate you say. You are an idiot, Cecile, and you always were, that is why you are a waitress." The woman spoke unemotionally, running a pencil up a line of figures. "Are you certain you only served them coffee for two?"

"Yes, I wrote it down."

The woman finished her calculations and returned to the subject of her customer.

"One cannot blame a storm for that. Be sensible girl; think. Apart from the hat being crooked which I admit one could attribute to the storm — my God that hat! — apart from that, she would have looked exactly the same when she set sail. It is difficult to imagine, but I assure you that at some point she has looked at that ensemble in a full length mirror and approved it. Not chic."

Mrs Thomas beamed happily towards the woman and signalled

for her bill. She was not by nature vindictive and although she had been hurt by the insults she was so delighted to have understood them that her first instinct was to pay what she owed and leave. The poor thing at the bar obviously lacked taste. The hat was an exact replica of the one worn by Celia Johnson in the film *Brief Encounter*. Trevor Howard had fallen in love with it and it frequently re-appeared on television to universal approval. It suited her. She had five of them, in different shades of good quality felt. This one was white with the bow tastefully contrasted in brown. She collected her things, straightened her hat and advanced upon the till. She would leave with dignity.

"I'm surprised you remembered the coffee," the woman said to the girl, glancing at the bill before presenting it to Mrs Thomas. "One day you'll bankrupt me with your stupidities and who will give you work then eh? – Madame 'as enjoy 'er meal?" she unwisely enquired of Mrs Thomas in English.

Mrs Thomas paused and abandoned her state of grace before launching into her first conversation in French.

"The soup," she said sweetly, "was quite tasty but it could have been hotter."

The tired girl's hands shot up to her mouth.

"But the omelette must be classed as a disaster. If you thought more about your kitchen instead of your till, you might in future consider moving your greedy arse and making sure that an omelette was served *baveuse*, as it should be, and not dried up and wrinkled like your poor, over made-up skin."

The woman remained motionless but the girl uttered a high pitched moan which showed some promise of developing into hysterics. Mrs Thomas had already selected a banknote which left an over generous tip.

"The change is for you, my dear, not for this rude bitch, make sure you get it."

She stumped happily to the door with her suitcase and umbrella at the ready. She delivered her parting advice in the open doorway.

"Black is a hard colour," she said, "for a woman of your age, but if you insist on dying your hair then you should be consistent, a grey moustache is unbecoming, not chic."

She thudded the umbrella open and sailed into the street. The girl, she decided, was not having hysterics. She was enjoying herself.

Outside the rain had settled into a sullen drizzle but the wind had dropped and with luck she hoped the weather would improve enough for her to stretch her legs. It was nearly four o'clock in the afternoon now that she had altered her watch one hour to conform to French time. Webber had worked well for her, not only seeing that her passport was rushed through in time, but booking her travel tickets and making sure that she had enough money in both travellers' cheques and French bank notes. Most of this she had secreted in a money belt which she was wearing next to her skin around her waist. The rough canvas chafed and irritated her as she walked but it felt secure and comforting. The Flandre-Riviera Express, with sleeping car accommodation only, would leave from the Gare Maritime at 19.30 and she was due to arrive in Cannes at 09.54 the following morning. From there, according to the Michelin map, Pegomas was only about eleven kilometers. She never believed in making plans ahead, she would decide when she arrived. Meanwhile she was in Calais, and with some hours to kill before she embarked upon the second stage of her journey.

The rain had stopped and although the fast scudding clouds still looked menacing she had no intention of sitting in a station waiting-room for over three hours. The Gare Maritime was close to the brasserie and she found a locker for her suitcase and confirmed the time and platform for her train at 19.30. She braved the local patois again and was advised by a helpful porter that she would be able to get food on the train but that in his considered opinion it wasn't worth the money. She would do better to buy herself some bread, cheese and fruit and he directed her to the Place d'Armes where she would find everything she needed and for a tenth of the price charged by the train robbers.

Half an hour later with a full carrier-bag she wandered down side streets and over a bridge until she found herself in the Parc St Pierre where, in pale sunshine, she was glad to rest on a park bench. The bench already had an old man respectably dressed in black seated at the other end. The sun had brought people into the park and she watched them with interest as they strolled round the gardens. It was odd to realise that every thought passing through their minds was in French. Her onslaught in the brasserie had revived her confidence in her fluency and whetted her appetite. Ever since her early days of dalliance with the boys of the Free French Airforce she had loved the language. It was a symbol of her youth, reviving memories of the delightfully outrageous suggestions the French boys used to make to her with pink, innocent faces and her mother beaming incomprehension as she washed up at the kitchen sink. Through the years she had kept it up, listening to the BBC news bulletins in French or escaping from the banalities of Woman's Hour to the limpid accents of Radio Paris.

She was grateful for the bench. On the whole her varicosed legs were not a handicap. She had decided long ago that so long as the elastic stockings made mobility tolerable she would ignore them. At night, on the advice of Sarah Collins, she slept with her feet slightly raised on a firm pillow. For the rest of the time she chose to accept her condition as a minor handicap of little importance. She missed Webber. It wasn't that she any longer had doubts about her mission, the homesickness had passed as quickly as the ravages of the rough sea crossing. She missed him, or more accurately she missed being able to talk to him.

The old man gave up the attempt he had been making at his newspaper crossword with a frustrated grunt and pocketed his pencil with resignation. She thought of Webber on the coach. A passable knowledge of the language, she thought, would hardly qualify her as an assistant puzzle solver but it did not deter her.

"Difficult?" she enquired solicitously.

"At my age, Madame, they are all difficult."

What age would he be, she wondered. Grey hair, untidily cut. He probably did it himself. A brightly healthy complexion with a dusting of white stubble hiding some nicks' from a blunt razor blade. The trousers of his suit, like the overcoat, were worn and shabby, at his throat he wore a hand-knitted grey woollen scarf. He looked neglected. A widower, she decided, and not used to taking care of himself, probably not as old as he looked, a retired bank clerk or minor civil servant. The brown eyes were kind and intelligent, the wind had made them rheumy like an old spaniel dog.

"Would you like an apple?"

"You are very kind Madame, but unfortunately – the teeth." He smiled charmingly, another disappointment he had learned to accept. "Madame is English?"

"Welsh," she added conversationally, "I am not nationalistic, but I am Welsh – from Cardiff – the capital."

"Ah yes, it is a seaport, is it not? That would account perhaps for your excellent command of our language."

Mrs Thomas beamed graciously and inclined her head in acknowledgment.

"Madame is on holiday?"

The clouds had thickened and obscured the sunshine. Instinct told her that unless she captured his interest the weather might deprive her of his company and she would have to retreat to the station waiting-room and the less comprehensible accents of the railway staff.

165

"Someone threw stones at my cat. I have come to France to discover the reason."

The brown eyes considered her gravely. She might be mad, of course, but somehow he doubted it. The clothes were bizarre, it was true, but she had quality. In his long life as a priest he had seen many sadly deranged women earnestly confiding or confessing hysterical fantasies, but this woman was not like that. Now he was retired. It was not of his choosing but, as his Bishop had said, one must make way for youth. If he murmured something polite he could leave her and go back to the Home and play chess or listen to Father Alfred, who was most certainly quite mad, discussing the life and work of St Francis de Sales.

"You wish to intrigue me, Madame, and you have succeeded. However the weather is not agreeable. Over there, past the Rodin statue and behind the Town Hall one finds a pleasant place for coffee and we could be warm. Would you consider it an impertinence if an old man asked you to take coffee with him?"

The café was bright, clean and cheerful without being too noisy. She wished she had found it for lunch. Like the Ancient Mariner, Mrs Thomas transfixed her listener, but Father Bernard was a willing victim and sat entranced. It was a decided improvement on the boring virtues of St Francis de Sales. It was sad but true that evil was more interesting than sanctity. But what a way to combat it! What an extraordinary way to conduct an investigation! In France, he assured her, it would be quite unnecessary to presume such innocence for lack of proof. The young man would assuredly be arrested and held to account before the full rigours of an Examining Magistrate and the truth would be shaken out of him like a terrier shakes a rat. Father Bernard's eyes gleamed with the light of battle in a just cause.

"And if he refused to confess?"

"He would be taken to the railway platform and questioned as the trains rushed in. He would be seated in his poor father's car and confronted with eternal damnation."

"And if he is mad?"

"Then your law would protect him, I have no doubt."

Father Bernard watched her and saw something like disappointment in her face as she looked out across the bustling café. His own expression was curiously bright and cheerful.

"It must be said that if I were a murderer I would feel much safer in your country than in mine," he said gently. "One must be practical."

Mrs Thomas looked into the intelligent brown eyes with respect and for once was silent.

"So, you are thinking I am an odd sort of priest eh? Is that not so? My daughter, I am not on duty you know! We meet on a park bench and we shall never meet again. My bishop would tell me that I am, in the depths, a pragmatist; that I believe practical considerations are sometimes – not always but sometimes – more important than dogma eh? Well perhaps it is true. Of what good would it be if I talk to you of Sin and of all the names I know it by when your train will leave in less than an hour eh? No, you have no time to listen to St Thomas or St Augustine. You will, if you find her, learn more from his mother than from them or from me. The church has her rules and so does the law but you have chosen your own rules because you say your law cannot help you. Eh well! If they are your own rules you can at least change them as you proceed, is that not so? And murder – for whatever reason – is not like cricket, my daughter. You will remember that?"

"I'll remember."

"Perhaps one day you will write and tell me what has happened? It would be a kindness to an old friend, eh? Father Bernard, Hospice Ecclésiastique will find me."

Mrs Thomas gathered her carrier bag and her umbrella and kissed him firmly on the cheek.

When she told Webber about it she decided that she would make Father Bernard much younger.

·

⚜TWENTY-FIVE⚜

HER SECOND CLASS ticket gave her a comfortable compartment which, later in the evening, the attendant told her would be converted into sleeping accommodation with two bunks, one above the other.

At 19.15 there was no sign of any travelling companion. The train was crowded with people pushing past each other in the corridor carrying suitcases and anxiously checking the number of the compartment. Most of them, she observed with satisfaction, were French so that with luck she would be able to extend her vocabulary. On the seat beside her sat her battered copy of Harrap's *Concise French and English Dictionary*, an old friend for many years past. At the bookstall she had bought a book in case the journey proved tedious. Modestly, she had not thought her reading sufficiently good to tackle a novel and had settled for a cookery book, *La Veritable Cuisine de Famille, par Tante Marie*. It would, she thought, make pleasant reading to see what the opposition was up to and would make an easy opening for conversation since whoever shared her journey was destined to be a woman. She had thought that in France they might have been more open-minded on the subject but the travel brochure which was enclosed in the folder with her ticket was explicit.

"Passengers travelling in the same sleeping car compartment must ALL be of the same sex or of the same travelling party."

Gradually the bustle of passengers outside in the corridor subsided as people found their allocated seats. The windows were lowered for last goodbyes and when, at exactly 19.30, the train shivered and glided out of the Gare Maritime she still found herself alone. It was disappointing but she resigned herself to a dull journey, and after a cursory inspection of the muddy waters of the Bassin Carnot she abandoned herself to a critical consideration of Tante Marie's thoughts on duck in red wine.

It had been a long day and without her knowing it the book drooped on to her lap and she slept. She didn't hear the door glide open and close and not until they were clear of the town and out into the open country did she open her eyes to find Webber sitting in the other corner.

"It's all right, don't panic."

"I wasn't going to but I'll listen. Except I'd like to know how you made it with your hip in the state it's in?"

"That's part of the story. I'll tell you as we go. More immediately it's the reason for taking so long to shove down the corridor. By the time I found you, you were out to the wide. Didn't like to wake you."

"Very thoughtful. I hope that's whisky you're pouring?"

"Duty free on the Hovercraft. I caught the first one I could. It's quicker than the boat, my only chance of catching this train. I was lucky the weather cleared, there was talk of cancelling it. I gather you had a rough crossing."

"Worse than the Big Dipper at Barry Island. My God, that's a big drink. Bad news?"

Holding on to his glass he leaned across and kissed her in sheer thankfulness for her common sense.

"Sort of, I don't really know. I'm not risking it anyway. So – first things first. After you left last night, Peter Collins called in with some pills Sarah had meant to deliver earlier and forgotten. They're good too, must be strong, and mercifully they don't quarrel with alcohol so, as you can see, I'm mobile again, good as new, well, almost."

"What time was this?"

"Almost as soon as you'd gone, about half past eight. He stayed for a drink. I told him about Mark."

"Everything?"

"As much as we know. I wouldn't have done but it led on from something he told me. Anyway, thank God I did."

"Go on."

"He was looking for a golf ball in one of those clumps of gorse bushes, you know what they're like, thick as a forest, some footpaths beaten down by the golfers but you'd have to have a pretty good reason for being in there unless you were a bad golfer. He never found his ball but he did find Mark Carter and a friend. Peter said they were quite respectable by the time he saw them. He thinks they were hoping he might have ploughed on and missed the clearing they were in."

"They?"

169

"Mark was with Annie Spicer. God knows how he got on to her but he has."

Mrs Thomas thought back to the time when she had first talked to Annie at Henworth Hall. "I told my Mam, I said, he's a proper little smasher, he could leave his boots under my bed any time." She said: "He wouldn't have to, it's just our rotten luck but Annie made the running there all right, she's always fancied him. How long ago was this – the golf course?"

"As far as I can work it out it must have been quite recently, Peter wasn't sure of the day."

"She could have told Mark about the letter then?"

"She did. I went down to see her when Peter left. She lives with her mother. Annie was out with her boyfriend, her fiancé, they didn't get back until two in the morning. I hadn't got much choice so I pulled rank and waited. I wrapped it up as diplomatically as I could but I had to know."

"She may not have remembered the address."

"No such luck, it was short enough: Villa Emily, Route d'Or, Pegomas, Alpes Maritime. She remembered it because Emily was her grandmother's name and Pegomas was easy enough. You're quite right, she obviously made all the running. Her mother blames the books she reads. A bit of a madam. Chatted him up in the newsagents while he was buying a magazine about boats. She mentioned the letter and was cute enough to realise that he wanted the address badly. He claimed he'd mislaid it and wanted to write to Mummy, so our little Annie says she might just remember it if she thinks hard. Hence the appointment on the golf course. She put it rather more innocently, but that's what happened."

"Did she tell him she'd given it to us?"

"She says she didn't and on the whole I'm inclined to believe her, after all it would have weakened her bargaining power, wouldn't it? The poor fiancé was a bit lost, I'm afraid. He came in with her when they saw the light on in the room and my car outside. She'll have some explaining to do even though I managed to avoid the gorse bushes."

"She'll manage. She's no idea what she's done, of course. What did Peter Collins have to say?"

"Nothing that I didn't know already. He started in psychiatry, I didn't know that. He says that doctors are hamstrung by the law and the law is as tight as a drum. We'd need much more than speculation or suspicion to get Mark certified. He doesn't have much faith in psychiatry, either. They like to slot patients into neat little categories and put labels on them. Trouble is, they won't stay labelled. The chances are Mark is paranoiac but we can't prove it. Peter thinks he could lead a perfectly normal life or he could kill again – that is assuming we're right."

"Any more?"

"He told me that Mark cast some doubts on Margaret's sanity and he's had patients who have done that before now. In itself it's not enough, but add it to all the rest . . ."

"So it's like sitting on a time bomb and we are back where we started. John, you should be in Flaxfield near Margaret."

"I went to see her first thing this morning. I honestly didn't know what I was going to say. Play it by ear, I thought. I get on rather well with her. Mark wasn't there. He left suddenly about three days ago. Business, she said, she's very loyal and discreet but she thinks he might be trying to raise money. There is an important sale coming up, she wouldn't elaborate."

"How was she?"

"Bright as a lark and happy with it, full of the joys of married life. Her actual words were, 'I can't believe my luck'. Try telling someone like that she's married a homicidal maniac."

"Has she heard from him?"

"A couple of phone calls just to say things are going to plan."

"You think he'll go to Pegomas?"

"Yes. He might be there already. You can dial through direct from France, no bother."

"I'm glad you came."

"I booked this train for two in case the leg perked up. Just as well. It was a bit of a rush. I drove down and parked the car at Dover. I was worried about you. Have you eaten?"

For a moment she regretted the carrier-bag of food although there was ample for both of them. His casual acknowledgment that he had worried about her and the fact that he was there in the train with her, conjured up romantic pictures of an intimate dinner for two with shaded table lamps, white jacketed waiters and wine.

There was wine in her carrier-bag, half a bottle of good claret, she had taken the advice of the man in the shop. Webber watched her as she laid out the simple food on a clean napkin. She washed the glasses and produced a corkscrew, moving round the rocking compartment as efficiently as if she was at home in her own kitchen at Flaxfield. They ate in silence and when she had cleared away they stood in the swaying corridor while the attendant transformed the carriage into a sleeping compartment. She was disappointed that he hadn't questioned their relationship. She had mentally rehearsed some crisp observations on morality and privacy but they were not necessary. The lavatory in the corridor met with her approval and by the time Webber returned from it she had already clambered up the ladder into the top bunk, her clothes hung neatly from the hanger provided and her feet under the bedclothes raised on a rolled up blanket.

Webber was tired and gave no protest, grateful that he hadn't had to climb up himself. He didn't bother to undress, took his pills and lay on his back with his hands behind his head.

"John."

"Umm?"

"Shall we find her, do you think?"

"I don't know. It's a chance, the only one we've got. She might talk."

"Suppose we find him there – Mark – have you got a gun?"

"You've been watching too much television. Go to sleep."

"Who's feeding Bunter?"

"Doreen and Jimmy."

"Did you give them his meal chart?"

But Webber was already asleep and presently as the train hurtled down through France, and dressed only in pink elastic stockings and a canvas money belt, Mrs Thomas slept too.

That morning after Webber had gone, Jimmy Trottwood came to run Margaret over to the shop at Dunwold. The local bus service was hopeless and when Mark had taken the car, Jimmy had volunteered to drive her while he was away.

"My dear, I'm sure I'm late, I've been cooking fish for an ungrateful cat. Best cod, dear, and he won't touch it; sulking because Lizzie's away. Do I smell coffee?"

"Probably, but it's all finished and washed up. Wait till we get to the shop and I'll make you some there."

The suggestion pleased him because he would be able to linger and chat with her. He was glad to get away from Doreen who, ever since they had seen her mother off on the bus, had been particularly tiresome.

In the car Margaret relaxed, that was the nice thing about Jimmy Trottwood, his chatter was undemanding, a pleasant background, like the radio when you were doing housework. Adaptable too, and like the radio if the comedy didn't amuse you, a flick would change him into a serious discussion.

"Why are you feeding Bunter?"

"Don't ask me, it's been one of those mornings. Up at dawn to get Lizzie onto the London coach. Does she tell us where she's going? No she does not, so of course that upsets Doreen. Has she consulted her loving son-in-law about her clothes? No she has not, but we'll draw a veil over that. Come to think of it a veil was about the only thing she wasn't wearing. Not a word about pussy-sitting. We were told that John Webber was on Bunter duty. Doreen waves a tearful farewell, no, not tears of parting, dear, Betsey knows her too well for that. Sheer frustration that's what the tears were, and off she trots down the road without a word to her loving husband – she looks just like her mother from the back have you noticed? Better dressed, of course, but the same determined sort of bounce, like a dog going off to dig up a bone. So back I go to Maison Trottwood for soothing coffee and toast only to find a note from John Webber saying he's been called away suddenly on business and will I feed pussy. He left me all Lizzie's instructions; recipes and a time table as long as your arm. I promise you that cat eats better than I do. Soon be there. Comfy?"

"Webber came to see me this morning too," she said. "He wanted to know where Mark was, at least I think that's what he came for. Jimmy, I don't know why, but I'm frightened."

There was something wrong. Badly wrong. He felt it too, now, and Doreen had sensed it. When he had gone round to his mother-in-law's house Doreen was already there, nosing around among her mother's things for some clue as to where she might have gone and why. He had put it down to her natural family inquisitiveness, but it was more than that. Doreen knew her mother better than anyone, and she was worried about her. And now Webber.

She saw the change in his face and felt guilty. It was really too easy to get sympathy from him. Unfair because he was so kind. It was the others who frightened her. They frightened her with their questions, both the ones they asked and the others she saw only in their eyes.

She said, "I don't mean frightened, I don't know why I said it. Poor Jimmy, I do use you don't I? Come on, I can't manage toast, we've only got an electric kettle, but you shall have your coffee at least."

In the shop she seemed determined, even pathetically anxious he thought, to demonstrate that there was no reason for her remark in the car. He let her talk while he moved round with his coffee, admiring the fine mellow quality of the furniture. She had been a quick and intelligent pupil. He remembered Mark's style

173

from the days of the Dunwold Fair and as she talked it was his voice that he heard again. More eager perhaps, like a child proud of its knowledge; proud of Mark.

Once when he recognised a small elegant davenport desk as a piece he had priced in another dealer's shop, he expressed surprise to see how small a profit Mark had put on it.

"No, that's the right price, it's a bread and butter piece, small profit, quick turnover. He believes in that, remember?"

"Yes, I remember," he sighed in mock self condemnation. "I'm different, I hate parting with anything, so I charge the earth for everything. I like to be cosy."

"More coffee?"

"Please."

She was glad she had managed to get the conversation on to a normal level so that he would forget her sudden panic in the car. That was her problem, and she would fight it and win. And when Mark came back, even if sometimes he was strange and withdrawn, she would give him courage to confide in her. She would fight and win for both of them. She had beaten her mother and she would defeat all the others.

These were the thoughts in her head while all the time she could hear her voice talking brightly and calmly to Jimmy with his sad clown's face even when he smiled at her. The shop, and the new world of profits and customers, and treasures owned by customers' grandmothers. Did Jimmy remember telling her once that Mark was a beautiful race horse? It was true, Jimmy had seen that right back to the days of the Fair. Jimmy had seen it. She didn't say she knew Jimmy had seen it because he loved Mark too, but she knew it was implicit between them. There was no need to say it. Wasn't she lucky? Jimmy, wasn't she lucky? Sometimes she felt there was nothing Mark couldn't do. They were going to learn to sail when the weather was better. It would be wonderful in the summer and a change from the shop. Already they had been to see a boat anchored in the creek. They might hire it if business was good. He might even cure the damp in the cellar. Not enough to be able to use it, perhaps, but enough to stop it rising up into the shop.

"Are you all right?"

"Yes of course." Why was he looking at her so oddly? She was talking too much. That must be a change for Jimmy. Her natural easy laugh didn't sound as she'd meant it to. She'd been talking too much and it had all been about Mark, everything was about Mark. What else in the world was there to talk about, for God's sake?

"Will you go to the sale at Saxmundham?" That was safe enough. Jimmy was bound to know about it. Don't mention the American desk! Don't worry, she had more sense. Mark would kill her if she let that slip out.

"A bit out of my league, dear, but I might. I love a sale, will you go?"

"Oh yes, Mark will certainly, he'll be back by then."

"Same time tonight then?"

"Please Jimmy, if it's no trouble."

"It's no trouble, you know that, my dear. I must dash for Bunter's elevenses and you have a customer."

It was Peter Collins who passed him in the doorway. He was glad she'd have someone to chat to.

৵ TWENTY-SIX ৶

Mrs Thomas woke with a sense of excitement. The Flandre-Riviera Express had carved its way through France in the night, Paris and the sleeping midlands already lay far above them to the north. Her watch showed that it was a quarter past seven. At eight o'clock the attendant would bring them a roll and coffee and shortly before ten o'clock they would arrive in Cannes. That would give them ample time to discuss what they would do then.

A glance over the edge of her bunk showed that Webber was already up and had tactfully removed himself to the lavatory in the corridor. Even in the closed compartment the air felt different and through the window the early sun shone out of a blue, cloudless sky on to a strange landscape of bare rocks and gnarled, dry trees. Dressing in the confined space of the upper bunk did not appeal to her. The blinds on the corridor side were down and the window looked out upon the privacy of the deserted landscape. The train had obligingly slowed down to a crawl and Mrs Thomas prepared to descend with dignity. Flushed with excitement for the day ahead, her legs rested by the night-long journey, she ignored the flimsy ladder and grasping the stout rail above the window lowered herself gently to the floor.

The station through which the train glided slowly without stopping was deserted except for the draped figures of two early morning nuns standing long-shadowed in solemn serenity on the empty platform. They did not move as the strange full-frontal vision, elastic stockinged and money-belted, drifted silently past their eyes, framed by the carriage window and lit by the early rays of the sun.

The train moved on and the vision passed. In unison the nuns crossed themselves. They never saw Mrs Thomas's face which did not descend below the window frame until the station and the nuns had slipped away behind her and she looked out again upon an innocent and deserted landscape. She would never know that from that moment she would be remembered in the prayers of two kindly Sisters of Charity, although in the days ahead she would have been grateful.

The Villa Emily stood in its own extensive grounds which lay almost at the height of the Route d'Or, the steep winding road that climbs up from the banks of the River Siagne outside Pegomas until the hairpin twists straighten out on the bare mountain road which leads on to Tanneron.

The villa was isolated, shaded by umbrella pines and the craggy outcrop of limestone rocks which encircled it on three sides like the arms of a giant nutcracker. Only a small area of the land in front of it had been rescued from the surrounding scrub and laid out as a terraced garden. Like the villa itself, the garden looked uncared for and wild. Joan Carter had rented the property from an agent in Cannes. She had taken care to cover her tracks and the rent was paid in the name of the woman Camous, the widowed caretaker who lived in the small lodge cottage where the long private drive met the main road some distance from the villa itself.

As the train carrying Webber and Mrs Thomas pulled into the station at Cannes, Madame Camous was in the villa talking to a plain clothes policeman and a uniformed sergeant.

"If she has been missing since yesterday why did you not inform us before?"

"She might have come back. One does not like to look a fool, Monsieur."

"Was she in the habit of disappearing without informing you?"

"No, and certainly not overnight. I telephoned you when I saw her bed had not been slept in."

"And as far as you know nothing is missing."

"Only Madame."

"Quite."

The inspector sighed. He was young for his rank, intelligent and astute. It was possible the woman knew more than she admitted. He would have been happier if she had been local, easier to frighten, but from her accent she came from Paris and they were a cagey lot. He watched as she sat stiff-backed in the chair opposite, shrewd, careful eyes, the nose large and ugly, the hair well cut and coiffured in an unsuccessful attempt to soften her face. He had seen the expression before; surly, uncooperative, but correct. Parisians disliked the police.

With his sergeant he had already made his inspection of the Villa Emily. Shaded by the steep rocks and the trees the rooms were cool, the furniture expensive but without style or personality. The Englishwoman's personal effects were expensive, too, but not lacking in taste. The large kaftan dresses in the wardrobes were silk with rich embroideries, everything she owned spelt money. Very occasionally the inspector's wife astonished him by treating herself to a pair of shoes which cost him almost his monthly pay cheque. This woman could have stocked a whole shop with similar pairs without effort. So what had he got? A rich, fat Englishwoman was missing. No sign of violence or robbery, although he only had the caretaker's word for it that nothing was missing. Later he would go through her papers in her desk, they might tell him more about this fat woman who hired an expensive villa and lived alone.

"Madame Carter – how old is she?"

The woman shrugged, "Who knows? A certain age perhaps."

"You have searched the grounds, of course."

She looked at him with open contempt. "They are not small, Monsieur, one could walk for many hours, it is wild up here, I am not a bloodhound."

For a moment his face flushed with anger and she added quickly, "I have called her many times before I telephoned you. I ventured as far as I could."

"There is no car in the garage at the back."

"Madame Carter does not own a car, she seldom ventured out and when she did she preferred to hire."

"Did she hire a car yesterday?"

"I neither saw nor heard one but I am a little deaf, so it is possible."

The inspector stood up. A fat Englishwoman of a certain age, a bit of a recluse. Thank God it didn't sound like a crime of passion. It didn't sound like any sort of crime to him. At least he would be spared a search of the wilderness.

"We'll just take another look round. It seems probable that Madame will come back safely. She has probably met some friends in Cannes and forgotten to telephone you, the English can be very arrogant, especially the rich, I believe."

It did not seem sinister or complicated. A few more questions and he could follow it up with a routine check later. She walked after him into the large sitting room to the reproduction Louis XVI desk.

"She had few visitors up here, I imagine?"

"Exercise your imagination a little more, Monsieur. She had many visitors."

He turned in the chair to stare at her. Her face remained impassive but she enjoyed his discomfort. It was not only the English who could be arrogant. He had assumed too much from the size of Madame's dresses and that she was no longer young – yes that was arrogance. He had a shock awaiting him.

"She liked men, monsieur, young men with hard bodies and no money. The beaches are full of them and at night they filled the bars – certain bars at least. It is not only girls who sell themselves for sex, monsieur. If one can pay one only has to pick up the telephone." She reached past him and opened a fat address book on the desk. "Perhaps you had better check the names. I have not counted them but there seem a great number of them, Madame disliked repeating herself. It was an appetite."

She was right, the names filled page after page, occasionally there were surnames, mostly a single Christian name. Sometimes five or six under one telephone number or the name of a bar or restaurant. He closed the book without comment, not giving her any satisfaction by letting her guess anything from his expression.

"Thank you, Madame Camous. You may return to your duties, but it would be best if you remained on call."

He watched her as she walked away and with her his hopes for a quiet family weekend.

"Sir?" the sergeant said in the silence of the room.

"We shall be logical, you and I, Dubois. First I shall telephone my wife and then you will speak to yours. At least we can warn them to abandon plans. Some of our colleagues will not be so lucky. We shall be busy."

"And this little lot?" The sergeant nodded at the book on the desk.

"Headquarters, and good luck to them, copies to the vice and the drug boys. We shall have to know the whereabouts of every single one of these creatures over the last three days. Meanwhile, I want a search party of men up here and fast. Dogs – the lot. If something has happened to her the chances are that she is not far away. Get a man at the entrance to the drive as soon as you can."

"You think she's dead?"

"With her tastes it doesn't seem like an elopement does it? You'd better send the woman in again. I won't get much out of her but I can try."

In Cannes Webber hired a car. They had decided that Mrs Thomas would drive because of his hip and once again she

179

astonished him by accepting the situation as of no more consequence than a journey around the lanes of Suffolk in the days when he had first taught her to drive. Demanding only a cushion to raise her head above the level of the dashboard and after a cursory inspection of the gears she headed the Peugeot westwards along the coast until, guided by Webber's map reading, she turned off under a bridge and drove north towards Pegomas.

Once it had been a small pleasant village in the hills. Now the traffic from Grasse thundered through it on the way to the coast, filling the air with noise and petrol fumes. The village square was a crowded car park and it took them a long time driving around a confusion of one-way streets before they were able to find a parking space in the square. They sat at a pavement café where the waiter had to cross the road to bring them their ham sandwich and beer. They locked their suitcases in the car but Webber carried a small handgrip containing Mrs Thomas's personal effects. It was heavy and for a wild moment he had a vision of her leaping into the Villa Emily with some lethal and unreliable fire-arm at the ready. He wouldn't put it past her.

"Binoculars," she assured him tackling the crusty sandwich with gusto.

That morning in the train they had decided to stick to her original plan and simply arrive at the villa unannounced. At least Mrs Thomas wouldn't be alone and they would retain the advantage of surprise. Confronted unexpectedly, Joan Carter might well say more than she would if given time to prepare. It was possible that if she were forewarned of their visit she would disappear again.

Mrs Thomas wriggled her bottom on the plastic chair in genuine anticipation.

"And if Mark is with her, what will you do?"

"What would you have done on your own?" Webber enquired with interest.

"God save us!" She considered. "Behaved like a lady and talked nineteen to the dozen I expect. Seen what happened – what else."

He nodded. "He wouldn't give trouble, he doesn't seem to work that way." All the same, he remembered Peter Collins' words: "They like to slot patients into neat little categories and put labels on them. Trouble is they won't stay labelled". "It has to come to a head soon," Webber said, "and whether he's there or not, this looks like it."

The Route d'Or, the waiter told them, was not far. A little way out of the village they would cross the river bridge and just beyond it they would find a signpost. It was the wrong time of the year he told them. In the spring the hill was a blaze of yellow mimosa. He wasn't sure about the Villa Emily, he had to enquire in the bar. It was the last one, or perhaps the last but one, before the road straightened out for Tanneron, they said. There would be a sign at the entrance to the drive.

The autumn sun was bright in the clear sky as they passed over the little river and turned the green car off the road to climb up the steep, thickly wooded hill by a long series of acute hairpin bends. The day had an air of unreality about it. They could have been any long-married pair of British tourists enjoying a late holiday. At each sharp elbow of the bends they looked down to the ribbon of the river in the valley with the dense trees broken by jagged rocks rising up to meet them. They were almost at the top when they saw the policeman standing guard at the turning on the right hand side of the road. Even before they were near enough to read it Webber knew that the sign behind him spelled the words Villa Emily.

"Drive on," he said, "don't stop."

At the top of the next bend, higher up and out of sight of the entrance below, they pulled off the road. They climbed up through the trees to a small clearing where below them they could see the villa and its grounds. There were five or six police cars parked outside the house together with an official looking bus. Long lines of uniformed men with dogs were fanning out from the villa like the spores of a fungus creeping on grass. Through the binoculars Webber could see a youngish man in plainclothes talking to a small group of people with notebooks and portable tape recorders. Webber felt sorry for him. There was no ambulance so that he guessed that it was all just beginning; the men with the dogs hadn't got far, either.

"Are we going down?" she asked.

Webber shuddered mentally, his pale blue eyes decisive. "Lizzie, Common Market or not, I'd sooner dive into a pool full of sharks. Two strange English people walking into that little mess! We'd be here for weeks – months if my laddo down there is hungry for suspects. God knows what's happened but I think we can guess. She's missing, that's what, my girl, and you and I are going home. If they've got Mark we'll soon know and if not, then the sooner we get back to Flaxfield the better."

"Short holiday wasn't it?"

"If you're very good you shall have a cup of tea on the way to the airport."

"I can't fly!"

181

"You can and you will. Thank the Lord I'm with you. Left on your own you'd be down amongst that lot like a dog after a rabbit wouldn't you?"

"Probably."

"Come on, your chummy waiter can tell you about the nearest airport. Nice I should think, not Cannes. We can take the autoroute, you'll enjoy that."

In Pegomas they learned that flights to London from Nice were fairly regular but the first possible one would not be until the early evening. They bought a paper but were not surprised to find no mention of the affair at the Villa Emily in it. Curiosity nagged at her like a physical pain.

"What is the best ladies' hairdresser around here?" she suddenly asked the waiter.

He pointed across the square. "There is only one, Madame." She rose before Webber could question her.

"We've got plenty of time before your rotten old plane," she said. "You cootch quiet by here in the shade, I'm going to have my hair done."

❦ TWENTY-SEVEN ❧

MADAME JULIE'S HAIRDRESSING establishment for ladies was pleasantly clean and intimate. There were three chairs with their attendant paraphernalia of mirrors and basins standing on the composite marble floor. In summer, when the tourist trade warranted it, she employed two local girls as trainee assistants. Out of season she ran the business by herself until the twelfth of December when she took her month's annual holiday which she invariably spent quarrelling with her mother in Paris.

When her eyes had adjusted from the bright sunlight outside Mrs Thomas saw that Madame Julie already had a client to whom she appeared to be administering some final touches. Madame Julie was a pleasant looking woman of about thirty-five. She wore no wedding ring and her hands danced a delicate and vivacious accompaniment to her animated conversation. Mrs Thomas recognised quality when she heard it and silently gave thanks. The woman, as she had hoped, was a natural gossip. With a smile and an elegant wave of the hand she invited Mrs Thomas to take a seat at the small glass table covered with magazines, indicating with the aid of her watch and the fingers of one hand that she would be ready in about five minutes.

It was a long shot, but Pegomas was a small community, and moreover a small community with only one ladies' hairdresser. It was a field of enquiry which would not have occurred to Webber, and indeed had it done so he could not have availed himself of it. Mrs Thomas picked up a colourful magazine. Her attention was immediately riveted by a blazing headline under a photograph of the Queen and Prince Philip.

THE CLANDESTINE ROYAL STUD.
SCANDAL AT THE PALACE OF BUCKINGHAM.

The photographer had caught the Queen frowning severely, Prince Philip beaming amiably. They were surrounded by ecstatic, barking corgis. The article itself was disappointing. It appeared that a footman had been hiring out the favours of the royal dogs while exercising them in St James's Park. There had been a cabinet crisis over the incident and the Archbishop of Canterbury had been called in to mediate. It seemed a very short five minutes when the other customer exchanged pleasantries with Madame Julie and left.

Mrs Thomas reluctantly abandoned the Archbishop reduced to tears by Mrs Thatcher at number 10 Downing Street and settled herself on the warm seat of the chair. She gazed briefly after the departing customer before smiling shyly at Madame Julie in the mirror. It was time for openers.

"I hope you won't think me impolite, Madame, but I couldn't help noticing that lady's hair as she left. I thought it was quite beautiful. When I think what we have to suffer in London! Madame is an artiste."

Webber sat under the red and white café umbrella. It was pleasantly warm and he was content to sit and wait for her. He ordered a beer without difficulty; gassy and too cold it was nevertheless welcome. He thought of Lizzie's progress across the square, bottom bouncing among the parked cars with unerring instinct for the shortest route between two points. Her appearance was no longer comic in his eyes. Yet she was comic, he thought, not just the way she looked and moved but in her whole attitude and outlook on life and on everything around her. Once when they sat in his garden after one of her best efforts in the kitchen he had told her that she was the only woman he had ever known who could reduce horror and murder to the same level of importance as a shopping list. To his surprise she had taken it as a compliment.

"Quite right, yes it's true that, I suppose. I've always liked a list, it's tidy."

It was that same evening too that she had mildly rebuked him for his cautious solemnity.

"Not that you'll change boy *bach*, or me for that matter. It's the way we're made, thank God, and if you were born and brought up in a Welsh valley you've got to learn to laugh or you'd go mad. When I was eight there was a memorial service in our chapel for a boy who'd been killed in a pit accident underground. I had to sing the solo in the anthem and my knickers fell down in the middle of it. I cried with shame for a week. Years later his mother told me it helped her more than the sermon. It didn't take the horror away but it changed it. I think I learned then that it was no good trying to separate things and I never have."

A slim elegant woman with a honey tan and a white silk dress came and sat at the table next to him and he caught himself instinctively pulling in his stomach. He never did that for Lizzie, but he knew who he'd rather be with at that moment. Where the hell was she? She'd been gone for nearly an hour already. Perhaps she was right and they should have driven up to the villa and told the local troops what they knew and why they were there? Or he could, even now, keep Lizzie out of it, pack her off home and speak to them himself. Not a chance, not a hope in hell, she'd never go back alone and once they got caught up in the French Connection they were no longer free agents. It must be something serious with all that heavy mob up there. If there was nothing in the evening paper he'd get Lizzie to telephone the villa from the airport but not until they were sure of a flight. It was at that moment that he saw her crossing the square towards him. She was carrying her hat, her hair was tight-curled and the colour of a new horse chestnut.

"Like it?"

"It's different."

"It'll be all right when it drops. Sorry I've been so long but we were getting on nicely so I had a rinse as well to eke out the time. I've just been on the phone to the villa. You were right, she's missing."

"How long were you speaking?" his voice was suddenly urgent.

"I don't know – about five minutes, nice little man, came from Cassis, that's quite near Marseilles, I thought I recognised the accent."

She hadn't seen him move so quickly for months. He grabbed her arm and guided her down the stone steps into the car park, praying they could get out easily. They were lucky and moved out into the traffic as he turned to see a police car skid to a halt outside the hairdresser's.

"Keep going but don't speed. If you see a road block stop and don't speak French, only English, we're tourists, and for God's sake put your hat back on."

There was no road block but he didn't relax until they had driven south to Mandelieu on the D 109 and joined the Autoroute to Nice. He made her keep rigidly to the speed limit. Once a police car overtook them, a big black Citroen travelling fast, but it took no interest in them. Webber grunted.

"That means they haven't got on to the car-hire people, not yet anyway."

"What are you going to do with the car?"

"The airport car park and hope for the best. They'll find it soon enough, not too soon, I hope."

"They had the phone call traced?"

"Yes of course – routine."

"I'm sorry, I didn't think."

"It's all right, later on it would have been a good idea. Was it worth it?"

"Well at least it confirms she's disappeared. Nothing else, not on the phone anyway. It was the police of course, I knew that, but I was too stupid to realise he was keeping me talking."

"We're not out of it yet. They might be watching at the airport. They won't have a description of me, I'll have a look round first and leave you in the car. I'll soon know if they're there."

"Mark was questioned by the police in Switzerland about the death of a German boy. It was an accident and they let him go. There's more, too," she told him.

"The hairdresser?"

"Madame Julie, yes. At first I thought Joan Carter might have used her, she's the only one in the village. She didn't, she had a woman come up from Cannes but Marie Camous did, that's the caretaker who wrote the letter. She knows Madame Julie well. They're both from Paris and quite chummy."

"You're driving too quickly – go on."

"Mark was on holiday with his parents. He was about sixteen. There was a girl in the hotel, a waitress or chambermaid I think. Both Mark and the German boy fell for her. Mark and the boy went swimming in the lake but only Mark came back."

"Any more?"

"Yes, Joan Carter hated Mark. She was frightened of him too but we knew that. Frightened but determined. She had a mean streak, she'd spend money on herself – boys mostly – but she wasn't going to let him get any of it. The other one was different – Billy, she loves Billy. She kept in touch with Monmouth, there were long phone calls."

"She seems to have confided in this caretaker woman – Camous?"

"Marie Camous, yes, two women together and one of them frightened, I can understand that. Camous got some of the picture from Joan Carter direct but she was a great eavesdropper too, she had enough English to listen on the extension phone whenever she could. That's when she learned that Monmouth

186

was going to bring Billy into the business. He's a trained accountant, his father needs him, cooking the books I shouldn't wonder."

"What did they think Mark's reaction would be to that?"

"Monmouth thought she was worrying unnecessarily, he thought marriage would calm Mark down. He's never believed Mark was evil, let alone potty. Unstable that's all, and that's his mother's fault as much as anything, he says. Monmouth disapproves of her private tastes."

"The boys."

"That's right, she's as keen as ever according to Marie Camous."

"You've had a right old chat haven't you! No wonder you took so long. How did you open her up, may I ask?"

"Easy once I found out she was a chum of the caretaker. She's mad about English Royalty for a start. I said I was a seamstress and worked for Joan Carter's dressmaker. I'd come down to let out her frocks a bit. Seemed a bit unkind but I thought it was safer than taking them in. I was very discreet, of course, but I did mention Lady Diana's wedding dress in passing. I just took it from there."

He absorbed her information in silence, fascinated as much by her method of obtaining it as by its content. He watched her as she drove; the hands high up on the steering wheel, head tilted up to see over the bottom of the windscreen, the white felt hat crammed down over the conker curls.

"I ask as a fellow professional," he began mildly, "and my question is purely technical. But didn't you find it odd that this Madame Julie would discuss such private gossip with Joan Carter's dressmaker? After all you might have been a great personal friend of hers. It does happen, I believe?"

Mrs Thomas sighed. "You didn't listen, John. I wasn't her *dressmaker*. I'm just an old reliable seamstress, nothing grand like a designer. I've never met Mrs Carter in my life, that's why it was so nice to chat about her. I get sent all over the place, New York, Venice, Sandringham—"

"Very clever, yes that makes sense—I'd keep a bit more distance from the car in front if I were you—tell me about your phone call again, how did Madame Julie react to that?"

"She never heard a word. She gave me the number to make a courtesy call saying I was on my way. The phone was in the office and she was clearing up in the shop with taps running."

"There was no mention of Mark arriving?"

"Not a hint. But she hasn't seen Marie Camous for over a week. Billy's been down, though. His mother behaves properly when he's there – no boys."

"That policeman, the one you spoke to at the villa, tell me what he actually said if you can remember."

"He hedged for a long time, said he'd go and make enquiries when I asked to speak to her. I see now he was keeping the line open as long as he could. When he came back he said she wasn't available, then he asked me who I was. I pretended I was an American friend of hers just calling up for a chat. That's when he said she was missing and there were grave doubts for her safety."

"He said that?"

"Yes, I expect he wanted to shock me into saying something. When he asked my name I hung up."

"You probably don't realise it but you are driving very near the edge of the road."

Webber was a poor passenger.

At the airport he left her in the car park and made a casual reconnaissance of the booking desks and the departure hall. There were some uniformed police in evidence but it was difficult to tell whether they were more than the normal compliment. He spotted three plain clothes men but again they could have been routine; anti-terrorist boys perhaps.

The first flight to London was fully booked and the one after that. The girl was kind and understanding. Webber let her see him limping, he was unwell he told her, and had to cut short his holiday. There was nothing she could do she said, unless of course there was a last minute cancellation. He cursed Lizzie gently, marvelling that she could be so clever and so stupid. If they couldn't get away now – and it looked very much as though they wouldn't – they would certainly be picked up for questioning and that might delay them for days. Days when his every instinct told him that they should be back in Flaxfield. His best hope, he decided, would be to telephone to London. He still had influential friends there in high places. If they couldn't arrest Mark they would have enough to hold him for questioning, they could certainly examine his passport. Even as the hope crossed his mind he knew that Mark would deny having left the country. The passport would be missing. He was about to go out into the car park when a commotion at the London departure desk held him back.

Two of the uniformed policemen were questioning a short, stout American woman with henna-red hair and a strident voice raised in outraged anger.

"Questioning! Questioning! What kind of a lousy country is this? You wanna search me? So go ahead and search me. Now I'm a terrorist already!"

The man with her, presumably her husband, was doing his best to calm her down and to talk to the plain clothes men who had moved in on the group. He was not having much success. His wife's face was by now as red as her hair.

"This is what you get when you vote in the Commies. Chutzpah! Listen, I want the American Consul and I want him fast!"

With luck, Webber thought, he might beat the consul to it. He had a brief word with the sympathetic girl at the desk and within minutes he was back with Mrs Thomas now wearing her plastic navy blue raincoat and with every coloured curl thrust underneath her hat. The girl had confirmed that the wretched Americans would not be on the London flight to Heathrow and that Mr Webber and his nurse could take their place.

Not until the plane left the ground did he relax. Not until the terror of the flight was over and they had landed safely was she able to give her attention to that evening's edition of the French newspaper which the air stewardess had given her to read on the plane.

❧ TWENTY-EIGHT ☙

IT WAS ALMOST a month later that Mrs Thomas sat down to write to Father Bernard at the Hospice Ecclésiastique in Calais. Winter had come to Flaxfield and she wrote at the table in front of the kitchen fire with her French dictionary beside her.

". . . please find enclosed two pairs of thick woollen socks. They are made from a special oiled wool to keep fishermen's feet warm. I remember you talked at one point about chilblains. Two of my friends here are doctors and they tell me you should have warm feet, Doctor Sarah says don't hug hot water bottles and Doctor Peter, her husband who is very practical, says that if you do get them you can paint them with iodine to relieve the itching. He will come into this letter later on. Do you sense that I am writing evasively because I am not sure how to tell you what has happened since we met and talked in Calais? It is not entirely so. I truly care about your chilblains.

I got to Pegomas but I never spoke to his mother. It is possible that you will have read some account of her disappearance in your own newspapers. In the same way you will almost certainly know something of the terrible events here in this quiet corner of England. Something, but not by any means all. Some of the facts never appeared in our own newspaper and television reports. Not because they were censored but only because they never came to light. You will forgive me, but from the little I have seen of your own newspapers, I have grave doubts about the version which may have been presented to you. What I write to you now is certainly not the full story for how could anyone know that? But it is a factual account of what I saw and some of that which I learned later. There will be more, I believe, as I move among my friends and acquaintances in the weeks and months ahead. It is a little like colouring the blank pages of a child's painting book, is it not?

190

When I got back here to the village there was what I can only describe as a most curious air of calm and normality. I'm sure I do not describe it so with hindsight for I remember feeling frightened of it, and why should one be afraid of normal peace and calm? The boy Carter had returned and been welcomed with every sign of love by Margaret his wife. The auction sale at the farmhouse, which I will have to describe to you, was not to take place for several days . . ."

When Webber and Mrs Thomas landed at Heathrow they were both exhausted. They booked into the airport hotel for the night and in the morning he rang the police in Dover and got them to arrange for a local garage to pick up the car and deliver it back to Flaxfield. It wasn't only the journey he wanted to avoid but the wasted time. He wanted to get back as soon as they could. At breakfast she showed him the report in the French newspaper. It was on the inside, "The Heiress and the Beach Boys. Mysterious Disappearance in Alpes Maritime. 300 Suspects".

"Should keep them busy for a while," said Webber wryly when she had read him the short account.

"They don't seem to have much doubt about it, do they?"

"Neither would I," Webber said grimly. "They've just got the wrong runners that's all. He couldn't have wished for a better smoke-screen could he? Lucky."

"We could be wrong, there's no proof."

"There never is with him." There was anger as well as frustration on his face.

There was nothing in the English papers.

In the forecourt while they waited in a small queue for a taxi to take them to the coach station in Victoria he suddenly said, "Lizzie, I think I must go to the Yard. Proof or not, I've still got some clout there–maybe not much, but some. Enough to get him pulled in for questioning, perhaps. If I lay out everything, right back to the beginning, they'll listen. They'll have to: they've got to."

Three taxis came and then they stood at the head of the queue. She thought of his words in the train after he had been to see Margaret. "Bright as a lark and happy with it." As he leaned forward to give the driver their destination she held his arm.

"No John, wait. Let me speak to her first."

191

By the time the coach dropped them at Flaxfield they had decided what they would do. However demanding they would say nothing to Doreen, and that meant not confiding in Jimmy Trottwood either.

"She's bound to ask questions," Webber said.

"Let her, I can cope with Madam. Jimmy's all right but she'd have it all over the village."

They telephoned the Collinses and arranged to see them that evening after surgery. Sarah Collins had seriously considered cooking a meal for them but remembering Lizzie Thomas's reputation as a cook her courage had failed her. She persuaded herself that a dinner party would suggest too frivolous an atmosphere for a serious discussion and made plates of cheese sandwiches with gritty parsley. It was a curious compromise. The four of them sat round the modern oak dining table in a room which smelled faintly of disinfectant and rabbits. Sarah had spent some time placing the bottles of wine and beer among the plates and paper napkins to make the table look appetising and had failed. Her husband's red wrists protruding from the frayed sleeves of his sports jacket and the gentle tone of tired patience in his voice gave him more the air of a disappointed schoolmaster than a doctor.

"Of course you don't like it. I didn't suppose you would, but those are the medical realities and I can't change them. If every single one of your suspicions were proved true I could pronounce him medically insane, but on the evidence of his behaviour as it is known to me and reported to me by others, he is a brilliantly accomplished young man with no more than a slight personality defect."

"Reported to you by others," Webber said. "Meaning Margaret?"

"I've seen her several times while he was away, yes. The shop was an excellent excuse to talk to her without making it look like a consultation."

"Still hearing voices is she?" said Mrs Thomas.

"Interesting that," said Peter Collins. "It seems she did actually have some such experience. I have to admit that I feel I know more about her than I do about Mark."

"The fact is," said Sarah, "that she simply didn't want to talk about him." She bit hard into a sandwich talking through a vehement scattering of crumbs. "I knew her mother well, she was an old cow, simple as that. Of course Margaret won't talk about him, and she wouldn't even if she had doubts herself. She's behaving like the mother she never had. She loves him and she's protecting him. You don't have to be a doctor to work out that. To her he's a brilliant child that people don't understand."

"His own mother didn't seem to share that view," said Webber. "You said 'slight personality defect'. How would you define that?"

"Lots of kids don't get on with their parents. Mark's dislike would seem to go deeper than that. You could say that it amounts to a mild persecution complex. That, and his suspicion that she had actively plotted against him, I would say go beyond the normal level. This is evaluating him through Margaret, you understand. Who knows? Perhaps he has cause – she certainly believes so."

Webber's grim face made Peter Collins repeat stubbornly, "A slight personality defect – no more."

"I keep thinking of what you'd said about the police in your country," Mrs Thomas wrote in her letter to Father Bernard and continued,

"It was a frustrating evening. All stupid talk and speculation. Dr Collins is a good kind man but I could have shaken him. Just now when I looked up the word 'shake' in my dictionary it was your voice I heard again when you said, 'and the truth would be shaken out of him like a terrier shakes a rat'. I hear it now when it is too late. I will defend myself and tell you that I meant to act and I knew what I was going to do. My mistake was in waiting. John Webber I defend too, for, but for me, he would have gone officially to his friends in Scotland Yard before we left London. Like me he knew we were right. The doctors were still living in an English village among kind neighbours and nice people and couldn't believe that such things could be true in spite of their cleverness and their books. But John and I we knew, and we were determined to go to them, to Margaret and Mark, and face them with everything we knew and believed. At first I had thought to speak to her alone. It was John who saw that it had to be with them together. In that way it would at least be out in the open. Now I shall never know what would have happened or what his reaction would have been with Margaret there beside him. What stopped us? . . ."

At that point in her letter Mrs Thomas wished she had not written the last three words poised so confidently at the beginning of a new paragraph. It would be a long tortuous explanation and remain unsatisfactory at the end of it, for the answer to her own

193

question did not satisfy herself any longer and would stay to reproach her always.

At the time it had seemed reasonable, even sensible, but however much Webber had since consoled her she found it hard not to blame herself for not acting on her first instincts.

It was Tuesday when they returned to Flaxfield and spoke to Sarah and Peter Collins. On Wednesday morning Webber told her that he had decided they should wait until after the Saxmundham sale on Thursday before they faced Mark. There were, what seemed then, sound practical reasons.

Having successfully evaded a series of probing cross examinations by her daughter, Mrs Thomas was able to take advantage of Doreen's sulky silence and tune in to her son-in-law's gossip of the village while she had been away. It was from him that she heard some of his impressions of Margaret. Margaret in the car as he drove her to the shop and back. Margaret in the shop itself and her new life as a dealer in fine antiques. Margaret talking about the sale and trying so hard not to let him see how important it was for Mark. Margaret and Mark. Mrs Thomas picked her way through all Jimmy said, making adjustments and allowances where she suspected his loyalty to Margaret's confidences had inhibited his chatter and then, through it all, like the faint squeak of trapped terror in a hedgerow, she felt she could hear Margaret calling for help.

"Why after the sale?" Mrs Thomas asked Webber.

"Because if you are right, and it's important for him, he's more likely to be off his guard when it's over. If we're lucky and I haven't lost my touch he might let something slip through, something, anything more concrete than we've got now, and he's more likely to do that if she's there with him. It's worked before, it might again."

"And if it doesn't?"

"God knows, open a box and have a look inside, that's all."

"You won't go to the police, then?"

"I spoke to an old friend last night, got him at home. He wouldn't commit himself officially, not in an hour and a half he wouldn't. Unofficially he was telling me to go ahead and keep him informed. He's a good policeman, we were together for about five years. I told him the lot and he listened. I wanted Mark pulled in but he can't do it on his own. I'd have to go to the Yard and lay it on the line officially and it seems that even then they wouldn't do it. Not without putting it all through the machine. Southall, Switzerland, France and all the stuff on his father. It would take

194

weeks, perhaps months. In the end they will do it, but by then it may be too late."

"At least he listened, but months!"

"There's something to be said for being out of the force. I don't have to wait. At least he'll know we're on to him, that's something, and he might crack, he just might."

So it was agreed. They would move on Thursday, after the sale. It didn't seem too long.

That day, Wednesday, Dudley Dear arrived unexpectedly. Margaret disliked him at once. He was driving an expensive new Rover and wore clever, casual clothes like the glamorous young men in the colour supplement advertisements. He found a free room at the Bull and announced his intention of attending the sale.

"It comes under the heading of moral support," he said.

She could hardly disapprove of him openly since he told them that after careful consideration he felt he could extend his financial backing, in fact he was prepared to double it. There would now be an extra twenty thousand pounds at Mark's disposal to bid with next day. She hated the way he did it. Over casual, like a slimy little uncle at Christmas, she thought.

"How very generous of you, Mr Dear," she said.

"Oh Dudley, please! Mark and I are old friends, I hope – no I'm sure – we shall be too. No, not generous, just common sense. You forget I've seen him at work. I don't call it generous to back a certainty! I'm lucky enough to be able to do it, that's all."

It would have been easier to accept him, she felt, if he had been more obviously homosexual. You couldn't mistake him but there was a careful veneer of respectability about him that she knew he used when he talked to normal people. Like a clever little monkey dressed up in a suit and pretending to be a man. It was difficult to see how Mark reacted to him. On the surface he was correctly grateful but no more.

It was Mark's idea to close the shop for the rest of the day. It probably wouldn't be a good idea for Dudley to be seen with them before the sale, or that he should sit with them during it.

"We're not likely to get anyone in today except dealers," he said, "and they'll only be trying to pick our brains about the sale."

Dudley drove them out into the country to show off the new car and then back the long way round by the harbour so that Mark could show him the boat anchored and empty in the estuary.

"But my dears, how exciting! It looks madly professional. Two

195

coats of paint and a saucy flag and I'd sail round the world in that."

They drove back with the light fading. She was glad when Mark pleaded tiredness and politely refused his invitation to take them out to dinner. She saw Dudley's conspiratorial look of quick sympathy as though he knew she had stopped Mark accepting, but she didn't care. It wasn't true anyway; Mark had made the decision himself and she accepted it without question just as she hadn't pressed him to tell her where he'd been when he had gone away. If he wanted, he would tell her. It was the only way to help him and show her love and confidence.

When Dudley dropped them at the cottage before driving off to the Bull in his new toy, she slipped her arm through Mark's as they waved him goodbye until the sale in the morning.

Mrs Thomas wrote in her letter:
"I would dearly like to know what they talked about that last evening they were together."

She stared at the paper in front of her. Then she took courage and gave Father Bernard an account of those things which she did know about. Even as she wrote she found them difficult to believe.

The short simple sentences stared at her. The sale, and the other horrors, it was all there. She tried to picture the face of a kind old man in Calais as he read it.

The letter caught the evening post.

❧ TWENTY-NINE ❧

THEY HAD PLANNED to go to bed early but he seemed to have forgotten that and they sat in the light of the log fire in pyjamas and dressing gowns. The mean little hot water tank that her mother had thought more than adequate was enough to fill one good bath but no more. She could never bring herself to use her mother's bath water even though it took hours to heat the boiler for another. Now with Mark she revelled in it. It had become almost a ritual for her. All the evening Dudley Dear's name had not been mentioned. Mark had seemed not to want to talk about the sale, whether because he sensed her dislike of Dear, or simply because he felt there was no more to be said about it, she couldn't tell. She herself had no intention of mentioning either subject and was genuinely surprised to hear herself suddenly ask:

"Where does he get money like that? Not from the BBC, surely?"

"Those butchers shops; his mother and father died."

"I don't like him very much."

"He's a bit creepy; no worse than most of them. I thought I might need the money."

In his dressing gown with his hair uncombed she thought he looked ridiculously young, like a little boy hoping his nanny wouldn't send him to bed too soon. In spite of herself it was almost a question a nanny might have asked a child in her care.

"Mark—did you try and borrow money from your mother?"

When he didn't answer immediately she had no feeling that she had broken all her own rules, only a sense of relief that she had asked him something she wanted to know and she was pleased that the question had sounded quite casual and unforced.

There was no sign on his face that she had displeased him nor did she feel that his silence implied either a disinclination or an inability to answer. It was simply a break in the conversation

197

without embarrassment. The rest of it raced on, unspoken in her head, the answer to a question he hadn't asked. "I *didn't* know, it was just something Peter Collins said when you were away. He didn't know himself, probably some patient's gossip which he'd misunderstood, he had this idea that you might have heard where she was. He didn't seem to think it was important." She heard too the light easy laugh she would have used as she concluded, "and neither do I".

When he did speak none of that would have made any sort of sense and it was wiped clean from her mind, like an unplayed and unwanted tape recording. Her first reaction, but only for the briefest moment, was that he was joking.

"Peg, let's leave it shall we? The sale, the shop, everything; let's just pack up and get out somewhere."

So this was the way the storm broke, not with shouting or tears but quietly in dressing gowns in front of a log fire. She had defeated all her own panics and doubts, even delighted in a perverse way in refusing to be drawn into confidences about him. Webber and Mrs Thomas, Arlene Weikel, poor kind Jimmy Trottwood, Sarah and Peter Collins all of them probing and picking away like the grubs in furniture, burrowing in the dark, destroying good sound wood.

"You're overtired," she said and was immediately angry with herself for its weakness and banality. "Why now – suddenly?"

He left his chair and came over to her, sitting on the floor and resting with his head against her knees his face turned to the fire.

"I shouldn't have gone to Dudley. It should have been just us. You were right, I don't like him either. It was greedy but I thought I'd make it certain and then you're not in control any more. I knew that rule years ago. Never make a deal before a sale, the time for deals is always later when you don't have to listen to anybody, then they have to listen to you. This is the wrong way."

A log fell down into the glowing bed of ashes with a brief shower of sparks. One of them landed on the carpet a few inches from his dressing gown and burnt itself out in an acrid wisp of smoke. He seemed not to notice it and she made no move, nor did she speak, afraid that if she broke his mood she would destroy the link he was trying to make. She felt oddly relieved and exhilarated as though for the first time she was about to see some hidden part of him that before she had tried to guess at and failed. If you didn't know you couldn't help. Some of Peter Collins' vague generalities came back to her. Brilliant people were special cases he'd said, but brilliance carried its own problems, even dangers. She had known he was talking about Mark, only turning it modestly into his own

198

reasons for opting out of his own professional rat-race. She remembered him, laughing and self mocking, when he'd said that he doubted if his London hospital would rate a country doctor as amounting to much with his rabbit shooting and golf. "But then you see I distrust specialists and of course there was Sarah, too. It's a quality of life, and we have it together." Was Mark trying to tell her that now?

"I don't care about the sale, it isn't important," he said.

"Mark, you'll have to help me more than that. I can't understand why it isn't important. You said yourself that it was important, that it would set us up in months instead of years. How can you say that you don't care about that any more?"

He twisted up on his knees, facing her. "Some things you can't explain, you only know they're wrong. Dudley is wrong, that was my mistake, but it's not too late. You don't know what people are like. They think money gives them rights and powers and you never get free. Before you know it you can be back in the middle of it all again, little schemes and plots, always plots. You saw him and heard him today with his stupid little bits of clever knowledge, and where's he got all that from? Books from the library? More likely he's been swanning round Christie's or Sotheby's chatting his head off."

She hadn't expected to find herself defending Dudley.

"Mark, it's his money too, he couldn't be so stupid!"

In the last of the firelight his eyes were bright and fierce but his voice was still gentle.

"Peg listen, it isn't only Dudley, and it isn't just the sale. No, listen to me! Peg it's us, I want us. Let's go *now*, just us."

So it wasn't a storm after all, she thought, and felt tears of relief quick in her eyes. It wasn't even complicated, let alone disaster. It was a simple cry for love and reassurance and that she could give him, and with it her strength which was, thank God, so much greater than his, a last minute panic that she could master just as she mastered the bank manager and all the planning of their lives together. She told him that, holding both his hands so that he could feel the force and truth of her love flowing into him. It was so simple, if he wanted her just as she wanted and needed him. With his knowledge and her strength there was nothing they couldn't overcome, nothing and nobody they couldn't fight and win. He was right to see that the sale wasn't important and right to see that they were – the two of them, and all the fears and panics in the world couldn't take them away from each other. But being together meant fighting together.

199

His head had dropped down and she cupped his face in her hands to raise it.

"Mark look at me. You can't go on running away for ever. You don't need to any more. You mustn't worry about Dudley. I'm sure he'll be all right, you know there's a lot to be said for having a rich backer! He won't give us any trouble, nothing I can't cope with, I promise. I can scheme and plot just as well as he can if I have to. Mark, I love you so much and everything is just beginning for us."

She had broken every rule she had made for herself for months past and left herself holding his face in her hands with only the firelight jumping in the blank of his eyes. Not so long ago she would have panicked herself into wondering if she had made herself sound cheap and ridiculous, a legacy of her mother's taunting.

"Poor Mark! Don't worry, you haven't married a bully, I promise. You know, the trouble with tense firelight scenes is knowing how to extract oneself gracefully. Would you like a whisky?"

He nodded and she poured them at the table in the corner.

"It's so easy in those dreadful late-night films, the camera just cuts to waves crashing on the beach or something significant like the two of us sailing happily with flying white clouds. Now there's a thought! I'll even learn to sail that horrid little boat, and enjoy it too. How's that?"

He stood up to take the glass and the strain had gone out of his eyes.

"The fire's nearly out," he said, "let's take the drinks up to bed."

∞ THIRTY ∞

On the morning of the sale the weather was overcast. It had rained in the night but by nine o'clock it had stopped. The wind was light from the northeast, damp and chill with the threat of more rain to come.

During the last two days the workmen had erected a large marquee on the back lawn into which they had moved most of the lots to be sold. Furniture stood around the canvas walls in a jumble with more at the back. Trestle tables at the sides and behind the rostrum were piled with the lost life of the house, ornaments, books, tea and dinner services, numbered and lumped together with Japanese swords and silent clocks. The loved rubbish and rarities of an old woman who, from the indifference or courage of age, wanted no more part of them.

At 9.30 a.m. the auctioneer made his final round of inspection with his clerk. There were three auctioneers in the firm but the other two were junior to Mr Gough and usually handled the sales of livestock and farm equipment. Mr Gough was very conscious that he was the grandson of the founder of Gough and Groucher and tended to keep the plum sales for himself. He was short, fat, forty-two and bald except for a grizzle round his ears and an island tuft deserted above his forehead. Some mornings he teased it up into the sad memory of a youthful quiff. On formal and important occasions like today he spread it flat for maximum coverage when it lay damp and lifeless like a squashed spider. He was followed by his clerk at a discreet pace behind him.

"Ashtrays," said Mr Gough. "No ashtrays, tell Herbert to bring some over, empty biscuit tins, they're in the store-room, tell him to bring the lot. Don't want them burning the carpet."

The floor covering on the damp grass was coconut matting but he always referred to it as the carpet.

"Just a minute! Don't rush off like a race horse. Where are the fire extinguishers? And the first aid box?"

201

"I'll tell him, Mr Gough. I'm afraid the old man is getting very forgetful."

The auctioneer grunted. Herbert remembered his grandfather and wouldn't retire.

"See if that extension phone on the rostrum is working yet and tell him to get a move on."

While the clerk used the telephone Mr Gough continued his inspection of the marquee, like a ship's captain checking the lower deck before action. He had several times refused offers to amalgamate with London auction houses. Financially tempting though they were, he was loth to abandon ship. It would have been very pleasant to afford glossy illustrated catalogues with full page colour illustrations. Secretly he admired their smooth expertise and sometimes made visits to their London rooms, studying their auctioneers like a provincial actor on a pilgrimage to the West End.

The clerk rejoined him as he stood contemplating the American desk.

"Quite a good sale, Mr Gough, rather better than our usual, would you say?"

The auctioneer considered upsetting himself and decided against it, no Commander in his right senses would invite indigestion before action stations.

"Not bad," he conceded, "not bad at all. There might be one or two surprises, I shouldn't wonder. It depends on the weather, of course."

"Ah yes," the clerk said, deferentially following his master's eye to the desk and emboldened by his confidence. "Style of Chippendale, very nice. How much will that make, Mr Gough?"

The Senior Partner kept his hands behind his back but narrowed his eyes at the desk.

"Little country piece, pleasant enough but late, of course. Caused quite a bit of interest. I've noticed that. That's something you'll have to learn, young man. Walk your sales, keep your eyes open." He paused majestically. "It wouldn't surprise me if that lot didn't go sky high."

"Really, Mr Gough?"

"It could make over a thousand. And with a little help from the rostrum," he added modestly, "it might even make two."

He glanced at his watch. Following the London custom the sale was advertised to commence at eleven o'clock precisely.

202

At 9.40 a.m. Jimmy Trottwood had finished shaving and regarded himself in the mirror above the washhand basin in the security of the bathroom. Not for the first time he was saddened by the injustice of life which allowed him to feel young and look old. Clothes, he decided, would help, and with the smell of bacon and toast ascending from the kitchen he selected a pair of dark grey trousers and a tweed sports coat in muted grey-blue checks. He always bought his coats a size larger than he needed and shortened the sleeves. It was an old trick learned long ago to disguise his waistline.

He and Doreen had closed the shop for the day to attend the sale. He believed firmly in the old dealer's axiom that there was a bargain in every sale and lived in hope that he might be lucky. Outside the sky was grim, the colour of slate. It was the worst time of the year, with winter stretching endlessly ahead and summer an impossible dream. The sale at least would be a pleasant social occasion even if he didn't buy anything. Unlike Doreen he refused to allow Mrs Thomas's secrecy to upset him. Secrets were something he respected with resignation when it became clear that they were not to be divulged. You did your best and then pressed on with daily chores. What, for example, was going on between Margaret and Mark? Oh well, perhaps the sale was more important than he'd realised. What they both needed was a holiday.

Not the yellow tie, theoretically it should have been cheerful and spring-like but it looked jaundiced and quite wrong. He selected his plain blue in knitted silk. A holiday? Perhaps he could suggest that Mark and Margaret might like to join them on a winter package-deal to a sunny villa on an island. Why not? After all they shared the same profession and interests. Doreen would complain about the cooking and moan about a busman's holiday. That wouldn't matter, he would willingly cook for them all, and sew buttons on if necessary. He saw Mark dashing early into a warm blue sea edged with deserted beaches of white sand. The girls could make busy little buying trips to the village or go sight-seeing, while he and Mark would sit on the stone terrace overlooking the sea and talk about antiques and sale-room bargains. There was an essential gentleness about the boy, an inaccessibility that was intriguing, even challenging.

"Your eggs are rock hard," Doreen informed him, "and if you don't hurry we shan't get a seat."

Breakfast at Henworth Hall had been more successful, not perhaps for the faithful residue of winter dieters, but for Dr Maguire's special guests, Arlene Weikel and Mrs Barnstable, it had been lavish. Maguire was accompanying them both to the sale and the Rolls had been ordered for ten thirty.

Arlene had quite taken to Jessie Barnstable. In spite of her age the old lady was good company, she liked to reminisce about the days when she had travelled the world with her husband, fêted by foreign governments anxious to buy his invention for their airlines. Arlene should have returned to London, as she had promised she would when the weather broke. There were two reasons why she had reneged and stayed on instead of supporting Walter Weikel in the boring series of dinner parties he seemed to think were essential to the successful launching of a new West End production. The first was simple. She disliked the author and his mistress whom Arlene considered even more unpleasant and unnecessary than the plot of her lover's play.

Her second reason was less clearly arranged in her mind but was nevertheless a more potent motivation. She had become fascinated by Mark Carter. He was an enigma and she found it difficult to keep away from him. It wasn't, she told herself, that she had totally dismissed Lizzie Thomas's single-minded investigation of the boy's character, but she had come to believe that her very single-mindedness might well have been counter productive truthwise. With a mother like that who wouldn't have a personality problem? Sympathy and understanding might well unlock doors slammed in less sensitive faces. Everything took time. In warm baths she somtimes dreamed of Mark making an insurance inventory of the antiques in her homes in America. A strictly business commission, of course. For a high enough fee he might well be tempted. His little mouse of a wife could come too if she wanted, although of course someone would have to stay and take care of the store.

At 10.32 a.m. Dr Maguire, with Arlene Weikel and Jessie Barnstable as passengers in the back, eased the Rolls away from the Palladian pillars of Henworth Hall and headed for the marquee at Saxmundham. A country house sale always attracted him and he had not neglected to view it and to question his new tenant about her expectations. Her response had been disappointing for the old lady had shown only a perfunctory interest. He hoped very much that her unnatural lack of enthusiasm was not an early symptom of incipient senility. It was very pleasant to have his two most expensive apartments occupied and so satisfyingly productive. At her age one could not rely on a long term tenancy, but one hoped.

Luckily Joan Carter still kept in touch by telephone. She did not divulge her whereabouts but she liked to know everything that was happening at Flaxfield and Dunwold and he was happy to oblige and proud of his ability to keep their contact secret. Business was business and it was always possible that if he could allay her rather exaggerated distrust of her son that one day in the future she might well consider taking up residence if a vacancy should unfortunately occur.

Maguire's local intelligence was excellent. A tearful Annie Spicer had been quizzed about the break-up of her engagement and Arlene Weikel's innocent reports from Dunwold had all been carefully assessed and conveyed to Joan Carter. Since then she had not contacted him.

At 10.48 the Rolls drew up at the farmhouse only three minutes before Aubrey Monmouth arrived with his son Billy and an ancient woman in a full length coat of Russian sable.

In the large entrance hall Mrs Thomas stood alone, quietly watching people arrive, local farmers and their strong healthy wives, greeting and chatting in loose familiar groups before echoing across the bare floor boards and out through the house to the marquee at the back. She had nodded briefly to Arlene as she passed through with Maguire and Jessie Barnstable.

The only furniture in the hall was a trestle table with leaflets scattered on it announcing future sales, and a longcase clock which the auctioneer had thought safer to leave undisturbed. "Never move a longcase if you can help it, temperamental, takes weeks to set them again. Leave it, buyer's problem then, not ours. They fetch more ticking." Occasionally when the footsteps were quieter Mrs Thomas heard it measuring the minutes to eleven o'clock.

She couldn't hear what Mark and Margaret were saying to each other. Webber was not with her. He had business of his own which they had agreed together and which could not have been undertaken at another time. "They looked nice," she told him later. "Both of them; she'd taken trouble with their clothes, clean and fresh. More like it was summer, I thought, they could have been walking in the sun, not jammed up with a lot of overcoats and scarves in October. I was glad to see them like that, standing in that hall, laughing and smiling together."

"But that changed when Monmouth and the others came in?" Webber asked.

She thought and shook her head. "No, funny wasn't it? Almost as if Mark had half expected it. Polite, almost formal, with introduc-

205

tions, and Margaret looking – not sure of things, but pleased that he still seemed relaxed. I couldn't hear everything, just bits. I stood and listened, none of them paid any attention to me."

"Like what?"

"Monmouth was very smooth. You've met him, you remember him. 'Mark my dear chap, how nice, I hoped you'd be here. I told Billy on the way down I thought you might be.' It all seemed so ordinary and normal, like we'd got it wrong, you and me, and the old woman in the sables smiling at everyone and not knowing who they were."

"And then?" Webber asked.

" 'Hullo Billy,' Mark said to him, quietly, but I heard. 'A day trip to the country?' Billy never answered because his father took over. He was beaming at both of them, as though he was proud and thought Mark would be too. He wasn't acting, he'd just got it wrong. 'Billy's coming into the firm with me, Mark. It's really too silly wasting his time adding up accounts for other people. Quite foolish.' That's when the old grandfather clock struck eleven but Monmouth said it was three minutes fast. He had a gold pocket watch, it was accurate to six seconds a year he said. Then they all went through to the tent."

Mrs Thomas found a seat slightly to the side of the rostrum where she could see both the auctioneer and most of the people in front of it. The first rows, armchairs and sofas from the house, were numbered lots to be sold themselves. Behind them stood lines of folding wooden chairs, uneconomically hired by Gough and Groucher because they had nowhere to store their own.

Her daughter and Jimmy Trottwood together. The little man staying at the Bull. Peter Collins and Sarah. Dr Maguire with Arlene and Mrs Barnstable. Aubrey Monmouth between Billy and the woman in the sable coat and, together opposite her across the tent, Margaret and Mark. Later the faces were to come back to her. Not moving and talking above the sound of the canvas walls cracking in the cold wind, but still and frozen, like a photograph you hid in a drawer.

At 11.00 a.m. precisely Mr Gough took command on the bridge. Quiet and efficient, slightly supercilious, like his heroes.

"Good morning ladies and gentlemen. Glass and cutlery – Lot one. Eleven sherry glasses."

"Showing here!" shouted Herbert, pointing at one of the trestle tables.

⁌ THIRTY-ONE ⁊

THE CUTLERY AND glass came up to average expectations, Mr Gough thought, nothing remarkable but sound enough, the old lady should be well satisfied. Not that she seemed to care very much. Sometimes he stole a quick glance at her but her pale watery eyes gave no hint of her feelings as he dispersed her life's possessions.

The wine glasses and brandy goblets edged into carpets and rugs; dinner parties into memories of incontinent dogs. Household linen and her husband's once clever fingers twisting and pulling at the sheets. Jessie Barnstable blinked with satisfaction and relief, not as Arlene mistakenly thought because of sorrow and regret. Possessions hooked on to faces and memories and without them memories had less power to hurt. It wasn't, she explained to God in her prayers, that she was ungrateful for her life with Robert, she saw the sale not as closing a door but as opening another on to a new and tranquil landscape for whatever time was left to her. Every time the hammer came down it lightened her load.

Prints and drawings; 12.07 p.m.

The money wasn't moving properly yet. So far it had mostly been what Mr Gough thought of as "farmers' fun". He knew most of the farmers there and their wives; they had money but they didn't let it go easily. He'd managed to get one or two private little battles going over the household linen but bouncing mythical bids off the canvas walls was hard work with only limited possibilities. The local dealers were slow too. Trottwood Antiques had bought a set of ornate Arabian pony harness.

"What on earth do we want that for?" hissed Doreen.

Betsey was going to adapt it for the rocking horse. It was certainly the bargain of the sale, he told her.

Mrs Thomas watched Aubrey Monmouth. So far he hadn't bid for anything. The superior smile in asides to his son, silent and

207

burly beside him, sharing the catalogue like a hymn book. Only the colour of Billy's hair like Mark, the rest all Monmouth. Monmouth with his great long neck coming up out of the blue striped collar, bending deferentially down over the head of the woman in furs sitting on his other side. Rosie Bierburger.

For the fiftieth time Arlene studied her with fascination. It was quite safe to look at her, Arlene knew she was half blind and had failed to adapt to contact lenses, only when alone would Rosie resort to spectacles. That last face-lift hadn't worked either, the welt must have gone by now. Could she be eighty? Sure she could, eighty-four on the left side, maybe eighty on the right; in a good light. But Rosie Bierburger in Suffolk with Monmouth, and in sables! Arlene was glad she'd come.

It was 12.49 p.m.

"Ladies and gentlemen. The furniture."

That was better, now they were moving a bit. Front rows showing more interest, too. There was money in the front, he'd seen it in Christie's and Sotheby's. Nothing he couldn't handle. The Regency sofa-table at one thousand eight hundred pounds was good, the set of dining chairs at three thousand two hundred, a bit of a battle to reach his reserve price but they'd made it.

"Lot one hundred and sixty. A mahogany desk. Style of Chippendale."

"Showing here!" Herbert bawled behind Mark and Margaret.

"Five hundred pounds?" Mr Gough's eyebrows rose gently towards the squashed spider.

Nobody moved.

"Three hundred then. Three hundred pounds?"

A market gardener from Walbeswick raised his hand. He liked the desk. His daughter was taking her A-level exams next year. She needed a bit of encouragement. Three hundred pounds was a lot of money but it was one way of getting rid of a bit of tax-free cash.

A dealer bid to three hundred and fifty pounds.

The market gardener raised his hand. Madge wasn't a big girl, she'd get her legs under that all right.

At five hundred pounds the dealer dropped out. The market gardener beamed fondly at his wife, flushed with success. Mr Gough was not pleased. Country piece it might be but it was worth more than that, and that sly smirk from his clerk was irritating too. Several farmers' wives at the back looked distinctly uneasy as he appeared to look directly at them when accepting bids. It was 12.51 p.m.

"At one thousand pounds then, going at only one thousand pounds," he raised his ivory hammer and changed his mind, deciding that he might as well push it a little more. Advancing in fictitious bids of one hundred pounds he stopped at one thousand five hundred pounds.

No one in the front had made a move.

Mr Gough had done his best but enough was enough. He prepared to buy it in at one thousand five hundred pounds.

"For the last time at one thousand five hundred pounds then."

"Five." Monmouth's voice was quiet but quite clear.

Relief gave the auctioneer courage.

"I'm sorry, I can only take bids of one hundred pounds, sir."

"Five thousand," Monmouth said smoothly. "I am bidding five thousand pounds."

The bid was genuine, Gough had enough experience to know that. The suit, the accent, everything was right. But why, for God's sake?

In the murmur of interest in the marquee the market gardener stood up to see who would pay that kind of money for his daughter's desk.

Without giving any further warning Gough slammed the hammer on to the rostrum and with elaborate calm told his clerk: "Sold for five thousand pounds."

Mark said politely. "I'm sorry, you can't do that. I'm bidding. The rules are quite clear. If there is a dispute you must put it up again."

Gough flushed and turned towards Monmouth.

"I'm afraid my young friend is quite right," Monmouth said. "His hand was raised before you closed the bidding."

He gave an odd little dip of his head in Mark's direction and then looked back at the rostrum. He hadn't expected anything less than a battle. They might as well get on with it. He prepared to enjoy himself. It would be very odd indeed if Mark would get very far against Rosie Bierburger's money. He hadn't really wanted to bring her into it but he respected Mark's knowledge of the market and after much thought he decided to play it safe. Better to settle for a fat commission than to stretch his own resources unnecessarily. After all the more it fetched the higher his slice. He really could not lose. Unless of course . . . the muscles of his anus retracted fiercely and involuntarily. He remembered his conversation in her suite at Claridges as she peered at the Polaroid photographs.

"Is this the best you could do?"

"Without alerting the rest of the trade – yes. Professional photographers in a country sale-room? I think not."

"I've seen worse pieces in Washington," she admitted at last.

She wanted it for the Bierburger Foundation, as he had known she would, but she wouldn't give him a limit. She trusted Monmouth as much as she did any dealer. Not much. It was not unknown for dealers buying on commission to arrange for an accomplice to bid him up to his maximum. Sometimes they even put their own things into a sale with a high reserve price on them. It was an easy way to persuade a rich but careful client to pay more than they would in his shop. They couldn't haggle in a sale-room. She was too old to be caught like that.

"Now hear this," she had said, "I shall be with you and I shall sit silent. You will bid until I break it, so listen good, and hear me well if I say quit."

"I understand," he told her. Suspicious cow.

She nodded, satisfied. That way she still had control.

The voices of the farmers and the dealers died away as the auctioneer opened the bidding again. Monmouth was bidding with the forefinger of his left hand, Mark with an almost imperceptible nod of his head.

From five thousand to ten thousand pounds took longer than it should because in sheer disbelief Gough had forgotten to increase the value of the bids and was still advancing in single hundreds. He had abandoned his original theory that one of these two must have an identical desk and was bent on making a matched pair. At ten thousand pounds he increased the bids to units of one thousand pounds. At fifteen thousand pounds he decided that, like the boys' magazine stories of his youth, the desk must have a cunningly concealed secret drawer crammed with gold sovereigns. The pace of the bidding remained constant, forefinger and nod counting the thousands like the steady beat of the longcase clock in the hall.

Mrs Thomas watching. The agonised shame on the face of Dudley Dear. Margaret, white and tense, like a mother searching for a lost child on a crowded holiday beach. Arlene never taking her eyes off Mark's face. The old woman next to Monmouth with her head sunk down into the sables, not moving, eyes closed as though she slept. Maguire rapt. The tent silent, only Gough's voice recording the bids, the smell of cow dung, wet clothes, cheap pipe tobacco, Gough fighting to control his voice.

In the car Mark had briefed Margaret.

"If there's a fight I shall stop sometimes. Don't worry, it will only be to make them think hard. I'll come in again – if I can."

210

At thirty thousand pounds Monmouth was worried. Mark might have hoped for an easy ride but he was a professional; he had come armed for battle. The question was, how much muscle had he got? And at what point would Rosie Bierburger cry quit? At thirty-five thousand pounds the ancient face beside him stirred in the collar of the fur, rising like a tortoise at the end of winter. Monmouth braced himself and went on bidding, the finger rising and falling, thirty-six thousand, thirty-seven thousand. Slowly Mrs Bierburger raised a lorgnette in a jewelled claw to inspect the young man who was bidding against her. Thirty-nine thousand, forty thousand, forty-one thousand. She moved on to Margaret's face and then at forty-eight thousand on to the auctioneer. It was genuine she decided; she was not being cheated. The hand fell back on to her lap and the head sank again into the fur.

At fifty thousand pounds Mark stopped. It was 12.54 p.m.

In the silence Gough tried to clear his throat but the sound came out like a whimper of relief. He wanted them to stop. It was a nightmare, where the bidding bore no relation to any known reason or sanity. He heard his own voice, small and frightened as though he expected the silent crowd to erupt and scream at him in disbelief.

"At fifty thousand pounds then, at fifty thousand."

Mark looked at Monmouth.

The hammer rose.

"Fifty-five," Mark said clearly.

For a moment it took Monmouth aback.

A woman's voice somewhere at the back cried out "Oh no!" The warning note of hysteria acted like a catalyst for Gough, returning him to reality. He did not understand what was happening but it was real and he was a man in charge of his sale-room. His face was moist with sweat, he could feel it running down his body under his shirt. The woman's cry had acted on the people in the marquee too, releasing a burst of pent up emotion in a sudden surge of voices, a movement of bodies, some of them standing on chairs to try and identify the centre of the drama. There was a smell of fear as well as excitement. You had to control it or you had a stampede on your hands.

"Ladies and gentlemen!" The voices sank and died away. "I must have silence for the bidding."

Six months before the clerk had been a schoolboy. He remembered the tone of voice, half expecting the senior partner to add, "I shan't tell you again".

211

Margaret wanted to touch Mark's arm, for support in his fight, for pride in him. She didn't because he would know it without that. She was proud of herself, too, because she had saved him from himself. Fifty-five thousand pounds was their total capital. From now on they would be using Dudley Dear's money, another twenty thousand pounds. It didn't matter how it ended. She and Mark would win whatever happened. She would make him understand that, she was stronger than he was.

Mrs Thomas watched, storing information for Webber. Jessie Barnstable struggling to understand, pale, not speaking. Arlene Weikel ignoring Monmouth, watching Mark.

Gough looked at Monmouth. "At fifty-five thousand then – it's against you sir? – thank you. Fifty-six thousand, fifty-seven thousand, fifty-eight thousand."

Rosie Bierburger was not unduly disturbed. She had long ago lost track of both her income and her capital, that was for lawyers and tax robbers but she was a shrewd, astute woman. She would not have people back home think her a rich old fool with more money than sense. Her American adviser had been asked to check the Polaroid photographs. His report had been succinct. "On October 21st 1978 an almost identical desk fetched one hundred and forty thousand dollars or seventy thousand pounds. That was in Christie's New York sale-room and it was a world record." He was presuming this one was genuine. It was; Rosie didn't need Monmouth to tell her that. Even so the price was surprising, surprising for a sale in a crummy tent. The kid in the white shirt had guts, knew what it was, too. He must be buying on commission. Pity; she could have let him buy it and name his price to her. That would have been quite acceptable and she would have paid it without a quibble. She didn't give a damn what she paid in private. Too risky, no, it was a commission and she would have to fight a bit longer. How long? And who in hell was he bidding for?

At sixty-eight thousand thousand pounds Mark appeared to hesitate. Not long; enough to break up the rhythm. When he started again Monmouth's finger continued to prod out the bids. Seventy-two thousand, seventy-three thousand. Monmouth felt the sable coat shift on the seat next to him.

It was coming to the end.

Arlene saw it in Mark's face too. It was a mask and it moved her heart. He was nearly spent up, she was sure of it, who else would know it if she didn't? She looked at Rosie Bierburger. God, but she was a boring old bitch.

At seventy-six thousand pounds Mark shook his head.

The jewelled fingers tightened on the handle of the lorgnette. The wrinkled face peered impassively through the tobacco haze. Arlene longed to bring the other side of that face up to eighty-four, eighty-five maybe. Make the old monster pay a bit more. She wouldn't stop now. It would be very sweet but she dared not even think of it. Walt would go mad if he ever heard of it.

"At seventy-six thousand then. At seventy-six thousand pounds."

Gough raised the hammer.

"Seventy-seven thousand," said Arlene.

The lorgnette swung round in a slow arc. So that was the mystery solved. The boy was bidding for Arlene Weikel! He had gone to her limit and now she had decided to carry on. Or had she? Arlene's composure had deserted her, Rosie, the seasoned campaigner of a thousand sale-rooms, saw the ashen face and the hand pressed involuntarily to the mouth.

It was Gough, uncertain of this new nightmare, who paused.

With the glasses still held on Arlene's face Rosie said, "Quit".

"At seventy-seven thousand pounds then. Seventy-seven thousand for the last time."

Some sound like a dry chuckle came from the old, malicious face. She lowered the glasses.

"Eighty thousand," she said. The voice was quietly contemptuous.

Then Gough completed the final ritual without any further interruption.

It wasn't the end.

In the uproar of voices that followed Mrs Thomas was the only one who saw clearly what happened.

She saw it because she had seen Mark Carter move like that before. She was powerless to move or warn. It was unbelievably quick. She never saw him pick up the Japanese sword. The razor-edged sword a Japanese Ambassador had presented to Robert Barnstable.

She saw Aubrey Monmouth half rise, oblivious of the boy in summer clothes behind him.

The look of quiet triumph on Monmouth's face was still there when his head landed on the coconut matting in front of the rostrum and came to rest smiling up at the auctioneer.

It was 12.58 p.m.

⚜ THIRTY-TWO ⚜

SURPRISINGLY CHRISTMAS AT Flaxfield seemed very little different from other years. The reporters and the television crews had done their work and moved on. Gradually the story dropped out of the newspapers, people still talked about it in the Bull and in their homes but the Christmas tree appeared in the square at Dunwold, and in Flaxfield the carol singers made their rounds as they did every year. Webber gave them five pounds. Betsey and Doreen stood at the door of Trottwood Antiques and sang with them; the rocking horse wore the Arabian harness and a hat trimmed with holly. Mrs Thomas had cooked bakestones for them and dispensed parsnip wine. At the Collinses there was hot rabbit pie and beer. On the terrace at Henworth Hall there was another Christmas tree and presents.

They sang outside Margaret Carter's cottage too but it was dark and empty and they moved on. In London, Dudley Dear was writing a book.

Father Bernard sent Mrs Thomas a Christmas card with a drawing of the Hospice Ecclésiastique on it, a grim ugly building with forbidding turrets. He enclosed a brief note acknowledging her letter. He was sorry he had not replied earlier but Christmas was a busy time and he had been given a locum tenens for a priest with bronchitis. "Quite a pleasant church," he told her cheerfully, "but the sins in the confessional are very mediocre, nothing to compare with those of Flaxfield." No, her letter had not appalled him, he was too old for that but he had to admit that he had read every word with absorbed interest. He realised that she had been under some considerable strain when she wrote and there were still some things which were not at all clear to him. When his temporary job ended in February he would write at length and, if he may, ask about them. It was very kind of her to send him such beautiful warm socks. The central heating at the

Hospice had broken down and Father Alfred was being very difficult.

At the end of February the Christmas rain had given way to deep, hard frost and thin powdery snow covered the fields of the fens from beyond Flaxfield to the sea. Mrs Thomas stuffed newspaper in the cracks around her kitchen window frame and sat at the pine table in front of the fire to reply to a long detailed questionnaire from Father Bernard. Life in the village had started to get very dull again and she answered it eagerly.

". . . To be honest, no I don't think your Father Alfred is mad, a little odd perhaps, eccentric might be kinder, you must not think me an expert in these matters! I don't suppose he meant to steal your thick socks but it was very nice of you to let him keep them. Only one pair, I hope? There are limits to charity! The weather here is so terribly cold that the sailors' shop at Dunwold had almost sold out but I am sending you four more pairs as a late Christmas present, two from John and two from me. He thanks you for your good wishes and says to let you know that his arthritis is much improved in spite of the cold. I am a great believer in the heat from coal. I make him sit in front of his fire quite naked except for his underpants to preserve his silly old modesty. Goodness what a lot of questions you do ask! But yes, certainly I love him. You must have guessed that when we talked. And him? My lovely old policeman with his dear fat belly and his limp? I don't know – yes I do, but he is not like me and would be shy to tell me.

After that horror in the sale-room I went to his home where we had arranged to meet and discuss our plans for confronting the boy next day. I can't remember how I told him what I had seen that morning but he held me in his arms for a long time and kissed my eyes as if to blot it out of my mind. That was delicate, wasn't it? He has a superior quality and it is enough for me. I'll bet you were formidable in the confessional box with your leading questions.

Questions, ah yes you must indeed have thought it strange that the reports in your French papers carried no mention of the other horrors, his father, the poor Indian girl or the dead boy in the Swiss lake. We kept quiet Father, John and I. The Collinses know of course, even the police – unofficially. You see, we said nothing because of Margaret. What good would it have done? If he had lived and come to trial then they would surely have proved only what was so obvious at the end, that he was indeed mad, poor creature. At least I believed it would. Some people don't agree and speak of evil. Shall we talk of that one day?"

The fire in the kitchen had burnt low. In spite of her Harris tweed trouser-suit and her fur-lined boots, Mrs Thomas felt the bitter cold. Bunter, the cat, moved politely to allow her room to shake more coal out of the hod.

"That will soon burn up," she assured him as she returned to read Father Bernard's letter again. She wrote:

". . . No, of course I do not think you morbid or idly inquisitive. I know you better than that – isn't that odd, since ours was such a brief meeting? You see my first letter was written so soon after it all happened and I'm sure I must have left you puzzled about so many details. Now it is calmer and I can think more clearly. First the cellar in the shop.

I do remember telling you that John had an instinct about it. That is why he didn't come with me to the sale. It was his one chance to examine it when he was certain they would not be there. Policemen are very good burglars! He got in through a window at the back of the shop and forced the cellar door. Father, let me explain. This is what we think (no, we are certain) Mark had planned. The plastic sheeting all over the floor and on the table under that strong ceiling light was to make certain there would be no trace left after he had dismembered poor Margaret. Those plastic bags half filled with heavy builders' rubbish were to put the pieces in after he had cut her up. That's what the old surgeon's instruments were for, of course, they were all neatly laid out on the table, ready and waiting. And the holes in the bags were to make sure they would sink when he threw them out of the boat. John thinks he would have sunk the boat too and swum back to the beach. (He was a powerful swimmer – remember the Swiss lake.) John brought the surgeon's knives and saws away with him so the cellar was innocent when the police examined it. Just a cellar with builders' rubbish like a hundred others. There was an axe in the cellar, too. Mad or evil, Father? She doesn't know anything of all this. What good would it do now?

In many ways she is a remarkable girl – a little more than a girl now. For her Mark Carter was a genius and he loved her. She even blames herself for not realising that he was on the edge of a nervous breakdown! Best leave it. Why should we kill her love as he would have killed her?

Mrs Barnstable died quietly a few days after the sale. Dr

216

Maguire and Mrs Weikel were with her. It was probably delayed shock I suppose, although I'm told she never referred to the saleroom – not once. That last evening she opened her eyes and said quite clearly, 'Robert was a terrible gardener'. Then she died. So that is something else we shall never understand, I suppose. Like the water tower. I'll come to that in a minute. I'll have to think a bit first.

The American desk? Yes, it went off to somewhere called Dead Neck Creek. That's where the David M. Bierburger Foundation has its home. An ironic resting place for it? Arlene Weikel says that Mrs Bierburger is not a nice woman. It was Mrs Weikel, by the way, who persuaded Margaret to come and recuperate at Henworth Hall. She lived in the very grand flat where Mrs Barnstable had been, and of course before her Mark Carter's mother had been there. Arlene insisted on paying for it. She is very rich and very kind – unusual? I knew you would pray for Margaret. I did too. 'God, give her strength,' I asked. He must have heard us. She is strong, stronger than I ever knew. I first met her just after her mother had died. I remember admiring her then, she had possibilities I thought, not an ordinary girl, a survivor. But to remain sane after all this! She talks about him all the time, she wants to, she talks of love, of what she calls 'his escape' and of her relief. Who among us would destroy that?

Fancy you seeing Joan Carter interviewed on French television! I never did meet her as you know. She was warned by Dr Maguire, of course, that Mark had left Flaxfield. She knew about Mark all right, she wasn't going to risk another encounter! Arlene had a Christmas card from her; robins and snow. Rather unsuitable we thought since she has gone into some sort of religious retreat on a mountain in Mexico. Lots of young men apparently, living on soya beans and worshipping the Sun God. You remember what she said on television about Mark? Well it was on her Christmas card too – 'After all, he was my son'. You are right, one must not judge but I find it difficult not to. I am not like you. Billy, her other son, has inherited his father's business in Bond Street. I believe he is marrying a woman who knows about antiques to run it with him. Pragmatist! (Touché?)

There remains the tower. I don't know Father . . ."

Mrs Thomas laid down her pen and poured herself a glass of malt whisky from the bottle that Webber had given her for Christmas. The telephone was in the cold hall so she slipped an overcoat round her shoulders to dial his number.

"John, were you in bed?"

"No, reading – anything the matter?"

"No, I just wanted to say goodnight. Don't forget dinner tomorrow."

"That's not very likely, now is it? Can we have roast beef?"

"Wait and see – how is your leg?"

"Fine – goodnight Lizzie."

"Goodnight love – see you tomorrow."

Bunter had come to the kitchen door to make sure she wasn't going out. Overcoats were ominous things sometimes.

She took up her pen.

". . . I don't know, because I don't really know Peter Collins. Sarah, his wife, is much easier. I don't think she really knows him, either. It is an old familiar pattern isn't it? Do you remember I said that it was a little like colouring the blank pages of a child's painting book? Well perhaps this one will remain blank, unless one day . . . This is all I know. I don't know if it will help you to decide what really happened.

In the tent that morning Mark walked out quite slowly. Nobody tried to stop him. Some people in the doorway even stood aside to let him pass. He got into his car and left – just as simply as that – he just disappeared. Peter Collins and Sarah took Margaret home and stayed with her.

By the evening the village was full of police cars and motor cycles. There was no sign of him. There was a report that the car had been seen on the road to Dunwold so they set up road blocks and sealed it off. There is only one road leading into the town, so it was easy. The police came to question Margaret, of course, but Peter and Sarah said they couldn't question her about where Mark might be, she was in a state of shock, they said. She did tell Peter and Sarah though, and Sarah stayed with her while Peter drove alone to the water tower. Now you know as much as I do. It was in all the newspapers and I'm sure in yours too. I can add a little.

It was very misty – thick sea mist like we often get round here. Dr Peter says the car was half hidden in a hollow dip with gorse bushes at the foot of the tower so he knew Mark was there. He must have been very brave to climb up those stairs to the platform at the top. Mark was quite dead, he said. It must have happened just before Peter reached him because the body was still warm and he could still smell the cartridge powder from the gun. Margaret said later that she had never seen it before. Peter thinks Mark must have stolen it when he collected the surgical instruments. It was Peter's rabbit gun and he kept it in his garage.

Is that a little clearer, Father? Perhaps you are a more skilful painter than I am? Or perhaps I am too close. In Calais you might be able to stand back a little and observe the tower from the Hospice Ecclésiastique. Dr Peter is not an ordinary man, but I am quite certain he is a good man.

Is your dining room still ice cold? Now listen, my old dear. It's very late but I have something to ask you and you will disappoint me dreadfully if you refuse, and John too.

There is a little man called Dudley Dear, he comes into the story earlier but you will have to wait until we meet before I explain that. Briefly, he knew Mark and has decided to write a book about him. He went to Pegomas to do some research, went to the villa and interviewed a lot of young men in Cannes. (I'll give you a laugh about that later.) The villa is empty now, of course, but he spoke to the housekeeper who says it is available to rent. I've only seen it from a distance but apparently it's very large and grand with lots of rooms and a swimming pool.

He's been down here to the village, too, poking around for 'background'. I don't think the book is going to be very good – or indeed accurate – it is to be called *Flawed Genius*. I find Mr Dear interesting. Some people here don't like him because they think he is writing his book to make money – trading in tragedy. There is much more to him than that. Like Margaret he needs to talk about Mark. He has possibilities.

The idea came to me quite suddenly. The village here seemed very dead and lifeless, the English are really quite awful in some ways. Give them half a chance and they sink back into their little homes and go to sleep in front of the television. I think television is like whisky, only good in moderation. People don't talk enough do they? Not any more. I love reading about house parties in the old days – not all that long ago either – when people had time to talk – like we did in the café. My last visit to France was insupportably short and I decided then that I would return.

So – I have booked the Villa Emily for six weeks! (A month is too short.) April and the first two weeks of May (the Mimosa will be out, think of it!). The house guests (house guests! There's classy, isn't it?) will be, John and me, Dr Peter and Dr Sarah, my son-in-law (a dear sweet man who might well be canonised one day), and my daughter Doreen (needs watching but I can manage her), Dudley Dear (the author), Margaret Carter and Mrs Weikel who, as we say in our Women's Institute, has very generously consented to pay all expenses. (Actually she admits that she is longing to send a card to Joan Carter addressed from the Villa Emily!)

Oh, and of course you! Now Father don't you *dare* thwart me! You won't have anything to do at all except pack (you won't need your thick socks). I am organising everything. There will be plenty of cars, people will want them for trips in the daytime. John and I will collect you at the Hospice and you will travel with us. (Dates and times later.)

Only think what a time we shall have! The conversations! (you and Dr Peter perhaps?) Crossword puzzles, no chilblains, no arthritis, good food, I promise you, (we must discuss Tante Marie, I have some bones to pick with that one). It's late and I'm tired but so excited, I do love it when things *happen*. I'm glad Margaret is coming — you will like her, I know. She is selling all her things — quite right; my son-in-law is putting everything into Christie's for her — anonymously, The Property of a Lady. We think it best, after all the publicity. She wants to drive down on her own. Father! You are quite outrageous! I'm sure she wouldn't dream of giving anyone a lift.

Goodnight my Father.

I must find someone to look after my cat.

Someone kind."